WALKING
DEAD
MAN

Also by Mary Kittredge

WALKING DEAD MAN

An Edwina Crusoe Mystery

Mary Kittredge

ST. MARTIN'S PRESS · NEW YORK

This novel is a work of fiction. All of the events, characters, names, and places depicted in this novel are entirely fictitious or are used fictitiously. No representation that any statement made in this novel is true or that any incident depicted in this novel actually occurred is intended or should be inferred by the reader.

WALKING DEAD MAN. Copyright © 1992 by Mary Kittredge. All rights reserved. Printed in the United States of America. No part of this book may be used or reproduced in any manner whatsoever without written permission except in the case of brief quotations embodied in critical articles or reviews. For information, address St. Martin's Press, 175 Fifth Avenue, New York, N.Y. 10010.

Editor: George Witte
Production Editor: Marie Finamore
Copyedited by Jolanta Benal

Library of Congress Cataloging-in-Publication Data

Kittredge, Mary
        Walking dead man / Mary Kittredge.
               p.   cm.
        ISBN 0-312-08333-5
        I. Title.
     PS3561.I868W35   1992
     813'.54—dc20   92-25159
                                                                        CIP

First Edition: November 1992

10 9 8 7 6 5 4 3 2 1

ONE

The guy was nothing. The guy was nobody. So it was perfectly okay to incinerate him.

Perfectly. Ricky Zimmerman strolled from the parking garage of the midtown hotel where, inside, the guy was eating breakfast. Steak and eggs, order of hash browns, couple slices of toast with jelly on the side. Nice glass of juice and a second cup of coffee, maybe, while he sat there looking at his newspaper.

All in all, it made a pretty decent last meal, and the guy was not going to feel anything. Ricky knew his business well enough to have taken care of that.

The first part of the device would kill the guy. The second, triggered in an instant by the blast of the first, would produce a human cinder identifiable only by dental records. That was the job for which Ricky Zimmerman would be paid, later today, ten thousand dollars, assuming he accomplished it, which he would in about fifteen minutes.

Perfectly.

Smiling a little, Ricky crossed at the light and entered a corner coffee shop. In the pocket of his jacket was a radio remote-controller of the type used to operate small gasoline-powered model airplanes. The spark needed for the model plane's engine ignition was provided by a charged coil, which in turn could be activated by a signal from the remote.

Ricky had replaced the coil with a battery, in his device. But the principle was the same: When he toggled the controller *on*, an electrical current would begin flowing in the device, continuing until it reached a gap. There a small bright spark would briefly appear—jumping the gap, completing the circuit, and igniting a bundle of substances so volatile the very thought of them made Ricky's smile widen noticeably.

"Real nice morning," said the waitress, fetching Ricky the Coke and doughnut he had ordered. She glanced wistfully out the big plate-glass window at the front of the coffee shop, opposite the counter where Ricky sat.

From here he could see the parking garage ramp, and up the avenue to the intersection. The guy's car had not appeared yet.

"Kinda makes me wish I could be out there," she added with a little laugh, pausing for Ricky to pick up on it.

Ricky didn't. This, however, did not deter the waitress. "You know," she continued, mostly on account of Ricky's smile, which she had utterly misinterpreted, "it's, on a nice morning like this, it's exciting, sort of." She let her hand rise and fall in a way she had seen probably in an old movie somewhere, a gesture which by its end was as limp as her hopes.

Ricky turned from the window to the bleached-blond waitress standing tiredly in front of it. She was young now, but she would be here, still dreaming, until her neck and the part of her chest that showed in the vee of her waitress uniform got all wrinkly and disgusting-looking. She would be here until her feet swelled up so bad, she couldn't even stuff them into waitress shoes anymore. By

2

then she would be old and defeated, plug-ugly, and have a voice like a metal grinder.

But hey, she'd bought that trip, hadn't she? Was buying it now, in fact, standing there wishing Ricky Z. or some other hotshot was going to stroll into her crummy coffee shop some morning, fall in love with her like a lightning bolt. Yeah, maybe forty more years the little waitress had in her. Only, not if she kept standing in front of that plate-glass window.

From the corner of his eye Ricky glimpsed the car ascending the hotel parking garage ramp, signal blinking as it prepared to enter traffic. It was the silver Mercedes to which he had attached his device, fifteen minutes earlier. Ricky slipped his left hand into his jacket pocket and came to a decision.

"Hell," he said suddenly. "I'm sorry, miss, could you come out here, please? I lost my contact lens, it's right here by the bottom of the stool somewhere. Could you help find it?" Ricky bent as if to search the floor for the nonexistent lens.

"Hey, waitress," rasped a man down the counter, "what's it, yah birt'day? How long a person's gotta wait, getta nudda cuppa coffee in this joint?"

Ricky straightened, swiveling to face the man, who in the full glare of Ricky Z.'s professional regard remembered abruptly that coffee was probably not very good for him, that in fact this entire neighborhood was probably not very good for him, and that he did indeed have pressing business elsewhere which he really should be getting to immediately.

A puff of spring breeze laden with exhaust fumes wafted in the door of the coffee shop as the man exited. Meanwhile the silver car completed its turn and proceeded up the avenue. Ricky kept it in sight while the waitress came out, full of concern for the lost contact lens.

"Watch out you don't step on it," she said as Ricky slipped from the stool to crouch beside her in the relative protection of the

3

counter. "That happened to my sister once, she was on the floor looking for it, and while she was looking for it she—"

The waitress smelled of cooking grease, hair spray, and cheap cologne. Three, two, one, thought Ricky Z., toggling the remote switch. "Hey," he said, "I didn't lose it, it's still in my—"

The explosion when it came was a deep bass *thump!* followed by the crash of the plate-glass window imploding. Ricky grabbed a handful of the waitress's hair, pushing her vigorously downward while the counter's half-dozen other patrons dove for the floor.

One guy who wasn't so lucky took a shard in the cheek; the rest, accustomed to random gunfire, speeding cabs, rampaging muggers, and bicycle messengers careening down walkways reserved exclusively for the use of pedestrians, had suffered no apparent injury, Ricky saw with relief as he lifted his head.

Having people die in your immediate vicinity was a drag, especially if it happened regularly. For one thing, it tended to make the authorities ask why, which in Ricky's case was perhaps the most pertinent and least welcome question they could possibly have asked. So far he had managed to spare himself this trouble, and as he peered around the debris-strewn coffee shop he was delighted to see that in the dead-in-the-immediate-vicinity department, his luck continued favorable.

"Jesus," blurted the guy with the bloody cheek in the eerie silence following the explosion. "What the freaking hell was that?"

Ricky got to his feet, lifting the sobbing waitress by the arm and avoiding the daggers of glass that lay everywhere, and peered through the jaggedly framed hole where the big plate-glass window had been. In the street, people were gathering themselves, looking dazedly about as sirens began wailing. Some ran toward the car, which was now burning hotly, orange flames pouring from its blown-open passenger doors. Others collected their pocketbooks and briefcases, snatching at scattered papers as they backed frightenedly away from the blazing wreckage.

None appeared seriously hurt. "It looks," said Ricky Z., biting his lip to keep himself from laughing, "like a car fire. Maybe the gas tank exploded."

The man with the cheek gash held a wad of paper napkins to his wound. "Take more'n a gas tank, make a car burn like *that*."

Suddenly Ricky did not feel like staying in the coffee shop. "Yeah," he replied. "I guess you're right." He dropped a five-dollar bill atop the glass bits on the counter and turned to leave.

But the waitress stepped in front of him. "I ain't takin' your money, mister," she said in the adoring tones Ricky Z. had always hated. You started hearing that voice out of a woman, any woman, right away you knew you had a sizable problem.

"You saved my life," she went on. "If you hadn'a gotten me out from behind that counter when you did, I would've been—I wouldn've been— Oh, my God."

Swiftly Ricky took control of the situation, reaching out to grasp her by her flabby arms. "You listen to me," he told her, "I didn't do anything. That was what you call your act of God, there, you gettin' away from that window before whatever happened out there happened."

Gulping, the waitress gazed up at him. Ricky had seen that look in a dog's eyes once, and had given the mutt a hard boot in the behind so as not to have to see it again. Here, though, he would have to use different tactics.

"You wanna thank me," Ricky Z. told the waitress, "you tell me you're gonna take the second chance the good Lord has given you. Hey"—he waved around at the ruined coffee shop—"you ain't doin' yourself no good workin' here. What're you anyway, twenty-two, twenty-three years old?"

"Twenty-four next week," she replied in a whisper. "I *was* gonna go to paralegal school, see, but then I kind of ran out of money, and—"

Ricky smiled encouragingly at this girl while wondering how

much schooling it could possibly take to learn to let a bunch of lawyers push you around. "Well, then, see? There you go. You gotta dream, something to accomplish in your life, now you gotta go after it, am I right?"

The other patrons nodded soberly, all obviously rooting hard for Ricky's pitch; any minute the bunch of them would break into a song, even the guy with the bloody napkin pressed to his kisser.

Ricky looked the little waitress in the eye. Her hair had felt like sticky spun glass in his hand, like he could actually have broken off big solid wedgy sections of it if he'd wanted to.

"Don't be thinkin' you'll see me again," he warned. "This ain't no movie, and I ain't no white knight. You want somethin' a certain way, you gotta make it that way, you understand what I am sayin' to you?"

Jesus, the time he was wasting on this happy horseshit. He had planned to be halfway to the bridge by now, on his way out of the city to the payoff spot. But there was no help for it; if he didn't resolve the situation here, give this female a dose of the romantic bushwa she was sticking him up for, she was the type who might do something really stupid. Call up the newspapers, tell them the story and even make them put his description in, maybe, so she could find him and reward him. And wouldn't that be something, though, Ricky Zimmerman's description printed in the newspapers?

Up the street the Mercedes continued burning merrily. Cop cars were diverting traffic at the end of the block. Ricky could hear the static their radios emitted. An ambulance siren whooped briefly.

"I . . . I understand," the waitress said. She straightened, lifting her chin, blinking back big shimmering tears. "Thanks, mister. Thanks a lot." Venturing a trembly-lipped smile, she put out her hand.

Ricky took it and held it firmly for a moment. It felt exactly like a fistful of limp, warm suet; when he dropped it he had to fight the urge to scrub his palm on his pants leg. "You take care, now," he said, and got the hell out of there.

Two hours later Ricky Z. was in his own car, a cherry-red Datsun 280Z with charcoal-tinted windows, antelope leather seats, a sunroof, a fuzz-buster hidden behind a blank dashboard panel, 480 watts of custom-installed JBL quadraphonic sound, and a cellular phone whose number no one knew except Ricky, since he felt its purpose was to allow him to phone other people, not to put him at the beck and call of any jerkoff who might take a sudden notion to phone him, any time of the goddamn day or night. The effect of four ten-inch speakers cranked up inside the 280Z was similar to that of a live rock concert being played in a metal garbage can, with the audience and the band all right there together *inside* the garbage can, but Ricky liked it.

He had quick-stepped the fifty blocks from midtown to the lot on the Upper West Side where, earlier in the day, he had parked the car. Despite its tempting appearance it remained unmolested, a circumstance Ricky thought might have something to do with his own quiet reputation as an up-and-coming young man who would just as soon rip your lungs out as look at you. Now he cruised west on the George Washington Bridge, headed for Jersey and his ten thousand dollars.

To his left spread the skyline of lower Manhattan, the wide deceptively blue expanse of the Hudson River on its way to the Atlantic, and the drab, congested sprawl that was Fort Lee, Weehawken, Hoboken, and eventually Jersey City. Up ahead and to his right were the Palisades, which was where Ricky was going; coming off the bridge he took the 9W exit, passing under the connector that would have taken him into Fort Lee had he happened to be feeling suicidal that day, and headed north on the parkway.

After another twenty minutes he left the parkway, doubled back a few miles along a two-lane road through the newly green trees of Palisades Interstate Park, and pulled into a scenic rest area overlooking the river. The area was little more than an oil-stained gravel patch with a scarred wooden picnic table and a couple of trash barrels overflowing with refuse. Someone had tried inexpertly to set the table on fire; its crossed legs were rounded and blackened stumps. The last time Ricky had been here the place had been deserted, and the time before that, which was why he had chosen it for this business he was about to transact.

But it was not deserted now. Unbelievably, a kid was sitting on the picnic table. When he heard the Datsun pull in the kid turned and stared at it, looking for all the world as if he thought he had some right to be here. In a moment, when the Datsun did not go away, the kid got down off the table and actually walked over to the car, coming to a halt a few feet from the driver's-side door and the rolled-up, charcoal-tinted window.

"Hey," the kid called, squinting at the tinted glass, which from his side was opaque, "that's a nice car you've got there."

Inside, Ricky Zimmerman stared in amazement. This kid had no idea whether Ricky might be sitting there leveling a .357 at him, ready to roll down the window and blow his freaking head off, which incidentally was precisely what Ricky felt like doing, only he did not have a .357 with him. This kid had *no idea* who he was talking to.

Still the kid stood there with a big goofy grin on his face, his dark, greasy hair tied back in a ponytail, wearing ratty jeans and a fake leather jacket that looked as if he'd stolen it off some trash heap. Pair of holey sneakers, no socks on his feet; the kid looked as if he'd slept in an alley last night.

Which, Ricky suddenly realized, the kid probably had, and if he, Ricky, were simply to remove the kid from the face of the earth it was unlikely anyone would miss him. Ricky considered this idea for several moments. Then, irritated, he reached out and snapped off the car's sound system, and the big booming quad speakers fell silent.

Outside the kid's dumb grin widened as he evidently regarded this as a hopeful sign. Of what, Ricky was not sure. He rolled down the window; the kid stepped forward eagerly.

"Hey, man, great car. Really excellent. *Superlativo.*" The kid made an A-OK sign with thumb and forefinger, meanwhile nearly dancing in appreciation, his gaze moving greedily over the cherry paint, custom magnesium wheels, retractable antenna, and other appurtenances with which the automobile was furnished. Peering past Ricky he took in the leather seats, the JBL quad speakers, all the many luxuries in which Ricky himself took so much pride.

Unwillingly, Ricky felt himself begin softening. Just then the kid stepped back and kicked shyly at the gravel with the toe of his sneaker, a look of practiced wheedling spreading on his face. Ricky snapped back to attention.

"Uh, listen, man," the kid said, "could you, like, let me have a lift out to the highway?"

Ricky mouthed the predictable words in his head as the kid spoke them. He had the little .25 automatic in the glove box, and he seriously considered reaching for it now, just getting the whole thing over with before his own business began. But he wasn't a crack shot, the kid would probably see it coming and run, and any minute the other car might drive in.

"Sure," he told the kid, "why not? Only I've got something to take care of here, first. And I need some privacy, you know? To get that thing taken care of."

The kid nodded sagely. "No problem, man. I was gonna start walkin' anyway. Other guy, gave me a lift, I fell asleep? Woke up, he had me out here." The kid shook his head. "Guy had the wrong idea, man, *absolutimento* the wrong idea."

Ricky laughed understandingly in reply. "You don't have to worry about me on that score. Listen, half an hour or so, I'll be along. We'll go over to the Boulevard, pick up some burgers. I'm heading back to the city, after. That suit you?"

At this the kid looked as if he'd died and gone to heaven, which considering his immediate future prospects Ricky thought was appropriate. Once the kid was in the car, it would be easy. Grinning, the kid turned and sauntered from the scenic rest area, disappearing where the road curved among the spring-green trees.

TWO

"I want to confess to a murder," said Theresa Whitlock, "but the police don't believe I committed one."

"Oh, I see," replied Edwina Crusoe, who didn't, and in whose experience it generally worked the other way around.

"Well, I haven't actually tried telling them yet," the young woman amended. She was blond, slim, and pretty, with china-blue eyes, a small freckled nose, and pink lips quivering miserably. Her blue-striped jumper with smocked bodice and puffed sleeves should have looked ridiculous on anyone over age six; on Theresa Whitlock, it was charming. Also, she had just finished weeping, and this made her look even more innocent and vulnerable.

All of which aroused Edwina's suspicions, and perhaps quite unfairly. But probably not, for Edwina possessed a sixth sense that invariably alerted her when, as her policeman husband, Martin McIntyre, would have put it, her chain was being yanked.

"Only," Mrs. Whitlock said, weeping once more, "when I *do* tell them, they *won't* believe me, and if they *don't* believe me I *know* he's going to kill me."

She dabbed the corners of her eyes with a handkerchief—Belgian linen, edged in perfect tiny stitches of silk, Edwina noted—and looked up imploringly. "The man I murdered means to murder me back. I've *got* to confess, to stop him. Will you help me?"

At this, Edwina inspected her visitor again. Having given up a successful nursing career for her present one as a private crime consultant (her card, Edwina thought, might just as well read SNOOP—MEDICAL/HEALTH MATTERS ONLY) she had no wish to begin rendering psychiatric diagnoses.

Still, she didn't have to be Sigmund Freud to know that a woman who thought a dead man could kill her had a screw loose, and a woman intent upon confessing to a murder, purely in order to discourage that dead man, was probably missing a few nuts and bolts as well, and possibly some important brain structures.

"Mrs. Whitlock," said Edwina, "I'm sorry, but I can't help you. My practice is limited to medical matters, you see. But I'll be happy to refer you to someone who *will* be able to—"

"I know, you think I'm crazy. But the phone calls and the letters—I tell you, I am not imagining them. And there've been . . . incidents. I've been mugged, and had my purse snatched. Our house has been broken into and vandalized. I found aspirin in my Tylenol bottle; I'm allergic to aspirin. It's as if he wants to punish me as much as he can before he . . . before he kills me."

"Letters?" asked Edwina, her curiosity piqued by the mention of physical evidence. Also, she had watched as Theresa made her speech. The young woman's eyes were those of a practiced, gifted liar: clear, limpid, and unwavering. But Theresa Whitlock was not lying now. "May I see the letters, please?"

Biting her lip, Theresa stared down at her hands. "I . . . I don't have them. They vanished. I put the first one in my bureau drawer; I didn't want my husband coming across it. The very next morning it was gone. There've been six, altogether, in the last few weeks, and I can't find any of them. Only once"—she opened her handbag—"there was this."

She passed a scrap of lined paper across the desk. ". . . see you bleeding . . . did to me . . . dead," read the torn fragment, which was scrawled in black ink in an angry, backward-slanting hand.

"How interesting," said Edwina, feeling in spite of herself the faintest bit chilled. "Do you by any chance remember the entire message? And do you know how this bit happened to become torn?"

"Yes, I remember. They're always the same. First he says he'll laugh when he sees me bleeding. Next, that I'll suffer for what I did to him. Then he says I'd better get ready to be dead. As for the tear, there's a plank of loose paneling in the den; I slid the last letter behind it, to hide it. The next day it was gone, like the others, and I was just so hysterical . . . well."

Theresa Whitlock gathered herself. "I went to my husband's workshop and got a crowbar, and pried the whole piece of paneling off the wall. This scrap had slipped down to where you couldn't see it, not unless you removed the plank."

She sighed, remembering. "It was a job getting that panel back on, the varnish touched up and the nails back in and all. I'm not," she added a little defensively, "as helpless as I look. I can take care of what I need to take care of."

I'll just bet you can, Edwina thought. "Only you can't take care of this."

"No." Theresa worked the handkerchief in her fingers. "I was so sure I'd gotten away with it, you see. I was careful not to leave the smallest clue. But he must have figured it all out, somehow. Or maybe dead people just know. Maybe they always know who killed them."

"Yes, perhaps," said Edwina, concealing impatience. "But knowing and doing something about it are two different things. I think

13

you may be the victim of an unpleasant prank. But I don't believe a dead man is going to murder you."

Theresa looked mutinous and opened her mouth to speak; with a gesture, Edwina silenced her. "Look, Theresa, even if you had killed someone—and you haven't yet for a moment convinced me that you have—it would take a good deal more than what you've told me here to persuade me that your victim is haunting you. As for the police, they'd laugh you right out of their sight. Don't you see how preposterous the whole thing sounds?"

"You don't understand," Theresa persisted. "All I want is for you to investigate a murder. When you do, you'll find that I committed it, just the way I'm saying I did. Then you can go with me to the police. That way," she finished, as if it were all very simple, "they'll have to believe me, won't they?"

She glanced at her watch and jumped up. "Oh! I've got to get home. We've got a new housekeeper, and today's her payday; she'll be wanting her money before she leaves." Pulling a checkbook from her bag, she scribbled out a check.

"Is this enough for you to start work, do you think? The murdered man's name is Thomas Riordan. You remember him; it was in all the newspapers. I'll come back tomorrow, to explain how I killed him. That way, you won't have to investigate so hard."

The check was indeed made out for enough to start work. In fact, at first glance it was for enough to start a small nation, with some left over for the purchase of a few colonies, besides.

"Wait a minute," said Edwina, "this is too much money. And I haven't agreed to work for you at all. As I mentioned, I only take *medical*—"

"Oh, thank you," said Theresa Whitlock, ignoring Edwina and babbling in her rush to get the words out. "I just know I'll be all right now. I can *feel* it." Saying this, she hurried out of Edwina's office; the door, weighted to close automatically, swung shut with its usual loud, hollow bang.

Edwina sat at her desk, blinking at the enormous paycheck. It might bounce, of course, but she thought it wouldn't; she'd had a glimpse at the checkbook balance. Upside-down reading being one of her specialties, she'd also seen the amounts of the two most recent deposits: ten thousand and forty thousand dollars, put in separately but within a few days of one another.

"Maxie," she said after a moment, "look at all this money."

The black cat raised his velvet head in inquiry, peering at the red leather armchairs positioned on either side of the marble fireplace, at the vases of fresh flowers placed about the room, and at his own stainless-steel food and water dishes, one of which at the moment was unfortunately empty. Finally he cast his gaze to the space above the mantel, where the oil portrait of Edwina's late father, E.R. Crusoe, hung in an ornate gilt frame.

Calmly the cat assessed E.R.'s expression, which remained uncompromising, and his posture, which remained unbending. In his day, E.R. Crusoe had counseled presidents, potentates, and prime ministers, as well as what he called tradespeople: steel magnates and oil barons, for example. All had found his comments useful, and had been willing, even eager, to pay him for them.

For his own part, E.R. had charged what he was worth, a tactic that had amassed for him most of the the best parts of Litchfield County along with enough cannily chosen stocks, bonds, and other financial instruments to make wealthy women of a dozen daughters. He had fathered, however, only one.

I don't *need* this money, Edwina thought. Besides, the story of the vengeful ghost was far too outrageous to be taken seriously, as was Theresa Whitlock's determination to confess to murder. The whole affair, in fact, promised generous portions of vexation, frustration, and exasperation, all of which Edwina decided to avoid by turning down the job.

She would give the check back, firmly and allowing no argument, when Theresa returned. Meanwhile, she supposed she had better be careful with the thing. Opening a drawer, she slipped the check into an envelope and tucked the envelope into a metal box; this she carried to the office suite's kitchenette, which in addition to the usual appliances had been furnished with a wall safe disguised as a trash chute.

Grimacing as always at this—someday she would lock a bit of trash into the wall safe, while absently tossing something valuable down the real chute—she had just finished turning the hidden dial of the combination lock when a loud rapping sounded at her office door. The rapping was urgently accompanied by the voice of Walter, the office building's elderly custodian.

"Miss Crusoe?" he called. "You'd better come out. There's a woman in your vestibule, and she's dead."

*   *   *

"Whoever shot her must have fired just as the door slammed," Edwina told Martin McIntyre several hours later. "She was dead a few moments after I last saw her. Otherwise, I'd have heard it; the vestibule is like a little echo chamber, and even a silenced weapon isn't completely silent, you know."

McIntyre, a tall, hawk-faced man with thinning dark hair and a habitually intelligent expression, nodded grimly. "What about the other way around? Can someone in the vestibule overhear what you're saying in here?"

They sat at the desk where Edwina had interviewed Theresa Whitlock. Now Theresa lay dead a few blocks away in the morgue at Chelsea Memorial Hospital, one shot from an unrecovered and as yet unidentified small-caliber weapon having been fired at nearly point-blank range into her forehead, killing her immediately.

"No," Edwina replied, "they can't. I checked that before I leased the place. Besides, nothing she said was worth killing for. None of it even made sense. Murder, revenge, and walking dead men coming to get her if she didn't confess to murdering a fellow named Thomas Riordan."

McIntyre looked thoughtful. "She say how she did it?"

"No, why?" She sipped the seltzer water he had brought her. As a homicide inspector, McIntyre dealt with violently dead persons almost every day; Edwina's line ran more toward the sort of live person who claimed to be able to cure things with vitamin injections, and who not only could not cure the things but did not even inject real vitamins. It was awfully good of him, she thought, to realize that she might feel upset—but then, McIntyre was awfully good.

He was also, at the moment, awfully skeptical. "Because *if* she did it," he said, "I'd like to know how she managed it. Tom Riordan's Mercedes was blown up six months ago by a bomb, and not just any bomb. This was the kind of a bomb takes a genius to make and a madman to dare planting it. Tricky, sophisticated, and volatile. And there's another thing."

"What's that?" Edwina asked distractedly, wondering what she could possibly have done differently for Theresa Whitlock. You could have believed her, for starters, said a voice in her head. Which was ridiculous, of course; Theresa's whole story was unbelievable. No one could blame Edwina for failing to take it seriously. And besides . . .

Of course, the voice in her head mocked, and besides.

"Riordan didn't die in the explosion," McIntyre said. "And with the kind of cash he took off with, we won't find him unless we get awfully lucky."

Edwina sat up straight. "How do you know that?"

"Dental records. Whoever was in his car when it blew up had nice teeth, but they weren't Riordan's teeth. Riordan's dental X rays and dental-work charts didn't match up with the remains. Score one for us: We managed to keep it quiet, so Riordan doesn't know he's a wanted man. Wanted," McIntyre added, "for murder."

"He set it up to look as if he'd died," Edwina mused aloud, "but to do it, of course, there had to be a body."

"Correct," said McIntyre. "He even made sure a lot of money got burned in the fire after the explosion, to make it look more believable. After all, who'd destroy a hundred and fifty grand on purpose? We think he figured the fire would be hotter, to get rid of the teeth so no one could tell it wasn't him."

"A hundred and fifty thousand, just for window dressing? He must have wanted to disappear very badly."

McIntyre nodded. "And if he didn't then, he sure does now. Riordan ever shows his face again, he'll wish he had been in that car. New York will get him for the homicide, and when they're done the tax people will be after him, and that's not counting all the other fishy stuff he was into. Tom Riordan had a jewelry store here in town, with a lot of big cash sales that never quite made it onto the books."

"So that's what he's living on, and why he had enough cash to leave plenty in the car."

"You've got it. If it hadn't been for those dental records, even I might think Riordan died in the bombing. As for who did, I'd say he paid some street bum ten bucks to drive his car around the block, except the teeth were in such good shape. Not your usual bum's teeth. But they never did identify the victim. No fingerprints to run, of course. Hell, there weren't even any fingers."

"Tell me about the bomb," she said. "You think Riordan had to hire someone to make it and put it in his car?"

"Absolutely. That was no amateur's device. New York had a good suspect for the bomb guy, figured they could nail him, maybe get him to tell us where Riordan went. Little punk named Ricky Zimmerman, only guy on the East Coast with the specific know-how, or so we thought at the time. But it didn't pan out."

"Why?" Edwina asked. In her mind's eye, she saw Theresa Whitlock's face looking relieved, even hopeful, perhaps for the first time in a very long time. *I know I'll be all right now,* Theresa had said. The memory made Edwina wince.

McIntyre laughed without humor. "Because when Riordan's car was blowing up, Ricky Z. was busy getting killed himself. Some other punk even littler than Ricky Z. got caught the next day in *Ricky's* car, doing ninety on the turnpike. State fellows look in the rear, there's Ricky folded up nice and neat where the spare's supposed to go, cute little bullet hole in his head."

He sighed. "And the kind of device it was, the bomber had to be there to trigger the ignition on the thing. So that ruled out Ricky."

"I see," Edwina said. "How thought-provoking. A woman says she's afraid she'll be murdered by a dead man. Moments later she *is* murdered, and now we find the dead man has a story of his own—that in fact, he may not *be* dead. Her handbag was intact?"

"A thousand dollars in it," McIntyre agreed. "No robbery." He wasn't investigating Theresa's death, for he no longer worked ordinary homicides; he headed a team that investigated serial crimes. Still, when he had arrived at Edwina's office, McIntyre's colleagues had, of course, answered all his questions.

"And if her death was to keep her from telling me something, it would have made a good deal more sense to kill her before she came in, not as she was on her way out afterwards," Edwina said. "Assuming, of course, that anyone knew she meant to talk to me at all."

Consideringly, she sipped seltzer water. "Now of the three people connected with Riordan's supposed murder—including Theresa, since she claimed so passionately to have done it, *and* Ricky Z., since last time I looked a medical examiner's time-of-death estimate was precisely that, an estimate—only Riordan himself remains alive. And that, I must say, I find curious."

McIntyre turned to gaze out the big office window, beyond

which the late-autumn afternoon was darkening to evening. "Your territory's been invaded, you're mad as hell about it, and you're looking for a good reason to do something about it. That about the size of things?" he asked.

"That's exactly the size of things, except that I've already got a good reason. I take exception to clients being murdered in my office." Angrily, she rummaged in a drawer for Maxie's leash and harness.

"Look, Edwina," said McIntyre, "there's nothing you could have done, and the department'll be working it up, you know that. Somebody might get lucky on it pretty quick." But he knew better than to try sounding convinced; an unseen assailant had committed an unwitnessed murder and made a fast, clean getaway—and this augured poorly for an imminent arrest.

"Well," she said, "thanks for trying to make me feel better, anyway. Come on, cat, Snoop Central is closing for today."

McIntyre got up, immaculate as usual in his gray suit, white shirt, striped tie, and oxblood wing tips. He smelled of Old Spice, lime soap, and cold fresh air; handing him the red leather leash and harness, she stepped past him to close the curtains and twist the knobs on the big silvered radiators to *off*—for if she did not, the building manager's idea of proper heat delivery would turn the office suite by morning into a set of chambers suitable only for the breeding and rearing of certain delicate reptile species.

Performing these automatic tasks, however, took little thought, so most of Edwina's brain remained engaged with the topic of Theresa Whitlock's checkbook deposits: nice round numbers totaling fifty thousand dollars, all in the previous week. It was as if Theresa had been preparing to engage expensive help, only she had not gotten help, had she?

Bitterly Edwina turned from the question, knowing it would return to haunt her; I didn't even tell her to be careful, she thought.

"Martin, do you think that check will be all right in the safe? It's only for tonight."

But McIntyre had turned his attention to the waiting Maxie, holding the harness as the black cat stepped into it. "You know, fella," he said, "you're a better citizen than lots of the people I meet all day. Hang on, and we'll clip your leash on, here."

At the snick of the clip snapping shut, the cat sat at attention. "Stay, boy," said McIntyre, letting the leash fall to the floor. Yawning elaborately, Maxie began washing his face while McIntyre walked away from him. When McIntyre reached into his pocket the cat's ears pricked up, but otherwise the animal made no move.

"Come, Maxie," said McIntyre from the kitchenette, where Edwina now stood frowning at the wall safe. Moments later the faint rattle of the leash heralded Maxie's arrival.

"Good boy," said McIntyre, feeding Maxie a liver treat. "In another month or so, we'll have you fetching the newspaper."

"Keep up that way," said Edwina, "and in a month you'll have him *reading* the newspaper. Martin, what *do* you think about this check? I'll be returning it to Theresa Whitlock's bank tomorrow, but I'd hate to have anything happen to it before then, and there have been a few break-ins in the building."

"It's too late for the safety deposit box," McIntyre said, giving Maxie's leash a gentle twitch. In response, the cat stood and waited. "But we could take it downtown, lock it in the safe in the evidence room, if you think that would make you feel any better."

"Well, maybe," she said doubtfully. "Fifty thousand dollars is a lot of money, though. I'm not sure I want Theresa's check out of my sight. I think we should just—"

"Dear God," said a man's voice from behind them. "Where did Theresa even *get* fifty thousand dollars? And why did she give it to you?"

The man in the foyer clasped his pale hands together. He was

21

in his early forties, wearing a fawn-colored corduroy jacket with sewn-on leather elbow patches, a beige turtleneck sweater, and a pair of dark brown, neatly pressed slacks. His shoes were thick-soled tan Hush Puppies, and on the little finger of his left hand he wore a gold signet ring with an enormous square-cut zircon set into it.

At least, Edwina *thought* it was a zircon; no one wore diamonds that size in public anymore except members of royal families, and even then only upon state ceremonial occasions.

"The door was open. They—they told me it happened here," the man uttered brokenly. "I have an office in this building, on the first floor. But I don't understand. What was Theresa doing here? How could this have happened? Who *are* you, anyway?"

"Perhaps you'd better sit down," said Edwina. Before you fall down, she thought but did not add. Stepping forward, she extended her hand, but he shrank back from it.

"You," he whispered, "must have done something to her."

"I'm Lieutenant McIntyre, New Haven Police," Martin cut in. "I'm very sorry about your wife. She *was* your wife, I gather?"

"Y-yes." The man looked from Edwina to McIntyre and back again. "I'm Perry Whitlock. You're the police? Are you here to arrest this person?" He ran a trembling hand through his black, curly hair. "I've just come from identifying . . . identifying—"

McIntyre guided Perry Whitlock to one of the big red leather armchairs by the fireplace. "This is my wife, Edwina Crusoe," he said, "and she isn't a suspect. Mrs. Whitlock was here in the office, consulting with Ms. Crusoe, before she was attacked."

Whitlock looked uncomprehending. "Consulting? But I don't understand. What kind of consulting? Are you a psychiatrist?"

"Did your wife need a psychiatrist?" McIntyre asked.

"No! No, of course she didn't, I just thought—well, she'd been distracted. She seemed a little worried, although she wouldn't say what about. But she didn't need treatment. What *was* she doing here?"

Whitlock got up and began pacing around the room, picking up objects and peering at them as if mystified by them, then putting them down again. He seized a cut-crystal paperweight, turning it this way and that in his shaking hands.

"I'm a private consultant to people who want information," Edwina told him. "Information on crimes, or on possible crimes, that involve medicine or health care. Bogus cancer cures, fake healing rituals, false professional credentials—that sort of thing. I have no idea how your wife chose me, and I wish I had asked her. There are a number of things I wish I had asked her, in fact. But she came to me because she was afraid."

Whitlock stared. "Afraid . . . of what?"

"Mrs. Whitlock told me she was afraid that someone would try to murder her."

Perry Whitlock looked at the paperweight in his hands, and replaced it carefully on the shelf. As he did so, Edwina saw his sudden pallor, the huge beads of sweat breaking out on his ashen forehead.

"I'm sorry," he began, "but I think I'm going to—"

"Martin, catch him quick," said Edwina, "he's fainted."

*　　*　　*

"This is kind of you," said Perry Whitlock from the maple rocker in Edwina's kitchen. After a hasty conference and over Whitlock's not-too-convincingly voiced objections, she and McIntyre had brought him home with them once he recovered from his faint. Because Edwina was a nurse, abandoning him could have exposed her to a lawsuit; the courts took a dim view of failure to help on the part of even ex-members of helping professions. Besides, while taking care of Whitlock couldn't bring his wife back, it was the next best salve for Edwina's conscience.

I ought, she thought again, to have believed her. I never should have let her walk out of that office without—

But here the voice of her conscience fell unhelpfully silent. Certainly she ought to have done *something* differently. If she had, Theresa might be alive. Only the specific nature of the something eluded her, as she began preparing dinner.

"But I really must be going," Perry Whitlock went on. "I've imposed on you nice people too much already. Thank you for all your help, and I'm awfully sorry I was rude at first, but . . . well. You understand, I'm sure." His voice broke. "You two have a lovely place here," he managed, "and I wish you all the best."

Rising, he scrubbed tears from his eyes with clenched fists. The gesture reminded Edwina of a woebegone child; a fresh wave of sympathy made her urge him back into the chair—sympathy and, she had to admit, something else: He was, after all, the husband.

"Perry, bringing you here was just common sense. Of course we couldn't let you stagger around alone; you might have fainted again, on the street. And since we didn't want to stay there in the office . . . Anyway, you shouldn't go back to an empty house. Are you sure there's no one you'd like to call?"

He shook his head distraughtly. "No. Theresa's parents passed away quite some time ago. She's an only child, like me. And my parents aren't well. I'll tell them, of course, but not just yet. As for friends, I'm not a social creature, I'm afraid. She was more out-going—Theresa was, I mean. She enjoyed seeing people. I wish now I'd gone out more with her. She'd have liked that."

His face crumpled again. "There's no one I want to have see me like this. Oh, God, I'm so sorry to do this to you."

At this, Edwina felt a pang of shame for her suspicion; the man was clearly devastated. "Perry, you are not doing anything to us, and you're staying for dinner. No, don't argue, just wash your hands and help me."

Whitlock looked up gratefully. "Yes, I'd like to help. I meant it about the house. Old, I'd say, isn't it? But it looks so . . ."

"So thoroughly and expensively remodeled," Edwina supplied crisply, "rebuilt from rooftop to cellar floor, and everywhere in between." She set out peppers, radishes, and a cucumber on the kitchen's butcher-block center island. "Here, Perry, you can put together the salad."

From the braided rug on the wood stove's hearth, Maxie uttered a reminder that his supper was due; when no supper was forthcoming he stalked off in search of McIntyre, whose pockets at least were sure to be full of little treats. Edwina watched his progress across the wide boards of the varnished pine-plank floor, wishing intensely that she had stuck to her guns on the matter of house redecoration.

In sketches, the decorator's plans had looked perfectly lovely— lovelier to look at than to live in, as it had turned out. The planks were cold in winter and clammy in summer; the woodstove reluctantly devoured expensive cords of hardwood but gave off little heat. The kitchen curtains were gingham and the walls handstenciled; the doors, equipped with historically correct latches, had a habit of swinging open when you wanted them closed and sticking closed when you tried opening them. The whole place was just too quaint for words, and Edwina thought that if even one more person told her how cozy it all was, she might begin shrieking.

Whitlock dealt handily with the cucumber, washing it and scoring it decoratively lengthwise before peeling and slicing it into pale, paper-thin rounds. Having something to do seemed to cheer him immensely, and he worked with confidence.

"You're good at that," she observed when he had carved the radishes into roses, torn the lettuce, and diced the peppers into bite-sized bits.

Whitlock smiled shyly. "Hobby of mine. I do—did—all the

cooking at home. This is a great kitchen, by the way. Wood is fun for atmosphere but it's the devil to cook on."

He gestured at the gas range hulking against one wall. An enormous old institutional model, it had been brought from the summer kitchen of the Crusoe family estate in Litchfield, and installed at Edwina's insistence, over the decorator's protests. Now its massive functional ugliness made it resemble the goblin in a fairy tale, an appearance Edwina found—in a houseful of museum-quality restoration and antique chic—both perversely comforting and childishly satisfying.

"Theresa said you had a workshop," Edwina remarked. "Is it a woodworking shop? Is that another of your talents?"

"Oh, I wouldn't call it a talent," he responded modestly. "I like making little things, out of metal, mostly. I made this ring, actually." He held up his left hand. "You see, I have a man who does the yard work, repairs, that sort of chore—we live out on Ridge Road, and in that neighborhood of course you have to keep things looking shipshape—and we have a daily housekeeper, so there's not much actual maintenance to keep me busy. Right now I'm working on a model of a famous sailboat, the *Galatea*. She'll be a beauty when she's done."

His face lit with pleasure for a moment at the thought of his project, then fell into somber gloom again; his shoulders slumped. The silence lengthened awkwardly as Edwina searched for some further topic upon which to engage him, but before she could find one he straightened to tackle the conversational gap manfully himself.

"So how did you happen to buy this old place?" he asked, as with a sharp paring knife he went to work on the cherry tomatoes. "Was it your dream house? Rural charms, and all that?"

"Not exactly," Edwina said with considerable understatement. "We'd decided to try living in the country, having a garden and

26

so on. And we liked this place the minute we saw it, even though it was a bit ramshackle."

Rather, McIntyre had liked it, and Maxie had adored it, bounding up the front steps at once and trotting ahead of them to explore the dilapidated rooms. Faced with their enthusiasm she had given in, allowing that perhaps in time she could learn to be happy here.

But she had not, although her husband and the black cat had settled in at once. Now the two males were out romping in the backyard, two inches of new snow being in McIntyre's opinion no obstacle to Maxie's obedience training. By spring he hoped to have taught the cat to catch a Frisbee.

Edwina wished that Maxie would learn to catch mice, with which the house still abounded, and wished even more for a dwelling with an elevator, a doorman, a balcony, and a taxi stand out front. Sighing, she finished assembling the marinade for the chicken, telling herself once again how fortunate she was and summoning up mental images of homeless people in order to convince herself.

"You don't care much for the place, do you?" Whitlock said. Opening the refrigerator, he selected six scallions, nipped their ends off, and began snipping them. "Don't answer," he added, "that was impolite of me. I guess a new house must take a little getting used to, though. Look at it this way, if you don't like it after a year you can always tear everything out and paint the whole place white."

She smiled. "You're perceptive. No, I don't like it much. I'm a city girl, or was one—I can't sleep without a few sirens in the street, and when something breaks all I want to do is call the super, not page through a book about home repairs, trying to figure out how to fix it. And around here, if you call a repairperson, you get a fellow with a cigar wedged in his mouth and a John Deere cap stuck on his head, who thinks loading a few tools into a van entitles him to charge the earth without bothering to do the job right. And heavens, what a spoiled witch I do sound. I apologize for it, Perry." Frowning, she whisked the marinade energetically.

But Whitlock only nodded in sympathy. "I like the country, myself. But it's not for everyone. What does your husband say?" He gave the salad a final toss, located as if by mental telepathy the drawer containing plastic wrap, and placed the covered salad bowl into the refrigerator.

You, Edwina thought, are rather skilled at getting people to talk about themselves, aren't you? "To tell you the truth," she said, "I haven't mentioned it to him. I know he's happy here and I hate to trouble him about it. But we'll see when summer comes; after all, I did promise to give it time. White's a good idea, though; maybe I'll try replacing all the gingham with unbleached cotton. Much more restful on the eyes."

As she spoke, Edwina covered chicken breasts with marinade: white wine, lime juice, capers, olive oil, and white pepper. To the mixture she added the secret ingredients: one tablespoon of plum jam, and one of crème de cassis. Gently, she turned the chicken pieces in the marinade, careful not to dissolve the fruit jam entirely. "I gather Theresa didn't much care for cooking? That is, if you don't mind my asking about her."

"Oh, no, I want to talk about her. I feel as if I'll never stop thinking about her. It's just that we were an odd couple."

Whitlock spread his hands in an I-can't-help-it gesture. "I mean, Theresa was young, full of life, and I really am the quiet type. And with the age difference—I'm forty-three, she was twenty-five—I was afraid, at first, that she might get tired of me."

"But she didn't get tired of you."

"No. She didn't. She said I was . . ." Whitlock broke down and wept unashamedly, burying his face in his hands.

"Excuse me," he said when he had finished, "but I just can't believe she's gone. We'd only been married three years, but you

saw her, you remember how beautiful she was. I wonder, do you—
Could I possibly have a drink?"

"Over there, in the cabinet under the dry sink. Ice in the freezer,
and the glasses are up there behind that door. Watch it, the cabinet
door sticks, and fix one for me, too, will you, please?" Edwina
measured water into a pan and a mixture of wild and brown rice
into a cup, and set the kitchen timer.

"The money your wife gave me—I'll be giving it back, of
course," she said when she and Whitlock were seated with their
drinks. Outside it was full dark; through the parted gingham she
could see fat snowflakes drifting lazily down through the reflected
glow of the yard lights.

November, she mused, wondering what the driveway would be
like in January. Already McIntyre was making hopeful noises on
the topic of buying a four-wheel-drive vehicle, than which Edwina
would rather just get a matched pair of draft horses and let them
tow her beloved little Fiat sports car about.

"But you really don't know where it came from?" she went on.
"She didn't, for instance, have money of her own somewhere?"

"She had all she needed," Whitlock replied, "and her own bank
account. But she didn't have her own money, not the way you
mean it. She worked for me for a while, but it was hard on my other
staff, my wife being in the office. It caused too much resentment.
And I didn't want her working for just anyone. She was . . . well,
don't get me wrong, but in some ways you had to make allow-
ances for Theresa. She just wasn't the nine-to-five type."

He sipped his scotch and water. "I never stinted her on a thing,
though. Clothes, travel, anything for the house, you name it. If
Theresa wanted it, she got it, no questions asked. But I didn't give
her fifty thousand dollars, and if she did have that much money I
have absolutely no idea where it might have come from. In a way,
it's almost more shocking to me than her death."

He shook his head in pained puzzlement. "Finding out a thing like that—it's as if there must be a whole part of her that I didn't know, that I never suspected or was let in on. It makes me wonder what other secrets she was keeping."

From the back of the house came the sounds of a door opening and the rattle of Maxie's leash. Then came the repeated slamming of the door, followed by muttered oaths from McIntyre, until the door finally consented to close. At last, the two appeared in the kitchen entry, McIntyre looking about happily for a drink and Maxie clamoring for his kibble.

"And," said Whitlock, "there must be a connection between the money and her death, don't you think? Two strange things—I can't believe they're not related, somehow."

"That," said Edwina, "may be jumping to conclusions. Your wife wouldn't be the first woman in the world with money no one else knew about. It isn't common, but it's not unheard-of—and it doesn't mean your wife didn't love and trust you, or that the money wasn't legitimate: an inheritance, perhaps. It just means she wanted something of her own, something she didn't *have* to confide in anyone. You can understand that, Perry, can't you?"

"I suppose," he conceded grudgingly while McIntyre, having dealt with the cat's needs, clinked ice into a glass. But Perry did not look at all convinced; in fact, he looked thunderous, and Edwina thought it might be a good time to change the subject.

"You know," she said, getting up to arrange some crackers and a wedge of ripened Brie on a plate, "I don't think you've told us what it is you do." People's occupations were a nice safe topic, allowing one to ask them plenty of questions without too much fear of stepping on a conversational land mine.

Besides, Whitlock was clearly well fixed financially, with servants, a house in a wealthy neighborhood, and to judge by the size of that pinky ring, enough cash to pursue expensive hobbies; gold was pricey enough, but the zircon was a beautiful stone and its cost must have been extravagant. She couldn't help wondering where the money came from.

"Yes," said McIntyre, seating himself at the table with them; across the room, Maxie crunched his kibble while aiming yearning little glances at the wedge of Brie. "I'd guess you're a college professor, or maybe a scientist," McIntyre went on. "Am I close?"

"I'm afraid not," Whitlock said, relaxing a bit, "although I don't mind your thinking I look like either one. Research and teaching are my second and third choices, actually, and I might still get a chance to do both someday.

"But at the moment," he finished, draining his glass and rising to mix another one, "I keep pretty busy being a dentist."

"Good Lord," said McIntyre abruptly, "I forgot, there's a call I have to make. Excuse me, you two, will you?"

"Prutt," said Maxie, which translated to mean that he was suffering from a cheese deficiency, and if he were not given some right now, he could not be responsible for the consequences.

". . . dentist," echoed Edwina faintly. Ordinarily, Maxie was not allowed Brie; the sort of low-ash, high-vitamin cat food he ate was quite expensive enough without adding any imported human luxuries to his diet. But to cover her surprise she busied herself by indulging him in a chunk of it, turning her back on Whitlock as she did so.

"You know," she managed when she turned again, "I always have been fascinated by dentistry. The technical aspects, I mean— forensics, especially. How people are identified by their teeth, and so on. Do you happen to know anything about that?" She watched him carefully for his reaction.

Whitlock preened, showing no sign of discomfort. "Well, I don't do that sort of thing myself, of course. I'm a family dentist, not a forensics expert. But I know the basics. When I was in training I studied it, and I like to think I learned."

"Really," Edwina marveled. "You know, in my line of work it

would be useful to know more about that. Just in case I ever needed to."

In her face, she hoped, was no hint of the fact that had sprung to her mind at Whitlock's revelation. It was the same fact, she was sure, that had propelled McIntyre immediately from the room so that she could be alone with the grieving widower:

Whoever had died in Thomas Riordan's car six months ago had been identifiable only by dental records.

"And it's not an easy thing to learn," Edwina went on, as persuasively as she could. "All those technical terms and such specialized knowledge."

Whitlock shrugged self-deprecatingly. "I could give you the outline in twenty minutes. As I said, I enjoy a bit of teaching, but you're sure you won't be bored? The nuts and bolts of it are rather dry. Cusps and fissures and surfaces, all of that."

Seating herself once more at the table, Edwina fixed upon Whitlock her most charming smile: the one, as she had been told by McIntyre, that could winkle the pearl from an oyster without opening its shell.

"Do," she invited, "tell me about it."

THREE

Arthur Feinstein approached dentistry with the delicacy of a jeweler and the energy of a stevedore, combined with a nearly maniacal perfectionism. When Edwina entered Arthur's treatment room the morning after the dinner with Perry Whitlock, she found Arthur peering through a Zeiss binocular magnifying-lens headset at a newly crafted gold onlay.

The onlay was fitted upon the third molar of a plaster mold of a half set of human teeth. Under Arthur's high-intensity work lamp, the gold winked prettily against the dull pink plaster. But the onlay was not a perfect fit, to judge by the frown lines in the flesh above Arthur's headset strap. To him, there were just two ways in which any dental onlay *could* fit: flawlessly and unacceptably. Anything besides perfection, he believed, was plain laziness.

"Can't have it," Arthur muttered. "Look at that little gap. Couple years, I'll be in there with excavating equipment." He removed the lenses, which resembled the protuberant eyes of some science-fiction insect, and scribbled impatiently on a notepad.

"What's the matter, Arthur," Edwina asked, "is the world not living up to your high standards again?" She seated herself in the treatment chair and smiled at him; sitting in a dental chair without having to have any immediate dental work done was, for Edwina, one of life's sweeter pleasures.

"Let's just say there are times I'd like to take a drill to a few things besides people's teeth," he replied. "No standards for the detail work anymore, you know that? Now I've got to call this patient in again, shoot her full of novocaine, and take another whole set of impressions. Boy, she's going to hate me."

"Doesn't like the novocaine?" Edwina asked sympathetically.

Arthur shook his head, sealing the rejected onlay and the note into a padded envelope. "Nah, the shots don't bother her too much. Took me a year, but I got her over that part of it." He slapped a mailing label on the envelope and tossed it in his out box.

"It's the goo we make the impressions with that half kills her," he went on. "This woman's got a gag reflex on her, you look at her cross-eyed and she's ready to toss her cookies. So I yank the temporary, stick a big glob of warm wax in there, the appliance alone is halfway down her throat, you can imagine how well that goes over. By the time the six minutes are up and the impressions are set, I'm about peeling her off the ceiling."

He punched the intercom. "Stella? Do me a favor, call Mrs. Anspach and tell her I need her back in for forty minutes. Oh, and get out that old Ouija board my kids used to have around here, and if you can't find it go out and buy one. Suzy's big on weird supernatural stuff."

He switched the intercom off and grinned. "Maybe I can get the spirit world to convince Suzy not to gag," he said. "But what's up, Edwina? Don't tell me you're finally ready to get rid of those wisdom teeth, come in for a little pre-op consultation." At the prospect, Arthur rubbed his pink hands gleefully together.

"No, but I might want a turn at that Ouija board," she told him.

Swiftly, she related the story of Theresa Whitlock's death, the teeth that could not be matched to dental records, and the coincidence—if it was one—of Perry Whitlock's occupation.

"Interesting," said Arthur. "Very interesting. Seeing as you're already in the chair, let me have a look at that amalgam on seven, why don't you? That's the one to the right of your right front tooth. Last time I saw it, seems to me it was iffy."

"Wait a minute, Arthur, I didn't come here to—"

"Open wide," said Arthur, whose powers of persuasion were considerable, especially when his rounded shape was viewed from a rapidly lowering dental chair. "Mmm-hmm." He tapped the tooth with an instrument. "Is that sensitive at all?"

"Ng-ngh." Edwina wiggled her fingers impatiently to let him know that, although she could not speak, she wished for heaven's sake that he would. *"Ahr-hur . . ."*

"Right. Perry Whitlock." Producing a shiny metal tool that looked irresistibly like a nut pick, Arthur began investigating the suspect tooth. "You know, this amalgam needs replacing, and I just had a forty-five-minute cancellation."

As he spoke he removed his fingers from her mouth, which she thought was really quite an astute move on his part since she had been about to bite them off.

"You just don't want to lose the fee," she said crossly. "You hate it when the office meter's not running, don't you?"

"A penny earned is a penny earned," Arthur agreed, his good cheer as always imperturbable. Slipping on a pair of thin latex gloves, he elbowed the intercom button. "Stella, can I have a three-surface amalgam tray in here, please? And pull Edwina's chart for me. Bring that in, too."

Looming over Edwina, he eyed her tooth with the look of a man intent upon eradicating, at once and permanently, one small bit of imperfection from the universe.

"But," he went on, "as it happens, I know quite a lot about dental identifications, *and* I know Perry Whitlock. So how about I don't eat this forty-five-minute cancellation, and instead of whistling while I work, I talk to you instead?"

"Fine," Edwina said, or would have if Arthur had not already gotten down to business, producing a syringe with a needle approximately the size of a railroad spike. Of course, the needle was not as big as it looked; sitting in a dentist's treatment chair, Edwina had noticed, had the effect of making all invasive instruments seem thirty times their actual size.

"All right, now," Arthur said calmly as he wielded the glittering object. For an instant Edwina remembered the horrible dentist of her childhood: no explanations, no painkiller, and no sympathy. His name and face remained engraved on her heart. Dr. Schultz had had a nasty habit of letting his bifocals go unwiped between patients, so that his eyes, looming hugely into hers, were magnified by lenses speckled with tiny drops of dried blood.

Sighing, she felt her adrenal glands kick in, speeding her heart rate and heightening her senses at a moment when she would most have wished them lowered. At the same time she hoped that Dr. Schultz—who must by now have been dead for at least twenty years—had gotten the eternal reward he so richly deserved, and preferably one with lots of brimstone.

Then Arthur was standing by the chair again: large, jovial, filled with confidence—so much of it, apparently, that he had plenty to share—and the needle shrank to stinger size once more.

"Just a pinch," he said. "Count three and it's done."

And as always, when Arthur said it, it was.

*   *   *

"Okay, the first thing to know," Arthur began a few minutes later, when Edwina's upper jaw felt numb and at least as large as a cantaloupe, "is that a normal adult human being has thirty-two teeth, and each tooth has five surfaces. Each surface has a characteristic pattern of fissures and grooves, almost like a person's finger-prints. So from just one tooth you can identify a person, if you have something to compare it with. Turn toward me."

Obediently, Edwina turned. A bit of unscheduled dental work, she reflected, was a small price to pay for one of Arthur's lectures; his fascination with every aspect of his subject made him a fine talker. Meanwhile, her interest in all that he was saying provided an excellent distraction from what he was doing.

"Huh, will you look at that." Arthur peered into her mouth. "Boy, you got in here just in time, you know it?" Squinting, he did something unspeakable—and, due to the effect of novocaine, also fortunately unfeelable—with a tiny pair of forceps.

"Ngha?" asked Edwina, whose mouth at the moment seemed ten times too crowded with cotton wads, a suction tip, a cheek retractor, and a dental drill: a high-speed, state-of-the-art dental drill whose strategically directed cooling spray of water, apparently, the suction tip was not quite adequate to control.

"Well," said Arthur, "another few months and I'd say you'd have been a candidate for major endodontal surgery. But don't worry, I think it's okay. Now, open wide again for a minute."

"Ngf-ngf?" Edwina opened wide again for a minute.

"Right," said Arthur, drilling with the enthusiasm of a man who has struck oil before and means most definitely to repeat the experience, "the next thing to know is that gold melts at sixteen hundred degrees Fahrenheit. After that, forget any idea of comparing dental reconstructions."

"Ngay-hunh?" The whine of the drill, Edwina thought, was the worst part; that, and the sneaking worry that somewhere down there in the hole Arthur was happily excavating lay a nerve that had escaped novocainization—a nerve, she feared tensely, that might make its presence evident at any instant now.

"Right," said Arthur, "cremation takes eighteen hundred to two thousand degrees Fahrenheit for one and a half to three hours. Which means—"

Blessedly, he lay aside the drill, began rinsing and drying the tooth.

"—*which* means unless there's some powerful accelerant and plenty of fuel over a long period of time, your average victim of your average domestic fire or garden-variety auto accident leaves a bunch of identifiable remains in the form of teeth, and bones, too, if there are any premortem X rays for comparison."

He painted the cavity whose filling he had just removed with something that smelled pungently of creosote, dried it with a jet of air, and stepped back to admire his handiwork.

"All right. Enough with the violent part; now for the part I really like. Let's fill that sucker back up and match it with your own pearly whites."

Behind her, a machine began blending the filling material with a sound like that of a tiny cement mixer. "So, if I'm the police and I have a tentative identification on a body," Edwina said, "I have the coroner or medical examiner take dental X rays of the remains."

"Right. Best way, you remove the jawbones, upper and lower, split them down the middle, and X-ray them from the side. Then you request records from the victim's dentist—X rays and dental charts, treatment notes, and impressions if there are any. Hold the pre- and post-mortem X rays side by side, compare the work with the dental charts—usually, it's pretty easy. It's especially easy if things *don't* match. Okay, open up again."

She opened up again, and he began packing amalgam into the tooth. The amalgam-packing instrument made, at each pass, a creaking sound much like that of a bone slowly being dislocated.

"So you can tell fairly easily who a victim *wasn't*—if there's no match—and if there is a match, you know who it was. But even if there is no match," Arthur went on, "you can tell a lot about a victim by the teeth. How old they were, what race, some of their habits like smoking a pipe or playing trumpet, even how much money they had. There, all done but the cosmetics."

"You said you know Perry Whitlock," she reminded him. Now that the tooth was refilled, Edwina felt pleased, dental treatment being a thing she would far rather remember from the past than contemplate for the future.

"Mmm." Arthur eyed the tooth judiciously, held up a color-matching chart, and began mixing pigment. "Decent fellow. Bit greedy. Four treatment rooms, he fills them up, runs from one to the next so the chairs never get cool. Not my style. Works for scale, though, on welfare and elderly patients, so that's a point in his favor. All right, let's make this look like a tooth."

Unable to speak while Arthur applied the white coloration in short, careful strokes, Edwina waggled her eyebrows questioningly at him.

"Whitlock takes," Arthur explained, "whatever the government sets as their reimbursement for work on indigent people, folks on welfare, all that. And what the government says the work is worth is barely what it costs to *do* the work, frequently. Lot of dentists, and doctors too, either won't take those patients or charge them something out of pocket on top of whatever Uncle Sam or the insurance company pays. Strictly speaking it's illegal to waive the extra, but doing it keeps a lot of people from having a toothache, is the bottom line. Okay, that's it. Good as new."

As the chair rose, Edwina felt the burst of optimism that always accompanied the end of a session of drilling, filling, or otherwise manipulating her teeth. Knowing this euphoria was purely the result of the endorphins and other brain-produced, natural antipain chemicals surging furiously in her bloodstream did not make the sensation at all less pleasurable.

"Do me a favor and stay away from peanut brittle for twenty-four hours or so," said Arthur, writing a note in her chart.

"Fine," replied Edwina, who would gladly have avoided peanut brittle for the rest of her life if it meant not having to have that filling replaced again, euphoria or no euphoria. "Anyway, the upshot is that dental ID is reliable? There wasn't likely to have been any mistake?"

"Not if people conform to the proper technique, which in a criminal matter I'm sure they did. Forensic odontology is a science these days. But you don't have to be a scientist to do the comparing part—here, I'll show you what I mean. Here are two sets of your own X rays." Arthur held the small squares of cardboard-mounted film up to the light.

"See?" he said. "There's the tooth I just filled, X-rayed six months ago. And there's the same tooth, three years ago. I don't think anyone could have any doubts about that."

"You're right. Even I can see they're the same. And that means Thomas Riordan probably *is* alive, which means he could have killed Theresa Whitlock. But if he is alive, then Theresa didn't murder him, so *why* would he— What's the matter, Arthur?"

"You didn't mention Riordan before," Arthur said. "That's who it was?" His tanned, rounded face—being no fool, Arthur vacationed frequently in Puerto Rico—was filled with the sort of interest he ordinarily reserved for a morning of root-canal work. "He's who they were trying to identify with the X rays?"

"Yes," she told him impatiently. "Why?" From the waiting room she heard a jangle of bracelets and the sound of Arthur's office nurse, making conversation with the next patient.

"Well," Arthur said, "gold is gold, whether it's in jewelry or in your mouth. And Tom Riordan was a jeweler, you know. Which means we knew some of the same people, even ran into one another here and there over the years. *And* the thing is, I happened to be passing Whitlock's office one day last year, when they were repairing Chapel Street. So I used to drive around past your building on my way to *my* office."

"Arthur, will you please get to the point? The novocaine is

wearing off now, and I don't want to be anywhere around you when this tooth starts to hurt."

"I'm getting there, and that tooth should *not* start to hurt, but if it does you are to call me immediately. There's only a prayer left between the filling and the nerve, so if you start having pain it means something, and I don't mean something good."

Having delivered this wondrous little bombshell, Arthur stripped off his latex gloves and began washing his hands. "Anyway, Perry's office has a door to the street, not just one from the building lobby, and as I was passing I saw Tom Riordan going in. The next week, same time, same place, I saw him going in again. And that, to me, suggests one thing: a series of appointments."

"Oh. But Arthur, that means—"

Arthur looked pleased as he sudsed himself to the elbows and scrubbed with boyish energy. "Yep," he said, "it means, unless I miss my guess, which I rarely do, you should excuse my saying so, that Riordan was a patient in Perry Whitlock's dental practice."

* * *

"Martin, don't you think that's rather odd? Perry told me all about dental IDs, and what he said matches perfectly with what Arthur said. But what he *didn't* say was, 'I had a patient whose dental records were examined for identification, just last year.' You'd think he'd mention something like that."

Twenty minutes after leaving Arthur Feinstein's treatment room, Edwina was in her own office, trying over the telephone to convince McIntyre that something was fishy. McIntyre, however, did not sound impressed.

"Look, Edwina, you don't tell stories about your clients, do you? Not to strangers, anyway. And Whitlock was upset. I don't think you can read anything into what he said or didn't say about that. He was down here giving a sworn statement this morning, by the way, the guy's still a bereaved-husband basket case."

41

In the background she heard the squad room: cops talking, typing, arguing, and mingling the most outrageously dirty jokes with the most outrageously grisly recent personal experiences. Police work, she had come to realize, was very much like being a hospital worker: See the worst, do your best, and in your off moments work at swallowing it all, like a python ingesting some enormous, unwieldy prey.

"And," McIntyre added, "he's got a nearly dead-bang alibi. He was in his office talking on the telephone when his wife died. His secretary could hear his voice through the closed door, see the light on the telephone console. Once she picked his line up by mistake and heard him directly, *and* from his private office there's no other door but the one she can see from her desk. So there's a few loose ends still to tie up, but down here, Edwina, they're pretty much ruling him out."

"Okay. Thanks for telling me." After this and an exchange on the subject of being extremely, ridiculously careful, with each of them promising to, Edwina replaced the telephone receiver and for a long moment sat staring at it. Then she opened the desk drawer, removed an aspirin bottle, and shook two tablets into her hand.

Arthur's insistence that the tooth should not hurt was, of course, nonsense; newly filled teeth were always sore when the novocaine wore off. Grimly Edwina carried the aspirins to the kitchen and swallowed them with a mouthful of tap water, wincing at the throb of pain as the cold liquid hit the fresh filling.

Meanwhile, what McIntyre had *not* said was how much he wished she would stick to her medical snooping and avoid the murder business. But she knew he did wish it; he had simply forbidden himself to talk about it, just as Edwina had forbidden herself to complain about the house.

"Look," she said to the silent telephone, "I'll poke around at this until another client walks in. The minute that happens, I'm off this thing. But at the moment there is no new client, and you can't expect me to sit here twiddling my thumbs. It simply isn't in my nature, Martin. Is it?"

Maxie, who had been asleep on the windowsill, raised his head irritably, as if to say that doing nothing certainly was in *his* nature, and could she please be quiet so that he could go on doing it? Leaping from the windowsill, he went off in search of a spot where a cat could get some peace and quiet, for heaven's sake.

Sighing, she crossed the room and placed her hands on the warm spot of windowsill Maxie had vacated. From the eighteenth-floor window she could see Long Island Sound, the rooftops and side streets of New Haven covered with fresh snow—the theory at City Hall being, apparently, that sooner or later the stuff was going to melt anyway, so why plow it?—and the buildings of Chelsea Memorial Hospital and Medical Center. Thoughtfully, she regarded the pale blue dome of the medical library, the Victorian pile of red brick that was the original Chelsea Hospital, and the steel and glass towers of the Howard Hughes Research Institute.

Over it all, snowflakes continued falling. Cars crept in the streets, and the only sound was the tinkle of steam moving in the office radiators. Frowning, she went back to the telephone and pushed buttons.

"I'd like to speak to Detective McIntyre, please. This is his— Oh, hi, Dick. He's just gone out? No, there's no message, I only wanted to ask him one more— Wait a minute, I'll bet you know the answer."

McIntyre's old partner, Dick Talbot, did know the answer, and was more than willing to tell it to Edwina. The punk who'd been arrested for speeding in Ricky Zimmerman's car on the turnpike six months earlier had been charged with murder. The defense attorney, one John D. Maxwell, had bargained the charge down very considerably, a task that turned out to be less than difficult considering the ghastly criminal record of Zimmerman himself, and the punk had been swiftly tried, convicted, and sentenced to serve no fewer than fifteen and no more than twenty-five years in the state penitentiary, where he remained at the moment.

"Which," Talbot said, "was no more'n he deserved, the fast-talkin', smart-aleck little bastard. Lied his face off, right up until the jury came back and told the judge that he was guilty. That shut him up for a while, that and the fifteen to twenty-five the judge smacked him with."

"So he denied it? He didn't say it was an accident, he just said flat out that he didn't kill Ricky Zimmerman?"

"Hell," Talbot growled, "he's driving the guy's car, swears up and down he didn't even know the body was in it. Meanwhile, he's got the weapon in his jacket pocket, got the nerve to try pulling it on the arresting officers. I don't know, Edwina. I don't know what's the matter with kids these days."

"Right," she sympathized. "I don't, either." As a matter of fact she *did* have a theory, but since testing it would involve the destruction of all the television sets in the world, she doubted it would ever be proven. Thanking Talbot for the information, she hung up.

Outside, the snow was falling faster, a dense, moving curtain of white beyond the office windows. No major weather had been forecast, which Edwina figured meant only a fifty–fifty chance that a paralyzing blizzard would blanket the East Coast by nightfall; these odds, however, were high enough to speed her decision about where she ought to go next.

The state penitentiary was eighty miles away, the morgue at Chelsea Memorial just eight blocks distant. Pulling on her coat and gloves, and ignoring the insistent beat of pain issuing from her tooth, Edwina set out for the medical center.

*   *   *

The first thing that struck her upon entering the hospital was how youthful almost everyone looked. Girls young enough to be her daughters were now old enough to be in nursing training, Edwina realized morosely and with only a little exaggeration, and the medical students, whom she'd thought were so intelligent and worldly when *she* was back in nursing training, now all appeared positively juvenile with their Adam's apples bobbing and their wrists jutting bonily from the too-short sleeves of their white medical jackets.

I don't belong here anymore, she thought as she signed the lobby guard's visitor book and offered her driver's license for identification. At one time, no guard would have dreamed of stopping her, much less of asking her to prove who she was; as nursing supervisor of Chelsea Memorial's evening shift, Edwina had been well known to everyone from the building custodians to the chief of medical staff. Only, she wasn't well known now.

Feeling blue, and with her plastic temporary ID card clipped to the lapel of her coat, she made her way to the lobby's rear stairwell, down a flight of yellow-painted concrete stairs, and into the hospital's basement. Here the smells of garbage from the open trash bay, frying fish from the main kitchen, sour mops from the housekeeping workroom, and sterilizing solution from the central supply department mingled in an aroma she found at once repulsive and nostalgic; over it all thrummed the workings of the enormous generators, concealed behind wall-sized metal panels that supplied heat and hot water for the medical center.

At the end of a long concrete corridor was the office of the pathology department; there was no one in the office, but she spotted a note on the desk. Scrawled in a handwriting she found delightfully familiar, the note entreated her to Ring Bell.

A small silver one had been provided for this; cheered, Edwina gave it an enthusiastic jingle and was rewarded in moments by Harry Lemon's masked, goggled face at the window of the door leading to the autopsy rooms. Nodding, he waggled five fingers; five minutes later, he fairly bounded through the door.

"Edwina! How wonderful. To what do I owe the honor? Sit down, let me look at you. It's been— Heavens, how long has it been?" Harry beamed.

"Too long, Harry," she told him, taking in his pink, plump face, thinning hair, and familiar chubby shape, clad as always in rumpled green surgical garb. "But what's all this about your moving to pathology? I thought you always said medicine was king of the specialties, that you'd never leave it again?"

"Indeed." Harry seated himself behind the desk, gestured her into the chair in front of it. "But when the king began to lord it over me, I decided a bit of fiefdom-rearranging was in order. The company of dead people is more restful, less ulcer-provoking, and in general eminently more rewarding than that of most live people I can think of. Yourself excepted, naturally."

"Naturally. And how long do you expect the company of the deceased to be rewarding? Since I'm sure it was your curiosity and not your antisocial personality that really motivated the switch."

She didn't bother mentioning the supposed ulcers; after two decades of hospital cafeteria food, Harry's stomach could have digested battery acid, probably right along with the battery it came in. He was now board certified in so many specialties that when he wrote for medical journals, it took half a column just to list all the initials and abbreviations he was entitled to.

"Oh, about two years," Harry said thoughtfully, and laughed. "After that I'm considering research for a while—epidemiology or virology, haven't decided which." He looked at her sharply. "Edwina, are you all right? Good Lord, you're white as a ghost."

"Fine," Edwina managed, feeling as if Arthur Feinstein's railroad spike had been driven, suddenly and without benefit of anesthetic, into the roof of her mouth. "I'm *fine*, Harry. I had a filling replaced this morning and it gave me a pang just now, is all."

She stood, removing her coat and steadying herself with an effort. "And I'm a bit overheated; it's warm in here with all this wool on." Venturing a smile at Harry, she sat down hastily again.

Rummaging in his bag, Harry produced a blood-pressure cuff. Advancing upon her, he brandished a thermometer. "You," he pronounced, "look absolutely ghastly, and I order you not to move a goddamned inch."

"Fine," Edwina repeated faintly. "Harry, do you suppose I could have a glass of water?" Surely she was not going to pass out in the morgue, she thought distractedly; that would be just too hideously funny.

Harry scowled at the thermometer, then fetched her a drink. "Temperature's normal. And so's your blood pressure. Did this dentist of yours prescribe anything for pain?"

"He didn't think I'd need anything." She omitted reporting the rest of what Arthur had said; if she did, Harry would send her right back to Arthur's office.

"Really, Harry, it's better already." She forced a smile; Harry looked unfooled. "And I didn't come here to complain about myself," she added. "I came to learn something. That is, I need to check with you to see if I'm remembering something correctly."

"A commendable motive," Harry replied with skepticism. "You are the worst liar I have ever met. I'm a doctor, for pity's sake, don't you think I can recognize real pain when I see it?"

In Edwina's experience, this ability was not common among members of Harry's profession—although, to be fair, she thought also that if the amount and severity of pain patients suffered were well and truly recognized by physicians, there would soon be no one left to care for the patients: The doctors would be too busy rending their garments, gnashing their teeth, and crying out to heaven in loud voices, protesting the injustice of it all.

From his bag, Harry withdrew a pad of controlled-substance prescription slips and wrote on one. "Here, get this filled, and if you keep on experiencing pain, do go back to the dentist."

Edwina blinked. The prescription was for a potent narcotic analgesic. "Harry, you're not supposed to have those slips."

"Correct," said Harry, looking unimpressed as he tucked the pad away again. "Now, what was it you wanted to know?"

*　　*　　*

Time of death, as Edwina had thought, was a difficult thing to estimate accurately. Witnessed deaths were an exception, but otherwise it was pretty much anybody's guess when the deceased had last drawn breath. But *educated* guesses could be made by taking several factors into account; these ranged, unfortunately, from the mildly disgusting to the positively revolting, and were not ones upon which normal persons ordinarily wanted to dwell at all.

Harry Lemon, however, had dwelt on them at length, and after that Edwina had run a number of additional investigative errands, with the result that it was much later than she wished when she finally headed out of town—or, rather, when she tried heading out of town.

Sighing, she peered through the windshield of the Fiat Spyder, past the flap-flapping of the wipers as they swatted away the falling snow. Applying the brakes very gently so as not to slide through the approaching intersection, she clasped her hands lightly around the steering wheel in order not to skid into oncoming traffic, or into a curb.

Meerowl, said Maxie unhappily from the floor of the little two-seater convertible, which he regarded as the perfect form of transport in summer when the top was down, but despised in winter with the windows up and the heater on. Hunkering forlornly in a mound of abject feline misery, he shot Edwina a look that translated perfectly to "Humans, pfui."

"Look, Max, if we don't do this now we'll be stuck in town tonight. If we hadn't stopped at the bank, the courthouse, *and* two branches of the public library we'd be home already, but now I'm not sure we're going to *get* home. So put a lid on it."

Cautiously, she pressed the accelerator; the tires spun and caught, and the car began moving forward. It was late afternoon, but the sky was already so dark that street lights along Whitney Avenue had come on; the side streets were closed entirely, and traffic crawled out of downtown as people tried to reach their own homes before nightfall, when even heavier snow was predicted.

"Blast," Edwina muttered as brake lights came on just ahead. A touch to the Fiat's brake pedal sent the car's rear end sliding, not that the brakes would have done much good; the street was so slick that what she was doing already more resembled skating than driving. Swallowing hard, she steered into the skid and felt the little car straighten grudgingly again as, up ahead, automobiles resumed inching forward.

"Livor mortis," she recited to Maxie, suppressing the urge to pull over and give up, "is a red coloration appearing in the dependent portions of a deceased body. It appears because blood pools on account of gravity."

Don't think, she told herself firmly. Just drive and keep talking; that'll keep you from spacing out. Stay alert and trust your reactions; you've gotten the Fiat through worse than this.

Maxie leaped into the bucket seat and tipped his head interestedly, seeming to feel that if she were going to tell him a story, he could certainly tolerate the ride better, and why hadn't she ever thought of that before?

"Fine," she said, shifting into second gear; since she was obviously not going to travel more than twenty miles per hour there was no sense lugging the engine. The car swiveled nastily as she let out the clutch pedal, then righted itself.

"Anyway, livor mortis appears a couple of hours after death and is fixed—that means it won't shift if you move the body—at eight to twelve hours. *Or* sooner if it's hot, *or* slower if it's cold. Which means livor mortis is useless for determining time of death. It is handy, though, for finding out if the body has been moved, because obviously if the livor mortis shows up on one side but the body's lying on the other, somebody tipped that body over, didn't they? Are you listening to me, Maxie?"

"Prutt," Maxie said contentedly, oblivious to the mortal danger he was in; Whitney Avenue had been bad enough, but now the little Fiat was battling its way up the ramp that led onto the Merritt Parkway. The parkway's design had been adequate when cars sped along it at the enormous rate of forty miles per hour; now such speeds were considered suitable only for the breakdown lane.

YIELD, commanded the yellow sign at the ramp's top; Edwina disregarded this, aiming the Fiat at a gap between two death traps disguised as automobiles: one a lumbering eight-cylinder sedan whose bald tires and shimmying suspension boded ill, the other a neat little VW Rabbit whose white-knuckled driver, an elderly man glimpsed briefly in Edwina's headlights, boded likewise.

By now it was full dark, and snowing so hard the windshield wipers could barely keep up. "Anyway," Edwina said brightly, ignoring the voice in her head that said she ought to have stayed in town after all, "next is rigor mortis, which is also pretty useless for determining the time of death, because it can appear instantaneously or after two to four hours, and can last six days, or disappear in twenty-four hours. After that is body temperature, which is obviously no help, because if it's hot the body stays warm longer, and if it's cold— Well, you get the idea."

Maxie made a sound in the back of his throat, as if to say that of course he got the idea, and by the way had she happened to fill the Fiat's gas tank, lately? Because *he* hadn't put any gas in, owing to the fact that he couldn't reach the filler pipe and wasn't allowed to carry money, anyway, and if *he* hadn't put in any gas and *she* hadn't put in any gas—

"Oh, blast," Edwina said, glancing at the fuel gauge, whose

needle hovered perilously near "E." "Well, I think we've got enough if only we don't get stuck anywhere."

At which moment, of course, and as if on signal, brake lights began flashing ahead. Soon the entire northbound side of the Merritt Parkway had come to a halt, while wreckers, squad cars, fire trucks, and ambulances crawled along the shoulder toward the accident up ahead. Switching on the radio, Edwina learned that the pileup had produced no fatalities, but that it was expected to take at least forty-five minutes to clear.

"Which," said Edwina, taking deep breaths and clenching her fists, as otherwise she would most surely have begun tearing her hair out, "brings us to the subject of decomposition."

Thirty minutes later, Maxie had heard about decomposition, chemical changes, gastric emptying, insect activity, and scene markers that contributed to the accuracy—or, more often, the inaccuracy—of a medical examiner's time-of-death estimate. Also, he had heard the Fiat's engine cough as its fuel line began sucking air, whereupon Edwina shut the ignition off at once.

"I may," she grumbled, "have to beg gasoline from someone, but I am not going to stand in a blizzard, pouring the damned stuff into the carburetor just to get the damned fuel pump primed again. Oh, damn and blast, anyway."

Maxie opened his mouth to comment, appeared suddenly to comprehend her look, and yawned instead. Then he stepped into her lap and began purring as if to say that he, at least, had perfect confidence in her.

"Right," she said irritably, placing him on the floor, "but some-times I think it would be easier just to act helpless and wait to be rescued. Stay here, damn it, I'll be right back."

Siphoning gasoline from one car into another while being pelted in the darkness by wind-driven snow proved as enjoyable as Edwina expected, but convincing the driver of the other car to let her do it at all was, if possible, even more charming a task. The other car's tank, as it turned out, was full, so the driver had no worry about that. He felt strongly, though, that no woman out of gas on a highway, *no* woman, could do more than smile and wring her hands together prettily, neither of which things Edwina felt at all like doing, and this confused him until with a ferocious flourish she produced thirty feet of oxygen tubing and a 250-cc plastic syringe from the Fiat's trunk.

Briskly she stuck one end of the tubing into the other car's gas tank, drew on the tubing's near end with the syringe until gasoline began flowing through it, and dropped the flowing end of the oxygen tubing into the Fiat's filler pipe. Ten minutes later the donor car's gas gauge was down a quarter, traffic was beginning tentatively to move, and the donor car's driver was gaping out his window in amazement at her.

"No, I ain't gonna let ya pay me, little lady," he said, "ya showed me a good 'un, there. Only where can I git some a that there tubing, and one a them suckin' gadgets?"

Edwina pressed these items hastily into his hands, thanked him again, and got back into the Fiat, which started at the first turn of the key. Her tooth, which had been quiescent for most of the afternoon, boomed murderously; all she wanted was to make it home, crawl into bed, and pull the covers over her head.

This, however, proved easier said than done, since when she did arrive home she encountered one final obstacle: the blasted driveway, which consisted of eight hundred feet of macadam, two S-curves, and a sharp left turn, all emphatically uphill and all covered at the moment by at least twelve inches of fresh, white snow.

Also, there was a set of footprints leading up it.

FOUR

The footprints, now filling up with snow, led first to the front door and then to the rear, where the back door stood open several inches. Light streamed from the downstairs windows while the alarm system, newly installed at great expense and designed to shriek at any intrusion while summoning security guards automatically by telephone, uttered not a peep.

They were not McIntyre's footprints: His long, determined stride was instantly recognizable, even through uphill drifts. Nor was his car among those Edwina had sighted abandoned in ditches, and McIntyre always slammed the door until it latched.

So: not McIntyre. Maxie protested, squirming from Edwina's arms and vanishing into the backyard darkness. Scrambling after him, she glimpsed smoke swirling for an instant from the kitchen chimney, before it was whipped away on the freezing wind.

And that, at last, was what decided her: Burglars might be stupid enough to burgle on a night like tonight, and they might even turn on a few of the house lights, the better to see what they were burgling, but she doubted any burglar would bother to fire up that infuriatingly recalcitrant woodstove.

"Who's here?" she called, pulling off her scarf and gloves and yanking off her coat. Her mother had house keys, and might have sent Mr. Watkins down here from Litchfield on some errand or another; having worked for Edwina's mother for forty years, Mr. Watkins knew better than to plead inclement weather when sent on missions of importance—such as, for instance, the purchasing of paper clips, or of pads of lined yellow legal-sized paper, or of the particular shade of blue Scripp ink with which Harriet Crusoe loaded her fountain pen, in order to write her fabulously popular and enormously profitable romantic-suspense novels. Harriet knew the code that disarmed the alarm system, too, and might have told it to Mr. Watkins.

Harriet might also, Edwina reflected, feeling vexed, have bothered to call and say that Mr. Watkins was coming. And what could Harriet be wanting here in the middle of a storm, anyway?

The alarm system had been triggered and reset, Edwina saw by the blinking ready light. Chastened, Maxie slipped in behind her and twined purringly around her ankles, then stopped to lift his head with a look of unhappiness. "Mumf," he pronounced, his yellow eyes narrowing and his nose wrinkling with distaste at the scent of a stranger. Not, his tail semaphored, Watkins.

"All right, that's it," said Edwina, striding along the hall toward the kitchen with Maxie trotting appreciatively behind. He did not care to confront an intruder himself, his jaunty attitude seemed to say, but if she were going to do it he would be more than happy to come along and watch, and even to cheer her on from the sidelines if necessary.

"Some help you are," Edwina grumbled. "I should trade you in on a rottweiler." Then she halted, for in the kitchen doorway stood a young woman she had never seen before in her life.

"Oh," said the woman, putting her hand to her heart, "what a fright you gave me! I didn't hear you come in."

Edwina eyed the stranger, noting that she was about twenty

years old, with a short mop of black, curly hair and enormous brown eyes. Her cheeks were still rosy with the cold she had come through and her lips were a deep, rich, red although she wore no makeup; still, she had a hungry look about her, as if she had missed a meal—or a few of them—lately.

Also, Edwina noted irritably as she brushed past, the girl was wearing a pair of what looked very much like Edwina's own slippers, and had already drunk what looked like most of a scotch highball from one of Edwina's own highball glasses.

"I'm sorry," she said evenly, "if I startled you. But this is my house, so I generally do walk in without asking permission. I'm allowed to do that, you see. Unlike yourself."

Swiftly, she surveyed the kitchen. A fake-fur jacket hung from a chair, dripping melted snow onto the pine flooring. On the counter stood a black drawstring satchel, made of material that was supposed to resemble leather but did not. Sticking from the top of the satchel was a pair of gloves meant for something other than making one's way through a blizzard. And drying before the stove, Edwina saw with the beginnings of a familiar sinking feeling, was a pair of short suede boots with rabbit-fur cuffs, which as winter footgear looked about as useful as an extra coat of toenail polish.

"The door," the girl ventured, "was unlocked, so I—"

"Pick up your coat and boots," Edwina interrupted, "and put them in the back hall where they belong. Leave the bag," she added as the girl made a move for it, "and while you're hanging up your things, you might rethink your story."

She reached out and took the glass from the young woman's hand. "The first thing we'll talk about when you get back is how you really got in here. And the next thing we'll talk about is why. Now, *scat*, before I call the police."

At the mention of the police, the girl's eyes widened and a little glint appeared in them. Her gaze moved once more to her bag and then to Edwina's face, her front teeth touching her lower lip briefly in calculation. "I didn't—" she began.

Seizing the bag, Edwina upended it over the butcher-block center island. Objects spilled out onto the smooth, scrubbed wood: keys, tissues, sales slips, pill bottles, costume jewelry, coins, an address book, a dozen or so shiny .22-caliber bullets, and a clutter of plastic cards, along with a small black handgun whose manufacture Edwina did not recognize. But she recognized the girl's look at the sight of it. Quickly, she plucked it up.

"You know," she said, "I've had a terrible day. I'm cold, I'm tired, and I have a toothache. So I think you'd better do what I say, before I lose my temper."

"It isn't loaded," the girl whispered.

Edwina checked, keeping her eye on the girl's face. Then she scooped up a half-dozen of the scattered bullets, opened the magazine, and slotted them in professionally. There were indeed a number of advantages to being the wife of a homicide inspector, she reflected, not the least of them being unlimited target-range privileges.

"Now it is," she said. She glanced at one of the credit cards, and then at another. There was a driver's license, too, and a library card, as well as a number of foil-wrapped condoms and some packets of moist towelettes. "Jennifer White," Edwina said. "Jean Wall, Janet Walker, Annette Whitson. Any preference as to which name goes on the complaint I'm going to sign against you, or should I just let the cops write you up as Jane Doe?"

"Oh, come on," the girl began, "you don't have to—"

"Be quiet," said Edwina softly. The effect was better than that of a shout: The girl's eyes widened as it occurred to her that she might have made an error in judgment, breaking in here.

"I'm sorry," she whispered. "I only wanted to talk to you. But when I got here, you weren't here, and . . . I was cold, that's all. I'd borrowed a car, but it slid off the road about a mile from here.

I thought I was going to freeze to death." She added defiantly: "I didn't take anything, or hurt anything."

"I see. Why didn't you come to my office? That would have been the normal thing to do. And how did you even know where I lived?"

The girl looked at the floor. "I looked you up in the phone book. There aren't any other E. Crusoes in it, and there was an address. I figured, what did I have to lose but a little time?"

Edwina considered this, meanwhile regretting the New Haven telephone book's completeness—it listed the numbers for small surrounding towns, not just the city—as well as her own rashness in letting her home telephone number be listed at all. Someday, she thought, I will stop pretending to myself that I am harmless, anonymous, and of little interest to the rascals of the world, and start putting up fences and really buying rottweilers.

"So, you started off in a borrowed car in the middle of a blizzard to visit me, without telephoning in advance, and without even knowing for sure that this was in fact my house," she said skeptically.

"I didn't want anyone to see me at your office," the girl replied. "I was afraid what happened to Terry might happen to me. Like I said, I was pretty sure it was your address, and I thought if I called first, you might not let me come out here. So I just—"

"Terry? Theresa Whitlock?" Edwina gave the girl another once-over, noticing the faded sweater and fraying rayon blouse she wore over cheap black stretch slacks. Three oval bruises showed on each of her wrists, as if someone had reached out and grabbed her, hard and recently.

"Theresa," the girl said. "Yeah, that's what she called herself since she got lucky. She caught on real quick to the way she had to act, after she married Perry. Although I've got to say, nobody ever had to teach Terry how to spend money, or how to behave like she always had it, either."

She looked at the glass of scotch standing half-full on the counter. "Can I drink the rest of that? God knows I need it and it's just going to waste."

Edwina nodded, and the girl drank thirstily, wiping her lips with the back of her hand when she had finished. "Sorry," she said when she saw Edwina watching her. "But some of us never had the chance to learn fancy manners. Or anywhere to practice them if we did. Kind of places I end up spending time in, you ask for a napkin, you might get it stuffed down your throat."

"Really," Edwina replied. "What kinds of places are those?" She knew the answer: A purseful of male contraceptives, moist towel-ettes, and ID with different names pretty much narrowed down the career choice the girl had made. Still, the frankness of the girl's answer came as a surprise.

"Crummy bars where I pick up guys," she said, "and the dumpy rooms I take them to, for money. That's how I met Terry, and that's how she met Perry Whitlock. Course, that's not how Perry tells it. Hear him talk, you'd think they got introduced at a church social, or maybe a dance at the country club."

She drained her glass. "Would you mind putting that thing down? Loaded guns make me nervous."

Edwina lowered the weapon. After a moment's thought, she slipped it into her skirt pocket along with the rest of the bullets scattered on the butcher block. The girl was not likely to try any foolish stunts now; the night, Edwina saw with a glance at the window, was getting worse, and although she had managed to pull the Fiat far enough into the driveway to keep it from being demolished by a passing snowplow, getting it back out again would be another story, even if the girl got hold of the keys.

"What is your name, anyway?" Edwina waved at the mess of things on the butcher block, to indicate that the girl should clear them up. "And how *did* you get in here?"

"My real name is Jennifer Warren," the girl answered as she

swept her belongings back into the satchel, "and I got in here the way Terry taught me to, by wiggling a stiff piece of plastic between the door and the frame until the lock snapped open. You really ought to get yourself some better locks, you know, a nice place like this. Somebody could clean you right out."

"And the alarm? It was set when I left. How did you manage to get around that?"

Jennifer Warren laughed. "I hate to tell you this, but if you're going to write the alarm code inside the front cover of your telephone book, you might as well just save your money and not buy any alarm. That was the first place I looked, and I still had fifteen seconds to spare before the thing went off. If I hadn't found it, I'd have had to beat it out of here, but I did find it. Anyone would, who knew what they were doing."

"I see," said Edwina evenly, cursing herself for another seven kinds of fool. She'd written the number down, contrary to the alarm installer's advice, as insurance against forgetting it.

"Oh, don't get bent out of shape," said the girl. "Lots of people write them down. It's dumb but it's not rare. And you'd have tried getting inside, too, if you were freezing out there."

In spite of herself, Edwina smiled; she had, after all, not been schooled in quite the same academies as Jennifer, whose hard-knock lessons, if those bruises were any proof, had continued right up until yesterday, or perhaps even this morning. And it was in fact freezing out there.

"You might as well leave the slippers on," she told Jennifer as the girl headed for the back hall with her coat and boots. "It doesn't look as if anyone's going anywhere for a while. I guess I'm going to hear your story whether I like it or not."

Jennifer glanced over her shoulder, her dark eyes unreadable but for a sudden look of pain. "You won't," she promised. "Like it, I mean. But somebody's got to hear it. I owe her that much. Terry," she finished softly, "was the only friend I ever had."

By six-thirty, sandwiches had been eaten, coffee drunk, and dishes stacked. McIntyre had not called, nor would Edwina expect him to; his own work would not stop for a few inches—or a few feet—of snow. Meanwhile her tooth went on throbbing, with the boring regularity of a metronome.

In her bag were the pills Harry had prescribed for her, but the pain was not really so very bad, and she did not want to sleep heavily with Jennifer in the house. A girl with that one's talents and experience, Edwina decided, bore watching however sympathetic one might be led to feel toward her.

Outside, snow continued falling steadily. The wood stove, persuaded into radiating heat by a diet of seasoned hardwood, made faint pinging sounds as of aluminum foil being crumpled. From the radio had come the news that the surprise snowstorm would not begin moving out until at least midnight; after that, Edwina had switched the radio off, and now the house was silent except for occasional sleepy twitters from Maxie, whose paws twitched energetically as he dreamed.

"What did you mean, that's how Perry Whitlock met Theresa?" she asked. "And why do you want to talk to me about her?"

Jennifer sighed. "Look, Terry was a hooker from the time she was fourteen, okay? Her folks were both drunks, Terry and a boyfriend took off, pretty soon she was on the street. He beat her up a few times when he found out, but then Terry found a guy who could beat her boyfriend up. And that was the last she saw of the boyfriend. She was nineteen when I met her. I was fifteen, and I'd gotten into a car with the wrong bunch of guys."

She looked up defensively. "Hey, how did I know? I'd only left home the week before, and I was hungry. They said they were going for burgers and they'd buy me some. Couple of hours later they pushed me out of the car. I was crying, my clothes all torn and bloodied up. Bunch of drunk college boys is what they were. Nobody on the street would even look at me. And then Terry walks out of a bar with some guy, she's all happy and smiling. Like he's the man of her dreams, you know. Terry was good at that. But when she saw me, she got rid of him."

Jennifer sipped from her glass of wine and glanced around the kitchen. Food and warmth had relaxed her enough to strip away some of her brash, tough-girl veneer, but she was still uncomfortable. As Jennifer nibbled unconsciously at a fingernail, Edwina saw how skinny her wrists were.

"Listen," she said casually, knowing the girl would be quick to take offense, "I don't know about you, but I like chocolate cake with red wine, and there's some in the refrigerator. Do you want some? I mean"—she smiled—"since we're trapped here in a blizzard, we might as well indulge ourselves."

Jennifer's look was all the answer she needed; the girl was famished—and, Edwina thought, not only for food. When they were settled again with slices of cake and fresh glasses of wine, Edwina returned to her gentle questioning. "So Theresa—I mean Terry—rescued you?"

Jennifer laughed. "Well, I wasn't going to let her. I was so ashamed, I told her to get away from me, and I'll never forget what she did then. She grabbed me by the ear, really hard. And she said, 'Girl, I just blew off a hundred bucks for you, and you're coming with me, now, or I'll slap you till your eyes roll back.' And then she took me to the emergency room, so I could get treatment and stuff."

"And dropped you off there?" Edwina nibbled at her slice of cake; somehow, even while she was talking, Jennifer had already devoured hers.

"Uh-uh. She sat there with me, told the cops I was her sister and I was staying with her, so they wouldn't take me and try to send me home. After that, I really was staying with her. We were roommates for a year, until she married Fairy Perry."

Edwina choked on a sip of wine. "Fairy Perry? That's what you called him?"

Jennifer shook her head. "That's what *she* called him, and she meant like the Fairy Godmother, only this one was a man. See, the thing is this."

The girl leaned forward earnestly. "Terry couldn't stay on the street forever, nobody can. But the difference was, Terry knew it. She didn't want to be an old, scaly-legged hag, doin' it with guys for ten bucks in the front seats of cars, someday maybe getting her throat cut, or maybe strangled."

At Edwina's startled glance, Jennifer shrugged. "Hey, it's what happens," she said. "Girls get old, or they disappear. And Terry said, 'Jen, don't just live for the moment like I did when I was your age. You need to save your money, plan a future. Get a handle on things.' "

The girl scraped her cake plate and licked the last bits from her fork. "I listened, too, because Terry was smart. We used to do stores, apartments, credit cards—you name it, we scored it. She wasn't just a girl who could only do one thing."

"Break-ins, you mean. Shoplifting. Credit fraud." That was where the girl had gotten the nerve and experience to disarm the alarm system; Edwina wondered what else Jennifer knew how to do, and remembered the weapon she'd carried.

Jennifer nodded. "Only, Terry had this one guy she worked for, she had to give him a lot, and also she had debts, because for a while she'd been heavy into drugs. So when Perry showed up, she figured he'd be her ticket out. And he was."

The fire in the wood stove was dying down. Maxie eyed Edwina to see if she would throw another log in; when she did not, he ambled off in search of a nice soft sofa to shed on. "I don't see,"

Edwina said, "what this has to do with Terry being killed, though, or with your being in any danger. If you are."

"Well, maybe I am and maybe I'm not. All I know is, Terry and I were like sisters. Even after she married Perry Whitlock, we kept in touch. She told me everything, or at least I thought she did. Then last week she called and said she was in trouble, bad trouble, and she needed help."

Suddenly the pieces of Jennifer's story came together. "She needed money, you mean. A lot of money, and not from Perry."

Jennifer nodded, swallowing the last of her wine. "I didn't believe her at first. Stealing, that's one thing, but killing a guy? And now somebody was going to kill her? I thought she was joking around, but then she started crying."

At this, Jennifer's cheap clothing and hungry manner took on an entirely new meaning; if she was telling the truth, Jennifer was not a bit poor. She simply never spent a penny on herself. But fifty thousand dollars? "How much did you lend her?"

"Ten thousand," Jennifer Warren said.

Edwina frowned; that wasn't much more likely. Jennifer had to have expenses. From the look of her, they didn't include drugs, but there must be some guy in the picture. Girls on the street just didn't survive without them, in part because the guys' recruitment methods tended to be so violently persuasive.

"And now you want the money back, is that it?" If it was yours in the first place, Edwina added silently; if you lent Theresa anything at all. But she refrained from challenging the girl, wanting instead to hear this little scam to its conclusion before deciding what to do about it.

"Well, getting it back, that depends," said Jennifer. "I lent it to her, I didn't give it to her, and I could use it. But what I really want to know is what's going on. For one thing, I don't know who else might know she talked to me. Maybe someone thinks she told me more than she did, and that scares me."

Jennifer got up and set her plate and wineglass in the sink. "I'll say this much, Terry was a good liar. She could make you think the sun rises in the west. But she wasn't lying when she told me she killed a guy. I don't know how she did it or why, but I know she did it, and I know *she* was really scared. And I think there was something more she wasn't telling me, but I never got a chance to ask her, because this morning I read in the paper that Terry was dead."

A little sob escaped her; she turned toward the window. It was a remarkable performance, if indeed it was one. At the same time Edwina remembered the sense she'd had of Theresa Whitlock: something wrong. Perhaps Jennifer had supplied the explanation: not that Theresa was lying in what she had said, but that there was something she hadn't been telling.

"I know you think this is all some kind of trick," Jennifer said, turning to Edwina again. "And that's okay. I'd think so, too, if I was you. But the way I see it, tomorrow or the next day the cops will know who Terry really was, how many outstanding warrants she had, how many prostitution arrests, thefts and loiterings and things like that she'd had racked up against her."

Her look hardened. "You know, after I was raped by those guys, Terry gave the cops her real address so they could get in touch. Call me, have me try identifying people. It was a big risk she took, doing that. Only they never called. They took one look at Terry and one look at me, and that was it. Like it didn't matter what happened to us, because they thought we were *both* hooking and we probably deserved it. It was like we were disposable girls."

"And you think that's what will happen again?"

Jennifer snatched up her bag, dug around in it, and produced a cigarette, which she lit angrily. "I know it will. They'll decide she was nothing but a gold-digging ex-whore with a string of crummy offenses and some kind of sordid secret life that got her murdered. The newspapers will lick their chops over it, the cops'll diddle around a little bit to keep Perry happy, and then everyone will forget all about it."

She blew a thin stream of smoke. "Everyone but me. So I think I want you to keep that money, Miss Crusoe, even though you think I only came here to weasel it back out of you. Terry took care of me when I needed her. Now I'm going to take care of her, and myself, maybe, too. I want you to find out who killed her."

"I see," said Edwina. "To avenge your friend's death, and perhaps protect your own life. But isn't ten thousand dollars a lot of money for—"

"For a girl like you," she had been about to say, but stopped in time; there was no sense rubbing Jennifer's nose in it.

But Jennifer showed no such sensitivity. "Hey," she said, shrugging, "unless all the guys in the world drop dead tomorrow, there'll be plenty more where that came from."

* * *

To her surprise, Edwina slept easily and well, but in the morning Jennifer Warren was gone. The bed in the guest room was neatly made, a damp towel and washcloth hung on the rack in the bathroom, and a pot of coffee had been kept warm in the kitchen. One cup stood in the sink, and a sheet of notepaper lay on the table; the note bore a telephone number, nothing more.

Outside the kitchen window the sky was gray, with a few last snowflakes spiraling from it. Jennifer's footprints leading out were the only sign that the driveway even existed. In the spruce tree at the foot of the drive, a cardinal stood out like a bright drop of blood against green branches laden heavily with white; beyond them, Edwina glimpsed the Fiat, nearly buried in a drift.

Jennifer's little gun, which Edwina had locked into the wall safe before she retired, would of course have to be turned over to the police; like the one that had killed Theresa Whitlock, it was a small-caliber weapon fittable with a silencer.

But the gun didn't fit Jennifer herself; thinking this, Edwina fed Maxie, pulled on a jacket and boots, and went out to find the snow shovel. The town plows had been through, spewing a ridge of salt-and-sand-impregnated slurry, and she attacked this first, working with a stab-and-hurl motion to dig deep bites with the shovel and fling each load away. Maxie followed gingerly, hopping from one bootprint to the next in an attempt to traverse the snow while avoiding all unnecessary contact with the cold wet stuff. As he reached her side, a bright red Jeep with its tire chains jingling and its horn honking came tootling up the road.

"Good Lord, Mother," Edwina said, leaning on her shovel to stare at Harriet Crusoe, who swung the Jeep zestfully into the space Edwina had cleared, gave the hand brake a decisive yank, and climbed energetically from the cab. The Jeep was equipped with an enormous yellow plow blade; also, it was equipped with Mr. Watkins, whose tan, wrinkled face Edwina thought looked mightily relieved as he slid behind the wheel where Harriet had been.

"Care to back 'er out, miss?" he called, with a wave at the Fiat, whose path to the roadway Edwina had nearly cleared. "And I'll 'ave a pass at this 'ere 'ill, if you like."

Edwina looked at Watkins, at the Jeep, and at her mother, who for a morning of Jeep driving wore a full-length silver fox coat, high black leather boots that made her legs look slender as a girl's, and a pair of black kid gloves that Edwina happened to know were lined with ermine. From the voluminously fluffy neckline of the coat peeped Harriet's trademark string of pearls, a strand of pink-white iridescent orbs too huge and perfect to be real, Harriet's funny little secret being that they were real.

"Darling," said Harriet, "do let Watkins be useful. He'll mope if you don't. You know how he hates idle time."

Edwina suspected that while working for her mother, Mr. Watkins rarely had enough idle time to find out whether he hated it or not. He did, however, like motor vehicles of all kinds, and the ones he could do big things with were the ones he liked best. Backing the Jeep into the road, he lowered the plow and revved the engine, a small implacable smile of anticipation on his face.

"Maxie," Edwina called, "come on, hop in the car. You and Mother and I will go for a ride, so we can stay out of Mr. Watkins's way."

Moments later they were heading down the road between tall maples whose skeletal branches dropped soft bombs of melting snow onto the Fiat's windshield. Bright sunshine flashed on flat white fields between mounded stone walls, creating purple shadows at the bases of the drifts. Behind a farmhouse, some children were out sledding, their primary-color snowsuits zipping gaily downhill and a brown dog gamboling in their midst.

"So, darling," said Harriet, settling herself. Her smile was serene, her white hair arranged in an elaborate, smoothly waved coiffure, and her face a youthful miracle of cosmetics combined with a diet-and-exercise routine so intense, it made Edwina wince to think about it.

But Harriet's eyes were no longer gazing at the scenery; instead, they were fixed upon Edwina with a look so piercingly perceptive that Edwina gave up all hope of pretense.

"I despise that house," she said, "and I feel absolutely dreadful about it. Martin puts up with plenty of things that I like, you know, and he doesn't say a word about them: My snooping into murders, for example, worries him immensely, but he doesn't ask me to give it up. It doesn't seem right for me to complain, and besides, it *is* a roof over my head."

"But," said Harriet knowingly as they rounded a curve and a frozen lake came into view; around it, pointed firs stood like sentinels, while at its center, from a black patch of open water, a flock of geese rose with a huge, slow flapping of powerful wings.

"But," Edwina agreed. The road straightened and ran across a low, narrow bridge. On either side, frozen cattails thrust up, their dark-brown, velvety heads waving stiffly as icy water rushed past their stalks somewhere below.

"You know," Harriet remarked after a while, "your father didn't like my writing novels. He thought even reading novels was a waste of time, when one might be learning another foreign language, or studying mathematics, or even practicing the piano. Something *improving*," she added, giving the word a wry twist.

Jarred from her own thoughts, Edwina sighed inwardly. No doubt one of Harriet's lectures would do her no real harm, but she wasn't in the mood for it. Then she sat up, realizing what Harriet had said.

"You mean, you did it anyway? In secret?" The thought of anyone defying E. R. Crusoe outright seemed so utterly unlikely, Edwina could not quite imagine any other way for her mother to have gone on writing—which, obviously, she had done: Harriet had at last count produced twenty-five of her gorgeously written and intricately plotted fictions, all set with a miniaturist's eye for detail in a different historical period and all built upon a single theme: the power of love.

Harriet's answering laugh was silvery. "Good heavens, child. Keep secrets from your father? It would have been a bit like trying to hide one's bones while standing before an X-ray camera, don't you think?"

Remembering E.R.'s chilly, pale-blue gaze, Edwina conceded the aptness of the analogy. He had been neither a cold man nor a cynic, but her father's capacity for accurate observation had been nearly infinite, or so it had seemed to a little girl trying for the first time—and the last—to sneak even the smallest fib past him.

"I told your father the truth," Harriet said. "That I regretted his disapproval, but that what I was doing was neither illegal, immoral, nor silly." She bit the last word off sharply. "And I was not about to trade concessions, either, let's be clear about that. I was thirty-five years old, the educated wife of a wealthy and brilliant older man who was away a great deal, and I had absolutely no work to do. You," she added indulgently, "were an easy child, and we were mobbed with servants."

Maxie stretched himself on Harriet's lap, luxuriating in the warmth of the fox fur. "What happened?" Edwina whispered.

Harriet lifted her immaculately coiffed white head. "I told him I was going to go on—he was livid, I recall—and if that meant he had to divorce me, he must do what he thought right."

"And he said?" High above, a red hawk flew in long, lazy circles, wings outstretched and unmoving as he floated, searching sharp-eyed for the twitch of a rabbit's brown ear or the scuttle of a gray mouse outlined against the snow.

"He said nothing. Not then, and not to me, for months. But the following June, *Heaven's Harvest* won the Prix de Flamme. You do remember that one, don't you? The one where a girl, Beatrice was her name, returns to live in her family's cottage in Cornwall to nurse an unpleasant cousin back to health, rather than marry the rich, attractive Lord Hiram Walkingstone in London?"

"Yes, the cousin was a cad, only she didn't realize it until it was almost too late." Despite her own thoughts, Edwina smiled at the memory; Cousin Harry had been so sweet and artless, and in the end so satisfyingly unprincipled.

"The best cad I ever wrote, I think," said Harriet happily. "The award ceremonies were empty without your father, of course; what did I need with five thousand dollars and a silver cup? But the night I returned from Paris—alone, as I had gone—he met me in New York. And he gave me these pearls."

She fingered the strand lovingly. "I shall never forget the night."

Edwina could barely believe her ears. "You mean, you won the prize and then it was all right with him? Just because you'd gotten important, and won something, Father was impressed? That doesn't sound a bit like him, you know."

Harriet Crusoe regarded her daughter with kind patience. "No, dear. It hadn't anything to do with winning a prize, or with anyone else's opinion of me. While I was gone, it seems, he'd read the book. Now, let's head home, shall we? Watkins is probably done by now, and I'm getting hungry."

"You realize," Edwina told her, "that what you've just said doesn't make things any easier for me."

"Yes, dear, I realize it. But the point is, you must do what you think right. And if you are really unhappy you must say so, for if you don't, you'll blame poor Martin, and then, like Harry Greene, you'll become a cad. Harry, you'll remember, blamed Beatrice for his inability to tell her he loved her, and you must remember all that came of *that*."

"Yes," said Edwina dutifully, "I remember."

They rode homeward in silence. "But," Edwina said at last, "I feel so spoiled, as if I must have everything all my own way. How can I demand one thing without offering another?"

Harriet snorted. "Good heavens, darling, it's done all the time. Take my word for it, Martin knew how stiff-necked and stubborn you are, long before he married you."

Uppon this comforting comment, the Fiat made its turn into the plowed driveway. "Meanwhile, why don't you tell me about this latest murder?" Harriet pressed her gloved hands happily together. "I do so love a juicy murder, and you do, too, don't you, dear? Yes, I believe you do."

Edwina stared at Harriet: wordlessly, shocked.

"One must be true to one's love," Harriet pronounced.

*　　*　　*

As it turned out, Harriet knew quite a lot about Theresa Whitlock's murder, the Litchfield press apparently feeling it owed its readers as much fresh juiciness as it could squeeze—or in this case, appropriate from the wire services. But she knew nothing about Ricky Z., and upon the unfortunate expert in the creation and utilization of illegal explosives—not upon Perry Whitlock or Thomas Riordan, to Edwina's surprise—she fixed with fascinated interest.

"Really," she drawled in the skeptical tones she reserved, usually, for the plot developments of authors less skilled than herself. "Why, if fixing a time of death is so uncertain, does anyone bother to do it?"

"Well, it can be important. It's a sort of useful legal fiction." Edwina poured coffee for herself, while Harriet sipped mineral water. Entertaining Harriet, as the years passed, became less and less a matter of offering food and drink, and more one of supplying a few small items of tableware for the provisions Harriet carried everywhere in her enormous handbag. Spread out on the kitchen counter were unsalted whole-grain biscuits, jars of wheat germ, vitamins, and brewer's yeast, and a plastic bag of dried banana chips.

"For instance," Edwina said, "it could make a difference in an inheritance case, to know which of two people sharing property died first, say, in an automobile accident. The heirs of the one who survived longest, even by a few minutes, might inherit, while the heirs of the other one could end up getting nothing."

"What a charming example." Harriet munched delicately on a biscuit that looked a fraction tastier than cardboard. "I don't imagine this Ricky fellow left much of an estate, though?"

"As a matter of fact, he did." Edwina assembled her own lunch, tuna salad on rye bread with alfalfa sprouts, the latter being her concession to Harriet's healthful example.

Outside, the driveway had been sanded and salted by Mr. Watkins, who was now puttering in the back hall; he would, he said, have that balky latch fixed directly, and were there any other repair chores he could put his hand to? As he was not, he confided, in the habit of eating lunch.

"Ricky had an insurance policy," Edwina went on, "with his mother and sister the beneficiaries. I have a friend who works in records at probate court," added Edwina, who had taken the trouble the day before to perform this research. "Three-quarters of a million dollars, which Riordan's lawyers immediately tried to sue for, in a wrongful-death action," she continued. "I got *that* part out of the newspapers; if the suit had gone on, it would have been quite a story. But since the medical examiner reported that Ricky was dead or dying at the time of the explosion . . ."

She stopped, noting the look of enlightenment on Harriet's face. "I wonder," said Harriet, "if Ricky's mother and sister knew how Ricky made his living? Because if they did, they might have taken precautions upon learning of Ricky's tragic death. Imagine, for instance, that he did kill this Riordan fellow, and they knew it. Then they might realize Riordan's survivors could target his estate, unless they worked fast to prevent them."

"Three-quarters of a million is a lot of money," Edwina conceded, seeing where Harriet was leading. "Enough so that a person might feel free to promise some of it to someone who helped keep Riordan's lawyers from getting hold of it."

"To someone," Harriet agreed, "like a medical examiner."

FIVE

Edwina thought it was perfectly understandable that prisons should be made difficult to get out of. She had not realized, however, that the really good prisons—the ones from which all thought of escape was a fleeting, infrequently recurring dream, rather than an actual physical possibility—were also extremely difficult to enter unless one happened to be wearing manacles, ankle chains, and a bright-orange government-issue jumpsuit with a number on the back and Velcro tabs in the places where buttons, zippers, and similar fastenings might otherwise be expected.

One phone call had repaired her ignorance. Persons wishing to visit inmates might apply for this privilege by completing a form available from the Connecticut State Bureau of Corrections, the processing of which form frequently required weeks or months.

Fortunately, however, the young man convicted of shooting Ricky Z. with Ricky's own .25-caliber semiautomatic belonged to a wealthy West Hartford family, so his defense had been top-flight: John D. Maxwell's reputation for courtroom theatrics was exceeded only by his considerable legal acumen.

It was true that Maxwell's efforts to convince a jury of his client's innocence had come to a premature halt on the morning when the prosecution, equipped with the murder weapon, the young man's fingerprints on the murder weapon, and the testimony of the Connecticut state troopers whom the young man had menaced with the murder weapon, strode smiling into court.

But Maxwell believed his client's version of events, or was wise enough at any rate to go on maintaining that he did while the client's family continued paying attorney's fees. So he listened carefully when Edwina told him why she wanted to see the young man as soon as possible.

"Interesting," he said. "You really think your client has something that might help my client find appeal grounds?"

As he spoke she could hear him pondering: favors wanted, favors owed, unknown favors possible in the unknown future. It was a hard life, being a defense attorney; the people one dealt with were often so eminently in need of defending, mostly for the simple reason that they were guilty. One couldn't afford to omit conferring a favor, since with it one conferred an obligation.

Edwina did not reply that as far as she was concerned, her client was a person who was surrounded by flowers and being viewed in a local funeral home. After some thought she had decided to waive her fee and to let Jennifer Warren find out later that Theresa's check had been returned to the bank. If it was money Jennifer was after, she could petition Theresa's estate for it, was Edwina's considered attitude.

Instead Edwina waffled, pointing out that until she knew more about what was going on in her own case, she couldn't tell if it would give any grounds for an appeal or not. But, she implied, she thought it might.

"That," she added, "is why I want to see him. To hear what *he* says." And to find out, she thought, if I believe him.

The upshot was that if Ricky Zimmerman *had* blown up Thomas

Riordan's car, it was probably because someone had hired him to. Logic suggested that someone might have been Theresa Whitlock; perhaps someone from her troubled background had introduced her to Ricky. Then Riordan, tipped off by Ricky, might have arranged another victim and disappeared himself.

It all gave Riordan a fine motive for killing Ricky, and for murdering Theresa Whitlock: the former to cover Riordan's own trail, and the latter for simple vengeance—since just because she hadn't really killed him didn't mean he wouldn't be pretty steamed about the attempt.

On the other hand, if Maxwell's client *had* killed Ricky, the whole theory went into a cocked hat, despite the events occurring just after Ricky's death—events that, as Harriet had noted upon examining Edwina's newspaper clippings, were curious indeed.

"Why not just go after this Riordan fellow?" Maxwell asked now. "If you think he's behind it all, then—"

"I would," Edwina replied, "only two states and a couple of federal agencies have been hunting him for six months. I don't think I'm going to succeed where they've failed. But if I could find out what really happened, I *might* pick up some new angle on where he is. And that *might* help get your guy out of prison."

"Tell you what," said Maxwell in the rich, mellifluous voice with which he was said to be able to hypnotize whole panels full of previously impartial jurors, "I'll talk to my client and his family. If they want him to meet with you, and he wants to, I'll see what I can do. No guarantees, you understand. But it is quite possible that we may be able to cooperate."

As he spoke she could hear his clock ticking; a billable hour, after all, was a billable hour, and each portion of one that Maxwell spent arranging a rendezvous between herself and his client would appear as a full sixty minutes when it was time again to add up his tab and present it for payment. Promising to call her as soon as he had an answer, John D. Maxwell hung up.

Putting down the receiver, Edwina looked around the bright, silent kitchen. It was nearly three o'clock; Harriet had gone, leaving behind the mingled scents of Pears soap and Joy perfume. When they had finished discussing Ricky Z., Edwina had returned to the subject of the house.

"I can get used to the country," she had said, "and to the quiet, and to having to drive everywhere I want to go, instead of walking. I can get used to yard work, snow shoveling, and doing repairs or finding someone who can do them. But—"

She gestured helplessly. "It cost the earth to have this house redone, and Martin would have heart failure if I tore it out again. He's so careful with a penny you'd think he'd hooked up with a poor woman instead of a rich one. But it's like living in a dollhouse, so sweet it makes my teeth ache." At the words her own tooth, quiet lately, gave a premonitory throb.

"Yes," Harriet said, "I see what you mean. Rather picture-book-ish, isn't it? Where," she asked, half-joking, "are the Ricky Zimmermans of the world when we need them? And what does Martin think about all this . . . this *decor?*"

To Harriet, the deliberate decoration of a room was one of life's inscrutable mysteries; rather, in her view, one simply collected things one liked, arranged them in ways that were agreeable and comfortable, and lived happily with the result. But when Harriet pursued this program, the result *was* agreeable and comfortable, not artificial, awkward, and reeking of recent deliveries from up-scale antique-reproduction emporiums.

"Martin remembers his three-room attic apartment," Edwina replied, "where he left behind the furniture he'd bought twenty years ago at garage sales. He hasn't said anything, but I'm certain he's in heaven; any upholstered chair whose stuffing isn't actually spilling out of it is an improvement to him, and so is anything that has an even halfway recent coat of paint on it."

Harriet had pursed her lips judiciously at this, but had made no comment; shortly thereafter she and Watkins had departed, the red Jeep zipping down the drive in a cheery jingle of tire chains with Harriet again at the wheel. No doubt by nightfall she would have bullied Watkins into teaching her how to operate the plow blade. Meanwhile there were several hours of daylight left, and the roads were now all passable. Checking the copies she had made of newspaper pieces about the Zimmerman cases—there had been one in criminal court and one in probate court—Edwina found the names and dates Harriet had pointed out to her.

Of these, the dates were most curious, for as Harriet had remarked, if Ricky's mother or sister *had* fiddled Ricky's time-of-death estimate then one or both of them had to have had a reason to do so. But how could they have realized Riordan's lawyers would come after the insurance money? And how could they have realized it so *fast*, in time to rig Ricky's autopsy report? Perhaps Ricky had told one or both of them whom he planned to kill.

Even more curious was the way Riordan's lawyers battened onto Ricky's estate. How had *they* known of any link between Zimmerman and Riordan, and how had they learned so quickly of the life-insurance policy? Odds were against any of them, lawyers or the Zimmerman family, having been tipped by police investigators; *their* business was getting information, not giving it.

Well, there was certainly something fishy, and one way—maybe—to find out what the fishy thing was. Pulling on her coat, scribbling a note to McIntyre, Edwina set off to visit Ricky Z.'s mother.

*　　*　　*

"Call me Willie, everybody does," Wilhelmina Zimmerman brayed.

The Zimmerman place was a red brick bungalow in a down-at-the-heels part of Brooklyn, the sort of neighborhood where forty years earlier little boys had played stickball, little girls had pushed doll buggies, and every child had possessed a skate key. Now each postage-stamp yard was enclosed by chain-link fence, the sidewalks were too cracked to skate on, and any kid walking down the street with a stick in his hand was begging to be attacked or arrested.

A bony, horse-faced woman with big yellow front teeth and black hair skinned back into a ponytail, Willie wore a man's flannel shirt, sockless sneakers, and faded jeans overdue for the washing machine; she came to the door with a cigarette dangling from her lips. But she greeted Edwina with every appearance of pleasure and admitted her at once.

"Sit," she bellowed genially, with a wave that threatened to overturn a lamp. "Want a beer?" She galloped out; moments later came the bang of the refrigerator door slamming, bottles clinking recklessly together, and glasses clattering onto a tray.

The lamp had seen better days, and so had the rest of the house. With ashtrays overflowing and the litter of daily life covering every available surface, however, it hardly mattered that the surfaces themselves were worn, stained, burned, cracked, or some combination of all of these. In the center of the room sat a color television, its battered cabinet heaped with old copies of *TV Guide* and its volume cranked to the maximum. On the stereo set, blessedly not operating at the moment, was a stack of old LPs, mostly Burl Ives and Tennessee Ernie Ford records. And in the air, amid stale cigarette smoke, hung a whiff of sweet perfume, or perhaps it was bubble gum.

"Here we go," Willie shouted; the tray crashed down.

"Thank you," Edwina said, stunned by the roar of a home shopping program. Plopping herself into a chair, Willie seized her bottle and guzzled from it, meanwhile staring avidly at the merchandise on the screen.

". . . this lovely twenty-four-piece silver-plated serving set!" the show's host yelled, displaying the hideous objects being presented for sale as an 800 number snaked past.

"Jeez, that'd look real gorgeous in here, don'tcha think? You want cheese an' crackers? I'm gonna have some."

Willie bolted to the kitchen again, returning with a box of saltines, a tub of bright-orange cheese spread, and a steak knife, which she stabbed into the gluey-looking substance in the tub.

"Help yourself," she invited, slamming her body back into the chair and returning her attention to the screen. "Hey, that is so rich-looking, dont'cha think that'd look terrific on me?"

Tentatively Edwina sipped her beer. The small house seemed to quake with the blare of the TV, Willie's bellowed comments at it and at Edwina, and with the thunder, from somewhere in another room, of a radio thumping out the steady beat of one Top 40 tune after another.

Quietly, she agreed that the feather boa being displayed on the screen—imitation ostrich feathers dyed exactly the same shade of pink as Pepto-Bismol—would look very nice on Willie.

"But that," she added, "isn't why I'm here."

Willie's greedy gaze did not waver from the television, and she did not answer. On a hunch, Edwina got up, moved to where Willie could not help seeing her, and repeated herself.

"I know," Willie replied. "You told me. Didn't tell me every-thing, though, I bet. You people, you never do."

She heaped a saltine with cheese spread and demolished it with her large, nicotine-stained teeth. "So now," she mumbled around the snack, "I just ignore you all when you come around asking me your silly questions."

Swallowing the rest of her beer, she reached for the remote. Stations whirled past in a blur until the screen went black and silent. "Don't get me wrong, I enjoy company," Willie added pleasantly enough. "And you ain't like some of the other ones, either, act like they're too damn good to sit down with a person."

Forcing a smile, Edwina took a sip of beer. Willie's voice held no rancor, but her eyes had gone flat and distant. When she spoke again, it was as if she were reading from invisible cue cards somewhere, and had read the same words many times before.

"He was a good boy," she recited, not seeming to realize she was shouting. "Never gave me a minute of trouble, and now he's dead. All these people keep comin' around askin' questions, wantin' to know all about crimes Ricky did. Ricky never did any crimes."

"People have been here asking questions?" Edwina shouted the words, and Willie nodded. In the corner of the ceiling hung an elaborate cobweb with a spider quivering alertly at the center of it; similar webs festooned the venetian blinds. Whatever she had done with the proceeds of Ricky's insurance policy, it didn't look as if Willie had hired herself any cleaning help—or gone on any wild spending sprees, either, despite her fascination with the home shopping program.

"First police," Willie said, "then FBI. Men from the army, thought Ricky stole some stuff. I told 'em all they were full of it, but they just kept askin'. Where did he go, what were his friends like? One of 'em had the nerve to ask me, did Ricky set fires or hurt animals when he was little. That guy was lucky I didn't give him a smack."

All this came out in Willie's normal speaking voice, which could in a pinch have been used for riot control. "Wouldn't it be easier," Edwina asked, "just to put your hearing aids in?" These appliances, she had noticed, were lying in a glass bowl filled with small household junk: old keys, loose change, rubber bands, and a bunch of hairpins.

Willie made a rude noise. "I don't need them damn things. 'Sides, now Ricky's gone I ain't got nobody to fix 'em for me. Fellow down at the store, all he's good for is sending 'em away. Get 'em back, they're no better'n before. Ricky," she yelled, "was good at that electronic stuff."

"Mrs. Zimmerman," said Edwina, feeling the time had come to fish or cut bait; for one thing, her own hearing couldn't survive much more of this, "you're right, I didn't tell you everything. I am an investigator, but not with any law-enforcement agency. I help people find out the truth about things, criminal things, usually, and I think the boy who's in jail for killing your son might not have done it. That's why I'm asking about Ricky."

Willie's dark gaze flickered appreciatively as she followed every word of this. "Well, I thank you. Them other ones was lying bastards. But Ricky didn't even live here anymore, just kept a little hobby shop down in the basement. Came by to eat sometimes, or get stuff out of a footlocker he kept down there."

Edwina sat up alertly, but Willie bellowed on. "An' his stuff is all cleared out, I put it with the trash, every damn bit of it. Felt bad enough without having to look at his things every time I wanted to go down there.

"So," she finished with a touch of disgust, "don't start getting all excited about goin' down there yourself and rootin' through. That's what they all wanted, but nothing was ever down there 'cept a bunch of model-airplane motors, wires and batteries and so on, an' now it ain't."

Drat, Edwina thought. "Mrs. Zimmerman, what did Ricky do for a living? For a job? I mean, he did work, didn't he? He had a car, and he must have paid the premiums on the life-insurance policy he left you . . ."

For the first time, Willie Zimmerman's brown eyes showed a hint of hostility. Still, she answered easily enough.

"He worked. For a demolition company, the kind that tears down big buildings. When you see on TV, some old hotel fallin' in a cloud of dust, bricks flyin' about a mile up in the air—well, that was Ricky. Only he got laid off."

"I see," Edwina said evenly. "Why was that?"

Willie's look chilled another fraction of a degree. "The boss didn't like him. Jealous, 'cause Ricky knew more than he did. So Ricky got laid off about a year before . . . Anyway, he was lookin' for work. You think somebody else killed him?"

Edwina relaxed; of course Willie didn't like talking about Ricky getting fired—not that Edwina believed this story for a moment, but it was pretty clear that Willie did.

"Right now it's just a possibility," Edwina said, "something I'm looking into. I have no idea whether or not I'm on the right track. You've been very helpful, though, and I'll let you know if anything comes of it."

She got up, thinking that Willie Zimmerman really was just as plain and harmless as she seemed. It wouldn't have been the first time a rotten son managed to fool a decent mother.

She moved toward the front door, where Willie's abandoned attempts at gracious living seemed symbolized by a small table covered with wood-grain adhesive paper. On the table was a yellow plastic doily with a black glass planter shaped like a crouching panther centered on it. Straggling from the planter was the pale, papery corpse of what had once been a philodendron.

"Actually, there was one other thing," Edwina said as Willie got up and followed her to the door.

To her left a narrow, shabby staircase led up, probably to the bedrooms; on each step lay a broken pair of shoes or a dirty item of clothing. To her right was a door, beyond which the radio continued blaring.

"I know you nearly had a problem with the lawyers of a man named Tom Riordan, wanting to take Ricky's insurance money away from you," Edwina went on. She glanced into the dusty mirror hanging slightly askew among some particularly venerable-looking cobwebs, just above the little table with the dead plant on it, and saw Willie's eyes following her words intently.

"And I was wondering if anyone asked you to give them some of that money. In return for making sure Mr. Riordan's lawyers couldn't get at it, I mean, by saying that Ricky had already died when Mr. Riordan was killed."

Well, she'd had to ask. But, spying a smudge of something on her cheek and leaning into the mirror to wipe it off, Edwina felt vexed at herself for having raised the subject. The idea of Willie faking her son's time of death had sounded perfectly possible, right up until the moment Edwina met Willie herself.

Now, though, it was ridiculous. Willie wouldn't have come up with such a thing, would not have comprehended it if someone else had, and wouldn't have gone along with it in any case. Stolid and simple Willie Zimmerman might be, Edwina thought as she dabbed at her cheek, but there remained advantages to such homely qualities; one might as well try corrupting a block of wood.

The smudge at last yielded to her rubbing. "I'm sorry," she began, turning back to Willie, and the words died in her throat.

Willie Zimmerman gripped the steak knife from the hideous tub of cheese, a look of bright purpose on her face. Willie's hand flashed up faster than Edwina would have thought possible; the knife's tip flew by, thudding into the wallboard behind her.

"Damn spiders," Willie said with satisfaction, dislodging the knife and with it the large brown creature she had skewered. The spider's legs twitched feebly and were still. "There wasn't any insurance money," she said, shaking the dead spider into the pot with the dead philodendron. "Insurance company screwed us out of it, said Ricky didn't fill out the papers right. So them lawyers was chasin' air, too."

"Oh. That's . . . too bad. For you, I mean," said Edwina, whose opinion of the other woman had just been changed utterly. There was probably a reason why a young man grew up to be an expert at blowing other people to smithereens, and in Willie's briefly unguarded expression she thought she had just glimpsed it.

"Sorry you gotta go," said Willie, not sounding sorry at all. As

Edwina reached the front step, the door slammed behind her and the porch light snapped out, leaving her in darkness.

* * *

"I don't know," Edwina said into the telephone. "Maybe she's a perfectly nice woman who just happens to have a thing about spiders, and she spooked me without meaning to."

She was lying on one of the two large beds in the garishly decorated motel room she had rented for herself; outside it was snowing hard again, and she did not relish the idea of six hours on a blizzard-choked interstate.

"But," she added, "I don't think so. I smelled perfume—Willie wasn't wearing any—or bubble gum—and Willie doesn't chew gum; she smokes. The music blaring out of the other room wasn't the kind Willie listens to, and I got the strong feeling when she talked about Ricky that she was saying what she was supposed to say. I think Ricky's sister was in the house, and I'll bet she'd told Willie what to tell me and what not to."

In the hall an ice machine clattered relentlessly; outside, trucks rumbled on the highway a hundred yards away. It was the sort of cheap, barely tolerable place McIntyre would have chosen to stay in, were he traveling alone, on the theory that tomorrow night he would be back in his own bed, and tonight would be just a memory, so what was the point of spending money on it?

The difference was that McIntyre could probably have slept directly on the highway, so long as the trucks were only rolling past him and not over him. His ability to become horizontal and unconscious at the same moment was, like his frugality, one of the little quirks Edwina found both irritating and admirable. She, on the other hand, had chosen the place simply because all the motels for ten miles around were just like it.

At the other end of the phone she could hear him now, moving about the kitchen as he put together his dinner: canned baked beans and potted ham on white toast, she suspected.

"There's something predatory about her, too," Edwina went on, as through the phone line came the clink of the can opener and the metallic *ka-chunk* of the toaster lever. "I wouldn't put it past her to have taught Ricky how to build all those bombs."

"Gave him a junior arsonist's kit for Christmas, you mean?" McIntyre chuckled.

"Right." She smiled. "So, what have you been up to?" She let her head fall back onto the pile of pillows.

"Well," he said, "I've been chasing a particularly nasty guy through six counties, and not quite catching him, and I've been keeping an eye on the Whitlock case for you."

"Thank you. And?"

"And it turns out Theresa had quite a thriving criminal career before she married Whitlock. Maybe she was turning tricks again, got involved in something a little too deep. Maybe she heard something she wasn't supposed to hear."

Ice rattled in his glass. "And if that's what happened, we might never find the shooter," he said. "The department won't allocate forever for that kind of thing, you know. Sooner or later it's going to be back-burner time if nothing useful breaks on it."

This was so close to what Jennifer Warren had said that for a moment Edwina was tempted to protest. But if it happened, it wouldn't be McIntyre's doing; it was just the way things went.

Also, it was all the more reason to keep at things, herself. From his tone, it sounded as if the Whitlock case had gone from boil to simmer in only a couple of days and would soon be cooling fast. *Disposable girls,* Jennifer had said; remembering, Edwina sighed.

"Oops," said McIntyre, "my toast's done. See you tomorrow?"

"Right," she told him, and hung up.

By now she was getting hungry, too; morosely she regarded the menu of the restaurant located across the highway from the motel.

Roast Beef With Hot Au Juice Sauce, it said. Chock Full O' Meat Caesar Salad. And her own personal favorite, the All You Can Eat Batter-Fried Clam Special.

Under the best of circumstances, all she could eat of batter-fried clams was none—the batter always outweighed the clam by a ratio of ten to nothing—and under the circumstances the word "meat" seemed suspiciously nonspecific: The motel was in an area where the restaurants were all reputedly controlled by members of famous crime families, some of whom were also meat wholesalers and others of whom were known upon occasion to need to dispose of inconvenient witnesses, and Edwina suspected that if she could make the logical connection, so could the meat wholesalers.

Thus she supposed that for tonight she would subsist on a Velveeta omelette, french fries tasting of clams, and a salad of limp iceberg lettuce and hothouse tomatoes daubed with Thousand Island dressing. She was preparing to go out and get this wondrous repast when the phone rang with a message from John D. Maxwell, who wanted to know if she would get in touch with him at once, to arrange an interview with his client first thing in the morning.

*   *   *

"I took the guy's car. I did. But I was gonna, you know, bring it back. And, like, I didn't know the guy was *in* the car when I took it. I mean, do I look like a body snatcher?"

Edwina thought Maurice C. Underhill III did not look at all like a body snatcher. For one thing, there was the problem of being able to lift a body, which Maurice did not look as if he could do. Six months in the Connecticut state correctional system had done nothing for his muscle tone; his pale flesh hung flabbily from his arms, and his cheekbones jutted from his face, which was notable for its almost complete absence of chin.

"No, you don't," Edwina said into the speakerphone.

86

Maurice's nose was long and pointed, twitching regularly as if he sniffed danger—which considering his present address and situation, Edwina thought, he probably did—and his eyes darted nervously beyond the sheet of wire-reinforced Plexiglas that separated the visitors' area from the long, narrow space, more a hallway than a room, where the prisoners sat. Even more than in his photograph, Maurice resembled a rodent of the nuisance type; his hands, improbably delicate, were like small pink paws.

"Anyway," he said, "Maxwell says talk to you, my folks say talk to you. But I don't know what to tell you, like, I ain't already said. I met the guy, he said he'd give me a ride, he's got this excellent set of wheels, only he says I should start walking 'cause he's got some business to do, first. So, hey, I start walkin'." Maurice fell silent.

"Go on." As she waited, Edwina felt weighed down by the mixture of misery, desperation, and fear that seemed to hang like poison gas in the visitors' area of the prison. The chairs, bolted to the floor, were filled with impoverished-looking women, mostly black and Hispanic, holding infants and toddlers up to the greenish Plexiglas.

From the other side, men gazed hungrily out, some placing their palms flat on the barrier or leaning up to kiss it; others slouched sullenly, their eyes hooded in fury as their wives or girlfriends chattered and cajoled, pleaded and wept.

"Maurice? We haven't got all day, you know."

"Huh?" Maurice's tiny eyes focused on Edwina. "Oh, yeah. I just kinda like, space out sometimes, you know? This place, I mean, it's *muy weirdoso*." He sighed dreamily, tugging at his earlobe.

Edwina wished that earlobe were a chain, attached to Maurice's light switch; the upstairs illumination he had evidenced so far was, to put it mildly, meager.

"Maurice. Then what happened? After you met Ricky Z. in the park, and he told you he would give you a ride."

"Oh. Yeah, after that." He concentrated with an effort. "Uh, I walked. Only, I got about a half mile and figured, why wear myself out? Guy said he'd come and pick me up, I figured, wait. Like, why walk when I could ride?"

Maurice frowned as if trying without success to puzzle out how he, an ordinary young man from a nice home and a good family, could have gotten into such bad trouble, so fast.

"Only he didn't come," Maurice said injuredly, as if it must all in some obscure way be Ricky's fault. "So I went back in, to look for him."

When Maurice was not speaking, he let his mouth hang open several inches, exposing small sharp teeth that some dedicated orthodontist had had a valiant but only partly successful try at straightening; now, no doubt because of the obstacles presented to a program of regular oral hygiene by bathrooms that doubled as gang hangouts, romantic-assignation spots, and unofficial but frequently utilized out-and-out execution chambers, Maurice's teeth were also covered with what looked very much like, but of course could not be, green moss.

This, combined with his slack, defeated posture and furtive expression, made Maurice Underhill III an even less effective spokesman for himself than he might otherwise have been. He was, Edwina realized, precisely the sort of defendant whom prosecutors and defense attorneys all got together and laughed at, when they gathered late enough at night for such trivial distinctions as guilt and innocence to have dissolved into an alcoholic haze.

Maurice was young, dumb, and in the right spot at the wrong time; he was also a rich white kid, and his conviction and long, difficult imprisonment would gain the prosecuting attorney some very welcome arguing points the next time some rabble-rouser decided to rattle a few of the rustier cages down at City Hall.

"Okay, Maurice," Edwina said. "You went back. Think, now.

The car was sitting there. Was the engine running? Was anyone else in the rest area?"

Maurice shook his head positively. "Hey, no. Like, the car was sitting there, keys in it, nobody else around. I thought I'd just drive it a little. I'd told the guy, *primo* car, man. He knew I, like, *appreciated* it. I didn't think he'd mind."

Maurice was perhaps the most unskilled liar Edwina had ever encountered. As he spoke, his gaze shifted evasively while his fingers fiddled with his earlobe, scratched his neck, and moved to his mouth, where his little rat teeth began nibbling on them.

"You didn't think he'd mind you taking his car for two days, leaving him in the middle of nowhere?" By now Edwina had had just about enough of Maurice Underhill III, who still had not grasped the simple reason behind his own predicament. At her words, his lip curled resentfully; it was not, he was about to protest, fair.

Swiftly she spoke again, before he could make her lose her temper; making people lose their tempers was the one thing, apparently, that Maurice was good at. Meanwhile she also revised her opinion of the fees John D. Maxwell was probably charging; whatever Maxwell was being paid to defend Maurice, it could not possibly be enough.

"Tell me, Maurice, did you think the state police would mind your driving the car at ninety on the turnpike? Did you think they'd mind your pointing a pistol at them after they'd pulled you over? Or did you think they'd understand you *appreciated* cars and guns so much that you simply couldn't help yourself, and let you get away with it?"

Maurice shrugged sullenly. "Hey," he muttered, "Maxwell said you were gonna, like, be on *my* side. It's not *my* fault the guy had to get himself killed, get *me* in all this trouble. Why doesn't somebody go looking for that *other* car, why do *I* have to get blamed for everything?"

Suddenly the horrid room with its noise and misery and bad smells seemed very clear and still. "Other car?" Edwina asked.

Maurice's sloping shoulder moved sulkily again. "Went in while I was walkin' out. Went out when I was walkin' back in. I figured maybe the guy went off in it, when I didn't find him anywhere around. Only, nobody believed me about it. What's the point of even *having* a lie-detector test," he queried in tones of deepest reproach, "if, like, nobody *still* believes you?"

It was, in fact, the one hurdle Maurice had managed to clear successfully. But since the test results could not be admitted as evidence in court, and because Maurice in every other respect seemed so thoroughly, obviously guilty, the lie-detector test had proved useless to his defense.

Now, however, Edwina applied her own test: "Maurice, *was* there another car that day? And do you remember anything about it?"

"There was a car. It was blue. That's all I remember. I wasn't, like, paying attention."

Edwina watched Maurice carefully. He was one of the least attractive youths she had ever met, but at present his eyes were not shifting nor were his fingers picking, tugging, scratching, or thoughtlessly investigating the contents of one nostril or the other. The wheedling, manipulative tone was gone from his voice, and his nose had stopped twitching, so for once he did not appear to be sniffing about for something new to weasel out of. Simply, Maurice sat there not yanking her chain.

"Are you gonna get me out of here?" he asked.

Edwina got up. There was only one good thing about this place, and that was the fact that she could leave it. Against her will, she began to feel sorry for Maurice, so devoid of any of the equipment he would have needed—mental, emotional, or physical—to make choices other than the ones he had made.

"I don't know," she answered. "What would you do if I did?"

His shoulder gave a morose shift, and at once he was the old Maurice again: a dreary, petulant juvenile who didn't understand why the world was so against him when all he'd wanted was to have a little fun. "Dunno," he muttered. "Hang around, I guess."

"I see. Well, you think about it and see if you can come up with something better than hanging around, all right?"

Maurice nodded. He'd heard all that sort of thing before. Edwina wondered if it might not be better to leave him here: Next time, he might do something worse than stealing a car and waving a gun in a trooper's face. Next time, the injured look in Maurice Underhill's eyes said, he might really kill somebody.

But this time, Edwina was pretty sure, Maurice hadn't.

SIX

"Harry," said Edwina into the telephone, "come and have dinner with me tonight. Please?"

It was late afternoon; arriving home from her prison visit, Edwina had found a note from McIntyre in place of the one she had left for him. The suspect he had been tracking was in the custody of a small-town sheriff, somewhere in upstate Connecticut; McIntyre had gone up there to collect him and would be home tomorrow.

But in the refrigerator were two sirloin steaks and an unopened bottle of Chablis, while on Edwina's agenda for the evening was a session of serious, determined brain-cudgeling, an activity she despised pursuing alone.

"Hmm," Harry Lemon said in the judicious tone he usually saved for a cell mass that might or might not be a particularly nasty brand of small-cell pulmonary carcinoma. "And to what, may I ask, do I owe this sudden impulse toward the care and feeding of the terminally reclusive—that is to say, my humble self?"

"Harry, if you'd accept more invitations, you'd get more of them," she said. "Besides, I really need you."

Harry's idea of a stimulating evening was a London *Times* crossword puzzle, the complete *Art of the Fugue*, and the tying of five hundred or so surgical knots in a length of suture silk, since according to Harry when it came to fine-tuning one's motor skills there was no such thing as too much practice.

"Yes," said Harry, "I thought I detected the tinny ring of the ulterior motive, and this, I confess, does cause me some alarm. You're not going to try wheedling more of those painkillers out of me, are you?"

"Oh, Harry, of course not; I haven't even taken any of them. I just need someone to nitpick the logical flaws in a little theory I'm developing, and you're the most nit—er, I mean, the most *logical* person I know. Other than Martin, that is, but he's out catching criminals."

"Ah," said Harry. "All right, then, I'll be there. Do chill those martini glasses, won't you? The heirloom ones, so fragile you could bite through them."

Harry sighed at the recalled pleasure of these useless but wonderfully lovely objects, all the more luxurious since in his own daily life Harry drank from plastic, paper, or foam and ate directly from the containers of the takeout food upon which, for the most part, he subsisted.

"I know the ones, Harry. I'll get them out now." Smiling, Edwina put the receiver on its hook and went to find the bottle of Beefeater's she saved for Harry's visits. It was, she thought, out in the back pantry with the bottles of claret, port and brandy, liquors she never drank and used rarely for cooking.

On her way she took also some old newspapers that Martin had been reading while she was away; stepping out the back door, she lifted the lid of the recycling container meant for cardboard and paper goods, put the newspapers into it, and turned. Then she stopped, deciding suddenly to mix those martinis now and to drink one very quickly, before the shock of what she was seeing managed to unnerve her for the rest of the night.

Slowly, she reached out toward the thing that was spiked to her back door with a hatpin. It was an old-fashioned, sturdy, elaborate hatpin, topped with a fanciful concoction of black jet beads. Impaled on the pin was a rat's head. That, she thought with the sort of distant, anesthetized perception with which one notices that one's car is stalled in the path of an onrushing eighteen-wheeler, must have taken some doing. Stuffed into the rat's toothy mouth was a scrap of yellow notebook paper.

Gingerly, Edwina removed the paper from the rat's mouth and smoothed it so that she could read it. The angry, back-slanted scrawl was familiar: too familiar. At the sight of it, Theresa Whitlock's frightened face rose in Edwina's memory; Theresa, who like poor awful Maurice Underhill had been telling the truth all along, only no one had believed her.

Get the idea? was all the scribbled note said.

* * *

"Let's just say," Edwina suggested to Harry when they were seated in the kitchen and supplied with drinks, snacks, and the comforting warmth of the heretofore incorrigible woodstove, which Edwina had persuaded into heating action by threatening to send it immediately to the scrap-iron dealer, "let's say Theresa hired Ricky Z. to kill Tom Riordan, only Riordan found out about it and used the opportunity to disappear."

Harry sipped, and munched a cheese puff. "Hmm," he said. "These are excellent. I didn't realize your skills extended to the pastry department, Edwina."

"They don't. Martin made these. I just defrosted them and baked them. Harry, what do you think?"

He took another cheese puff. "I think it doesn't really account adequately for Zimmerman's death, or Theresa Whitlock's, either.

95

Even if Riordan were very angry, he'd hardly have come out of hiding just for revenge against her; it would be too much of a risk. And there's no reason to assume it was Zimmerman who tipped Riordan off to the car bomb—maybe Zimmerman thought Riordan *was* in the car."

He drank more of his martini, holding the delicate glass by its slender stem and savoring the entire experience. "I will, however, consider the muddying of the waters by the Zimmermans. In view of her son's likely friends and associates, and her own probable awareness of them, I doubt Mrs. Z. *or* her daughter would have needed to pay anyone to fudge the time of the boy's death. I think a word to the wise would have sufficed—a word, perhaps, like 'kneecap.' But how do you know the time of death really *was* fudged, Edwina—and why would they do it?"

Edwina tasted her own martini cautiously, having already drunk one for medicinal purposes before Harry arrived. The rat's head was gone from the back door; considering the way she felt about the house she thought it made an unusually appropriate door ornament, but one could hardly leave it there for Harry to come upon unawares, and besides the present unseasonably early cold weather could not be expected to last forever.

So, after taking a good stiff drink and a dozen Polaroid photographs of the thing—it was evidence, although of what she was not yet sure—she had marshaled her resolve, seized the shaft of the hatpin with a pair of pliers, and pulled. The pin came free easily; so, unfortunately, did the head, which slipped off the pin and fell at her feet with a thump. Now it reposed in the trash barrel, wrapped in newspapers, so Maxie would not find it and decide that someone had brought him a new toy.

"They'd do it," she replied, "to make sure they got to keep Ricky's life-insurance money. And the reason I'm pretty certain *someone* did it is this: When Maurice Underhill says he saw Ricky Zimmerman alive, it was hours *after* Riordan's car blew up—*not* before, as the medical examiner's report had it. And Maurice has no reason to be lying about the time."

"Therefore?" Harry asked, accepting this much.

"Therefore, Zimmerman could have set the bomb, and probably did; that links Zimmerman to Riordan. Theresa's link is looser, but she says she killed Riordan, so I think she hired Zimmerman."

"Hmm." Harry tipped his head inquiringly.

"Even fishier," Edwina went on, "is the timing of what happened afterwards: Riordan's lawyers went after that money before the body in the bombed car was even identified—or as it turned out, not identified. They thought that Riordan was dead and Zimmerman killed him, but how did they make the connection so fast?"

She munched one of McIntyre's cheese puffs, which indeed were delicious, although how one could make anything less than delicious out of equal parts butter and cheddar cheese creamed together with a little flour, she failed to comprehend.

"It was almost," she said, "as if Riordan himself had told them what happened. And then Thomas Riordan vanished, which to me points at Riordan for Ricky's death *and* Theresa's; the link is circumstantial, I will grant you, but I still like it a lot."

"Well," Harry offered, "what if Ricky's mother or sister knew he was hired to kill Riordan? When they heard Riordan's car was bombed and Ricky was dead, they put two and two together—and they figured sooner or later Riordan's lawyers would, too."

She frowned. "But it was sooner, not later; it explains why they acted fast, but not why the lawyers did. And why *would* Riordan come after Theresa after all this time? Revenge *is* a skimpy reason to take such a risk, especially since Riordan's dropped out of sight so successfully, otherwise. But she knew his handwriting—the same writing as in the note I received, which I find unnerving. Now *I'm* being menaced by a dead man."

"No," Harry said, "you're not. You have at your table an expert on the habits of the deceased, Edwina, and I can tell you positively that the deceased have no habits whatsoever. There is only one thing a dead person can do with any effectiveness, and it is not something I care to discuss so near the dinner hour."

"Harry, I meant it metaphorically. Although," Edwina mused, "for a living person, Riordan certainly has managed to lie low. Two people he might like to have dead *are* dead, and notes in his handwriting have shown up, but otherwise there hasn't been a peep out of him for months. I wonder . . ."

But Harry wasn't listening. "Speaking of dinner," he said, looking about hungrily.

"Oh, heavens." Edwina jumped up. "This gin has rotted my brain. Sit," she commanded as Harry made to rise, "finish those cheese puffs, and pour yourself another drink if you like."

"Indeed," Harry said happily, following these instructions as he lounged at ease in her kitchen rocker, clad in his usual garb of green scrub suit, white athletic socks, and penny loafers. His round, amiable face was pink with gin and with the warmth radiating from the wood stove—she would, she reflected, have to threaten that stove more often—and his pale-blue eyes were contemplative.

Strolling in, Maxie spotted the large warm object reposing in the rocker and settled upon it; Harry's fingers with their clean, square-clipped nails moved casually over Maxie's head. In response, the black cat rolled his yellow eyes, stretched to the fullest extent his musculature would allow, and collapsed in sybaritic pleasure.

Ordinarily, Edwina would have found this sight delightful, but she could not find it so, now. Scrubbing the skins of the potatoes that she planned to bake, halve, empty of their white meat, and refill to bake again once the mashed meat was fortified with butter, salt, sour cream, chives, and fresh Parmesan, she wished she could forget about the rat's head.

But she couldn't; its message was clear and direct, and too ominous to ignore. Distractedly, she lifted her martini glass, and drank more at one time from it than was wise. As she did, the glass clinked against her front tooth; pain shot thrillingly up her face, into her eye socket, and from there into her brain.

"Oof." She swallowed the rest of the martini; if ever there was a time for painkiller, this was it, only she wasn't going to mix pills with alcohol, so she would have to stick with alcohol.

"You," said Harry with a fine gift for understatement, "look uncomfortable." He peered narrowly at her. "Hmm. Yes, I think I see the trouble. You're going to have to go back to the dentist, you know. But for now, get an ice cube from the freezer and rub it hard into the soft spot between your thumb and first finger."

This sounded ridiculous; icing her hand was unlikely to affect her mouth, other than to increase in number and variety the swear words apt to come out of it. But her choices were limited: She could try Harry's idea or fall moaning to the floor. Breathing carefully to limit air movement against the tooth, she tottered to the freezer and fished out an ice cube.

"Rub it hard," Harry instructed. "Hard enough so it hurts more than you want it to."

Sinking into a chair, Edwina did this. At first there was no response except more pain from the triangle of flesh between her thumb and forefinger; gradually, however, an amazing thing happened. The misery in her tooth began subsiding, first to an ache, then to a twinge that, while still significant, felt almost like pleasure compared to the original, bone-rattling anguish.

"Harry, that's astonishing. How does it work?"

"Gate control," Harry pronounced, "and how gratifying to see it in action." His face radiated the unalloyed pleasure of a man for whom pain relief was a sort of grail, right up there with the universally effective antibiotic, the even halfway effective antiviral, and the incisionless, instantly reversible vasectomy.

"The gate-control theory of pain," he explained, "says you can't get two of the same kind of thing through the same narrow gate in the nervous system at the same time. And although no one knows what *kind* of thing a pain message is, or where the gate is, or what controls it, either, in practice the theory works fine. If you want to block a pain message, send another pain message. Send it forcefully, repeatedly, from the right spot, and *voilà*—no more pain."

The microwave oven pinged; Edwina got up to attend to it. "How *long* does it work? That is, once you've blocked the message—"

"Sometimes," Harry replied, "it never comes back. I do not," he added severely, "expect this to be true in your case."

Earnestly he sat forward. "Unless you have that tooth fixed soon, you may expect to experience symptoms including more pain, fever, malaise, putrid discharge, halitosis, and such technically interesting complications as abscess formation, bone infection, sinus involvement, spinal-cord inflammation, and potentially irreversible septic shock, along with a deep, ongoing sense of your own idiocy for not having prevented these developments in the first place."

He paused for breath. "Do I make myself clear?"

Edwina gulped. The experience of being scolded by Harry was rare, chastening, and instructive. When you were ill, he didn't just want you to get better; he insisted you get better, and was perfectly willing to swat you firmly and repeatedly with the verbal equivalent of a rolled-up newspaper in order to accomplish this. To Harry, illness was not a misfortune; it was the enemy, and you were his battleground.

"Yes, Harry," she said, "I understand. I'll phone Arthur tomorrow. For now, though . . ."

Easing Maxie to the floor, Harry got up. "For now," he said, "let's finish cooking dinner. And afterwards, I want a look at that rat."

*   *   *

"Hmm," said Harry when the dinner had been eaten, the wine drunk, the dishes cleared away, and the coffee poured. Also, the rat's head had been resurrected and laid out on fresh newspapers, in the middle of the kitchen's butcher-block center island.

"First of all, this was your standard city rat," Harry said, "the kind that infests alleys and eats garbage and so on, not the variety people purchase and keep as pets for some bizarre reason known only to themselves. It is a remarkably *clean* rat, though. You don't happen to keep a scalpel in the house, do you, Edwina?"

Edwina forced from her mind any thought of shuddering or of making disgusted noises. Examining a rat's head was probably not Harry's idea of much fun, either, but he seemed to think it was important; besides, one properly allowed the guest his choice of activities for the evening, and Harry had chosen this one.

"No," she said, "but will a single-edged razor blade do?"

"Perfect," he said when she had fetched one from the utility drawer. "You see, this head has been severed neatly, quite low on the spinal column. So I think I may be able to determine . . ."

Against her own will, she watched fascinated as he exposed the spinal bones of the deceased animal. Even a single-edged razor, when wielded by Harry, seemed almost like a magical tool; he touched its sharp edge purposefully to the tissue, against the grain of the muscle fibers, whereupon the flesh fell away cleanly on either side of the incision he was creating.

"Yes," he said. "All the cervical vertebrae intact, without a sign of crushing injury. That means the animal was acquired by capturing it alive, not by prying its neck from a trap."

"How do you know it wasn't poisoned, or found dead? And what does any of that mean, anyway?" Edwina asked. On the floor Maxie paced impatiently, appearing to believe that once the humans had finished playing with his toy, he would be allowed to play with it.

"Have you ever observed a dead rat, anywhere?" Harry asked. "Other, that is, than in a trap? No," he answered himself, "you haven't, because rats are scavenging machines. *Omnivorous* scavenging machines, among whom the line between eating and being eaten is vanishingly narrow. Perhaps someone poisoned it after its capture, but not before. Now, just one more little scrape, and . . . yes, I thought so. Observe."

Harry stepped back, revealing what looked like a nightmare's anatomy lesson. The rat's head had been divested of its skin, and the bony front portion of its long, back-sloping skull had been exposed.

"Harry," said Edwina, beginning in spite of his artistry to feel thoroughly repelled, "I don't see the point of—"

"The point," Harry replied, "is that no point was necessary, other than to fasten the thing to your back door. See here, the puncture in the frontal cranium? That's where the hatpin was put through the bone, but there aren't any fracture lines around it. So the implement wasn't driven through in crude fashion; rather, it was inserted, via a perforation created for that purpose. Also, the spongy consistency of the tissue suggests it has been frozen until quite recently—in order, I would guess, to preserve it. All of which, to me, implies several things."

He wrapped the object neatly back up again, deposited it in the plastic bag she had provided for him, and began washing his hands vigorously at the sink.

"First," he said, "someone went to some trouble to get this rat at all. Capturing and transporting such a feral creature is unpleasant, difficult, and risky. Its bite can be wicked, and it can transmit some wicked illnesses. The parasites it carries can be dangerous, as well. But someone really wanted it—most likely, I should say, because the severed head of a Norway rat is one of the most naturally communicative objects produced by nature."

"To send me," she murmured as Maxie twined disappointedly at her feet, "a message."

"To send *someone* a message," he corrected, sudsing himself to the elbows. "That's the other thing: The head was preserved, which means it may not have been acquired for you specifically. It was gotten and saved for when it might be needed. For some sort of ongoing program of intimidation, perhaps."

He toweled off vigorously. "Now, let's extrapolate to the person with whom we're dealing, shall we? You did not, I gather, notice this object when you arrived home; therefore someone crept up to your door, attached it, and crept away unnoticed while you were in the house. Therefore, the person in question is daring and stealthy."

"And angry," Edwina said. "It doesn't only feel as if I've gotten a nasty message. It feels as if it's an enraged one."

"Very angry," Harry agreed. "Whoever it is doesn't just dislike something you are doing. He or she is furious with you. But what disturbs me most, I think, is the careful preparation of the object along with the elaborate decorativeness of the hatpin. Driving a nail through the thing would have done just as well."

Edwina nodded unhappily. "I see what you're getting at." She spread the Polaroids out on the table. "I remember thinking someone had gone to rather a lot of unnecessary trouble."

"Unnecessary, but enjoyable. Here we have someone who can plan, who takes risks, who is stealthy, and who has raised anger to an art form. Someone who takes pleasure in doing something unpleasant, doing it elaborately and meticulously.

"In short," Harry finished, "I believe that here we have more than a cruel prankster, or even a garden-variety murderer. Here, I think, we have a sociopath, and such persons do not quit or lose interest. When their purposes are thwarted, they escalate the frequency and intensity of their attacks."

"I see. So you think I ought to give up trying to find out who killed Theresa Whitlock, and let it be known to all concerned that I *am* giving up? To get out of this person's line of fire?"

Outside the kitchen windows, the night was clear and still. A full moon made skeletons of maples, and dark, looming presences of the evergreens, over the blue-white snow. Against her expectations Harry had drunk only two martinis and one glass of wine, and was now pouring himself another cup of coffee, all of which put paid to her private hope for an occupied guest room; soon Harry would be driving away quite soberly and responsibly, and she and Maxie would be alone.

Which, she thought firmly, is just as it should be. It is my house, after all; I may despise it, but I can defend it, and myself. Still, the thing on the door had rattled her.

"No, I don't think you should quit," Harry said, breaking in on her thoughts.

"Oh. But Harry, if you think it's so risky, why—"

"Because," he said simply, "I doubt your quitting would help. Once you've attracted the attention of a person like this, it's damned difficult getting rid of it. Putting the word out that you've quit could make things worse, if for instance it were perceived as a trick. No, I think someone will have to learn who this person is, and stop him. Or," he added, "her."

He set his emptied coffee cup carefully in the sink. "But until someone does, remember: You aren't dealing with a common criminal here, at least in my opinion. Sorry to be the bearer of bad tidings, but I don't like the look of this, and my only real advice is that you should be careful."

Unhappily, he regarded the grisly snapshots. "Yes, I advise you to be very careful, indeed."

The Colt .38 Detective Special was a six-shot revolver with a glossy blue-steel barrel, checkered zebrawood grips, and a red ramp front sight. A light, classically attractive weapon with a moderately heavy pull and a respectable kick, it was reasonably accurate when equipped with 148-grain semi wad-cutters, the ammunition of choice for professional target-range practice, of which Edwina had so far completed 250 increasingly successful hours.

When loaded with 129-grain Federal Hydra-Shock hollow-points, however, the Detective Special was something else again. Opening the small cardboard carton of twenty hollowpoints, Edwina slotted six of the dreadfully deadly nickel-plated brass projectiles into the cylinder of the revolver and snapped it closed.

Thoughtfully, she hefted the weapon. It felt heavier, loaded with hollowpoints: not the way it felt on the target range at all. She supposed it must be the weight of responsibility; one did not, after all, propel Federal Hydra-Shocks at 1500 feet per second into the body of a human being without considering the consequences.

Chief among these was a nearly certain end to the existence of the targeted human being, owing to the tendency of hollowpoint ammunition to explode immediately upon being surrounded by human flesh. It was this tendency, desirable or undesirable depending upon which end of the barrel one found oneself staring down, that Edwina sat considering as she gazed at the Colt .38.

At the foot of the bed Maxie stretched, luxuriating in the knowledge that, with McIntyre away, he would be allowed to stay. Setting the .38 on the bedside table, Edwina snapped out the light and got into bed herself.

She had locked the doors and windows, banked the stove, and checked to be sure the bedside telephone extension was properly connected. Also, she had constructed an alarm of emptied tin cans stacked one atop the other against that easily unlocked back door, in case the electronic alarm should be defeated again.

Soon her eyes adjusted to the darkness, and the room faded back up into visibility like a black-and-white photograph being developed. Maxie was a solid black patch; chairs and bureaus appeared made of charcoal. The house gave out the tappings and creakings always produced by old houses in the dead of night, but otherwise remained silent.

At 2:29 A.M., Maxie crept up and settled himself in the crook of her arm; at 3:14, the furnace purred briefly and shut off with its usual tinny bang of heating ducts contracting, and Edwina made her usual middle-of-the-night resolution to find out if it couldn't be stopped from doing that, for heaven's sake.

But nothing else happened; the telephone did not ring, no car approached the house, and no footsteps sounded anywhere in or around it, stealthily or otherwise. Moonlight whitened at the edges of the windowshades, and faded as the moon began setting; presently, the clock's glowing red numerals read 4:51, which was when Edwina began to think that she might sleep.

It was also when the back door eased open and sent all those carefully stacked-up tin cans clattering down.

SEVEN

"You could have killed me," Martin McIntyre remarked from behind his morning newspaper.

"But," Edwina replied, feeling as if the wall of newsprint were constructed instead of concrete and barbed wire, "I didn't."

Instantly upon finding that the intruder was McIntyre, she had lowered the loaded weapon she was gripping. Moments later the electronic alarm had begun shrieking, each of them being so thunderstruck at the unexpected sight of the other that neither had thought to disarm the device within the required forty-five seconds.

There had been no chance of her shooting McIntyre; if he had been an armed burglar, in fact, he might have fired while she was identifying him, a point she felt he appreciated insufficiently but one that had made a considerable impression on her. There is not much time, she thought—for the episode, while brief, had been instructive—during which it is both useful and legitimate to fire a weapon.

At any rate, and shivering with the burst of adrenaline her

nervous system had received, Edwina had phoned the alarm company to say that everything was perfectly all right—this was not an entirely honest assessment of the situation but she didn't think the alarm people wanted to hear about the look on her husband's face—while McIntyre caught his breath and tried not to break his neck, making his way in through scattered tin cans.

The effect on both their tempers had been unfortunate. Now, though, it was nine in the morning, and each of them had regained a measure of composure. "You still," she ventured, "haven't told me why you didn't stay there overnight."

McIntyre turned a page of his newspaper and concentrated on the sports section.

Fine, Edwina thought, picking up the want ads and staring unseeingly at them; be that way. Sunshine streamed through the white ruffled tie-back curtains the decorator had thought would be lovely in the dining room, amidst the authentic Colonial drop-leaf table and spindleback chairs, the pickled-pine hutch with hammered-tin frontispiece, the eighteenth-century hooked rugs and cross-stitched samplers, and the antique pewter displayed on the sideboard—display being the operative word, and the reason Edwina despised it all so heartily.

She took another calming swallow of coffee and tried again. "Martin, how was I supposed to know it was you? Would you have preferred I pull the covers over my head and let some burglar or worse have the run of the place?"

Of course he had been startled, trying to come in without waking her, to find her in the hallway poised in regulation firing stance. But she didn't like being made to feel such a criminal, nor did she enjoy having such a dim view taken of her explanation—for the news that a rat's head bearing an ominous note had been nailed to the back door had served only to sour McIntyre's disposition further.

"I didn't want to stay," he said, neatly avoiding her other

questions. "Room smelled like shower mold, coffee tasted soapy, and it turns out the reason the sheriff grabbed the guy might not even hold up. So I got the guy and got out of there."

"Which was?" At least he was speaking in whole sentences. "The reason the sheriff grabbed the guy, I mean," she said.

"Which was," McIntyre replied, putting down his newspaper, "that the guy's a black guy, walked into a diner and ordered coffee and pie. And in the immortal words of the sheriff—who, by the way, is pretty much funding the whole town on the illegal speed traps he brags about setting up—well, what he said was, 'We don't get many niggers up here, so I figured I'd shake this one up, he'd go home an' tell all his little brown cousins they'd better pick some other town to try an' dee-segregate.' "

McIntyre shook his head. "And all the time he's talking, he's nudging me. White man to white man, you see. And I'm just thinking two little words: unlawful arrest. I think we can still get the guy on our charges, but it sure isn't going to make the process any easier."

Edwina took an unthinking bite of her toast, remembering too late that she ought not to disturb that tooth. But it functioned without protest; perhaps it had only needed to settle down, after all. "What did you say to the sheriff?"

He sighed. "That's the other reason I left. Here's this cop, wouldn't know the Constitution if it bit him in the elbow, he's got his fat thumbs hooked in his belt loops, trying to josh me. So I kind of lost my temper, and after that—"

Edwina tipped her head at her husband. He had not quite lost his temper at being confronted in his own home with a loaded .38, although he was still—understandably, she had to admit—a little testy about it. But he had lost it over the abuse of a suspect's civil rights.

"—after that, I told him he was an ignorant disgrace to his goddamned uniform, and if he'd handed me the dirty end of the stick I was going to personally come back to his little hick town and hand it back, and that was when the hospitality shut off."

She couldn't help smiling at him, but he did not smile back. She wanted even more to put her arms around him, but something in his manner said that might not be a good idea, either.

As if to confirm her perception he got up, gathered his breakfast dishes efficiently, and carried them to the kitchen. She heard him talking on the phone out there; when he reappeared, he was wearing his suit jacket and carrying his briefcase.

"I've got to go," he said. "The guy said some things on the way back last night; I want to type up some notes. Then I've got to see the ADA, see if we can straighten out the probable cause, try to get some lab tests ordered on the guy."

She nodded. "Martin, I'm really sorry about this morning. But I waited. I would never fire blind, you know that. You do know that, don't you?"

He frowned briefly. "You did the right thing, Edwina, right by the book. I shouldn't have made the crack about maybe killing me, that was out of line. I know you're safe with the weapon."

He laughed without humor. "And if I didn't know it before, I guess I know it now. So quit worrying about it, okay?"

"Okay," she replied, but he was already gone, and a moment later she saw his tall, dark figure striding down the driveway to where he had parked near the road so as to come in quietly.

Great, she told herself, picking up her own cup and plate and loading them into the dishwasher; now he thinks he's married Annie Oakley. With the dishes from last night there was a decent load, so she added soap powder and turned the machine on; an electrical appliance running made the house feel at least halfway inhabited.

Which was the way it was going to feel all day; if we argued all the time, she thought, maybe I'd be used to it by now, but we don't and I'm not. Glumly, she snatched up Maxie's catnip mouse, his rubber porcupine with the squeaker inside, his wire jingle-bell ball, and the old red wool sock, tied in a knot and faded from years of washings, that he preferred above all other toys, and flung them into Maxie's toybox, at which point Maxie strode into the room, noticed that his toys had all been put in the box, and patiently began removing them again.

Two hours later she had straightened, dusted, polished, or wiped every household surface even nominally requiring these attentions; Harriet's housewarming gift had been a year of weekly visits from a professional cleaning service, so there were not many. But she found that sitting still did little to mobilize her thinking processes and even less to eradicate the gloom she was experiencing, while cleaning at least felt virtuous.

When the house had been set to rights—bed made, hampers emptied, Maxie's food and water bowls washed out—and the scent of fresh coffee had begun mingling sweetly with the smells of chlorine scouring powder and lemon furniture polish, she seated herself once more at the dining room table, to see if any useful thoughts had been generated by all this labor.

And, as it turned out, some useful thoughts had. They were not, however, pleasant thoughts. First among them was the clear realization that she had better find whoever had nailed the rat's head to the door and end that person's interest in her quickly; if she did not, the effect on her peace of mind—not to mention the effect on her marriage—would be disastrous.

Give head, note, & photos to police, she wrote on the legal pad she had brought with her to the table, *& explain same.*

Next came the business of questioning the medical examiner who had established Ricky Z.'s time of death. This at first look had seemed a simple enough matter. Now, however, she realized that one could not just telephone such a person to ask if he or she had taken any bribes—or been victimized by any threats—in the matter of Ricky's autopsy report. Admitting such a thing, after all, would be admitting to participating in a felony.

Nor was one likely to succeed by asking these questions in person. It would be better, in fact, if the medical examiner did not know what one really wanted. But how, when one came right down to it, to see or speak with such a person at all? A medical examiner was a fairly large cog in the bureaucratic machinery and surrounded, no doubt, by a network of obstructive underlings.

And there it was: underlings. In every office, there was always someone whose business it was to be the gossip, who saw all, heard all, suspected the rest, and—with the proper inducement— might be persuaded to talk about it. *Locate & question underlings,* she wrote, feeling she was making progress. This notation, however, raised another problem.

"Maxie," she said, and the cat looked up alertly from the catnip mouse he was in the process of dismembering; dispatching the old one, he had found, was the quickest way of getting a new one. That it was also the most efficient way of distributing a quarter-cup of powdered catnip all over the freshly shaken rag rug she had spread neatly in the kitchen doorway did not appear to concern him, or if it did he was managing to rise above this worry. "Maxie, if you were an underling, what would I have to do to get you to talk to me?"

Frowning, Maxie seemed to consider this question. But he could not answer it, of course, so after a moment Edwina returned to scribbling thoughtfully on the legal pad, while from the kitchen doorway came the sound of the catnip mouse's body being rent open, followed by a loud feline sneeze.

A moment after that, however, the tearing sound stopped and was replaced by a rattling noise. Edwina was about to get up to see what it might be—despite his masquerade of mild-mannered domesticity, Maxie could wreak more mayhem in less time than any other household pet she had ever seen—but then the rattling noise stopped, too, and Maxie's head began butting her ankle.

"Mrr?" he queried, stepping delicately back and forth so as to provide the maximum amount of irritating distraction with the minimum amount of feline effort.

"Maxie, can't you see I'm trying to think, here? Go play." Underlings, she thought, and scribbled this word again on the yellow legal pad. *Talk,* she wrote, and connected the two words with an arrow and a long, unhappy-looking question mark.

In his well-trained fashion, Maxie responded to her rebuff by leaping to her lap, turning around three times, and proceeding to knead up a comfy little nest by digging into the tops of her legs with his front claws.

"Ouch!" She tossed him to the floor. "Max, what's got into you?"

Springing to the tabletop, where he was so absolutely not allowed that Edwina merely stared openmouthed at him, the black cat walked onto the yellow legal pad, circled, and sat firmly down upon it. "Meow," he said resolutely, leaping down, trotting to the kitchen door, and pausing to look over his shoulder in beckoning fashion.

"I don't know what you're up to," Edwina said, "but I hope you've got a good excuse for yourself."

Then she stopped at the sight of the kitchen floor, which was carpeted with cat kibble. Maxie had pawed open the cabinet where his kibble was kept, dragged the bag out, and scattered the contents by the simple method of, apparently, hauling the bag around and around the floor by its end until the bag was empty.

"Maxie, what in the *world* did you think you were— Oh."

Bending, she examined him: ears alert, eyes clear, tail erect, and expression intelligent. His lips, narrow and pale pink against the lush blackness of his coat, curved enigmatically in a feline smile. "Maxie, did you do this on purpose?"

Maxie yawned hugely. Then he sighed, tired but gratified after a job well done. He did not move an inch, however, from where he sat presiding over it.

"Food? You think I can get people to talk with food?"

That, of course, was silly. First of all, she hadn't said people; she'd said *underlings*. And Maxie's vocabulary was limited almost exclusively to verbs: Words like sit, stay, and come were indeed within his grasp, but nouns—especially the unfamiliar, multisyllabic ones—were beyond him.

Besides, although she supposed the principle was sound, she could not imagine herself in a medical examiner's office, feeding chunks of salmon—or, God forbid, those horribly red, vividly meatlike little processed-liver treats—to some gabby clerk, secretary, or other minor, self-important functionary no matter how voluble, well-informed, or cooperative. Gossips weren't even motivated by liver treats; rather, in her experience, they ran on self-importance, lack of confidence, and spite.

Still, there were all those kibble bits. "Prutt," said Maxie, and nibbled one. Then he strolled back into the dining room, where he deposited himself in the plywood bed lined with an old sleeping bag that McIntyre had spent one whole Saturday afternoon constructing for him. Sighing, he fell asleep.

Slowly, Edwina picked up a kibble bit. In her mouth it felt like a small mealy stone, and tasted like Harriet's whole-grain biscuits. Actually, it tasted good.

Still chewing it—the kibble bit's texture was crunchily substantial and its flavor faintly sweet, almost like toast with honey—she went to the telephone, punched out the number for the main switchboard at Chelsea Memorial Hospital, and waited for the operator to come on.

*　　*　　*

Five feet tall and ninety-one pounds fully drenched, as a nursing student Hilary Bendel had resembled a child playing dress-up; her rounded face, wide blue eyes, and yellow, farmer's-daughter-style braids had done nothing to dispel this impression. The sight of Hilary brandishing a hypodermic had caused more than one unnerved patient to grab in panic for the call button, and she had been banished from surgery training due to her inability to reach the sterile instrument tray.

But nearly twenty years later Hilary was director of nursing at Chelsea Memorial Hospital, and she no longer appeared childlike. What she looked, in fact, was nine months pregnant and ready to deliver at any moment—which, from the expression on Hilary's face, would not be anywhere near soon enough for her.

"Ugh," said Hilary, sinking into the chair behind her desk. On her office walls were diplomas, commendations, awards, and photographs of herself with two small children, a man who looked pleasant, and a dog whose grin nearly rivaled Hilary's own.

"Whoever said pregnancy is a natural process," she remarked, "probably thinks being pressed to death by a stone is a natural process, too."

"Hilary," Edwina managed, "you're so . . . so grown-up." Then she did begin to laugh, and after a moment so did Hilary.

"I should hope so," Hilary said, smoothing back her yellow hair, which had been clipped, sometime in the improbable process of her maturing, into a chic little cap that made her face look narrower and her blue eyes, if possible, larger.

"But I'll tell you," Hilary went on, "after my first pregnancy I swore that if I could see all those obstetrics patients I'd nursed before I had a kid, I'd get down on my knees and and beg them to forgive me. 'Push, Mrs. Smith,' " she chirped in falsetto imitation. " 'If we wait just a little longer for our anesthetic, we can push *even harder* and have our baby *even sooner*. Won't that be wonderful?' "

Hilary made a face. "Wonderful, shmunderful. The minute the baby's born, it starts to cry and it doesn't stop for twenty-one years. Actually, it doesn't even stop then; it just isn't allowed to cry on you anymore."

Hilary was the only other truly rich girl Edwina had ever known on a continuing basis; the rest, immured in a sort of fly's amber of wealth, power, and privilege, had regarded Edwina's career choice as social suicide, or at best as a sort of chichi, holier-than-thou grandstanding.

Hilary was also the most down-to-earth person Edwina knew. "For this kid," Hilary went on, "I told my OB guy I want a spinal anesthetic the instant I come through the doors, and if I don't get it I'll bash my head against the wall until I bash myself unconscious. That put a look on his face, the schmuck. If he weren't so good in every other way, I'd give him a kick in the right place, sometime, let him experience for half an hour what his patients go through for eighteen or twenty-four."

The look on Hilary's own face, however, made it clear that she meant perhaps one word in twenty of this. Clearly she adored her work, her husband and children, and almost anything else she happened to lay her enormous pale-blue eyes upon.

"So," she continued, "what brings you to the wilds of good old Chelsea? Some nifty skulduggery, knowing you, I'll bet. But better tell me quick, I'm in labor and I might have to get out of here fast. My other babies took days, but . . ."

Hilary actually used words like "nifty" and "skulduggery." "You mean . . . you're in labor *right now*?" Edwina asked her.

"Hey, this office is lots more restful than eight hours at home with two toddlers. A three-year-old and a four-year-old—we call them Slash and Burn, for short. High on the list of skills for supervising them is the ability to wield a bullwhip. Mmph."

A strange look passed across Hilary's face. Absently, she

straightened a stack of already-straightened papers. Then she got up, sat down again, and got up again.

"You know, Edwina," she said, "there is a wheelchair in the corridor. I wonder if you'd mind bringing it in." She clutched her middle. "Immediately, I think," she added.

Swiftly, Edwina did as she was told. "Hilary, are you sure you're going to have the baby now?"

"No," snapped Hilary, shifting herself with some difficulty into the wheelchair. "Actually, it feels more like I'm going to have a rhinoceros. Blast, they told me a third one always comes faster. How are you at imitating an ambulance siren?"

"Not very good. Here's your handbag. Anything else you need?" Maneuvering the wheelchair quickly around Hilary's desk, Edwina headed for the corridor.

"Yes. Distraction. Lots of it. Tell me what you came here for." Hilary spoke these words in a grim voice, her pale hair plastered to her forehead and her knuckles whitely gripping the wheelchair's arms.

Edwina rushed the chair down the corridor, toward the lobby and the elevator. "Hilary, that can wait. Later, after the baby's born, I can—"

"Start talking, damn it," Hilary grated out. "Start talking and keep talking to me until I'm on that table. I'm not kidding, Edwina, I need something to focus on here. Please."

The elevator slid open. Blessedly, the car was unoccupied. Edwina whisked the chair onto it, pressed the floor button, and watched the doors slide closed nearly onto the nose of a large, outraged old lady in a flowered dress and black orthopedic shoes.

"Well!" the lady huffed, jerking back just in time.

"Okay," said Edwina. "I need the dirt from the medical examiner's office. If there is any. And not only do I not know the medical examiner, I don't even know where his office is, or if it *is* a he. But I need to know if someone fixed a certain official time of death falsely—was paid to do it or threatened to do it, or something—about six months ago. And you're one of the only people I know around here anymore, so I came to ask you about it."

"What if someone did?" Hilary's voice sounded strained but under control as the elevator doors slid open and Edwina sped the wheelchair out.

"If someone did, then the dead man—a fellow named Ricky Z.—was alive to murder another person. And that means this Ricky fellow could have been hired to do it by yet *another* person whose murder is the one I am investigating. And if she did hire him, I might be on the right track, but if not, then I'm not."

Edwina halted the wheelchair before the nursing desk of the obstetrics and maternity ward. The secretary behind the desk looked up, glanced at Edwina and at Hilary, and spoke in a businesslike voice. "Clipboard, please."

"We don't have a clipboard," Hilary told the secretary, who was about nineteen years old. The secretary's short black hair had been arranged, apparently by combing the equivalent of airplane glue through it, so that it stood straight up from the top of her head like the hair of a cartoon character suffering from extreme fright.

"We didn't go through the admitting office," Edwina said, "we came over here from—"

"Can't admit you if you don't have admitting papers," said the secretary. "You get them in the emergency room at night, at the admitting office in the daytime. Go to the admitting office on the first floor, left side of the lobby. They'll do the blood work, the lab work, the paperwork . . ."

The secretary was wearing a short-sleeved black leotard top under a neon-pink jumper. She was wearing a bracelet made of numerous linked safety-pins. Bright pink beads had been threaded onto the safety pins. The secretary's earrings were large pink-and-black ceramic cubes, and her fingernails were enameled in pink; her eyelids, shadowed in rose, brown, and a peculiar shade of turquoise, resembled a couple of day-old bruises, and her lips were vermillion, as were the triangles on her cheekbones.

"Young woman," said Hilary as Edwina was opening her mouth.

Something in Hilary's voice—the suggestion, perhaps, of Hilary's skill at bullwhip-cracking—made the secretary look up again. "I *told* you . . ." the secretary began in long-suffering tones, but before she could go on, Hilary was speaking once more.

"You get a nurse up here to this desk right now," Hilary told the secretary, slapping a business card up onto the counter, "and then you call my doctor. You tell him Mrs. Bendel is here, and she is going to have her baby *at once.* And *then* you are to get a comb and a washcloth, some soap, and a towel from the clean utility room, and wash off that war paint and comb the stiffener out of your hair. This is a hospital, not a nightclub."

The secretary blinked. With her mouth slowly opening and closing, she resembled some brilliant species of tropical fish.

"Snap to it," spat Hilary, "before I deliver this baby on your desk."

Hurriedly, the secretary got up and scurried down the hall in search of someone to take charge of the situation, Hilary's tone evidently having made some sort of impression on her. Being told in no uncertain terms what to do and being expected to do it, Edwina had found in her own years as a nursing administrator, often had that effect upon nineteen-year-olds; it was such a new experience for them that they complied with one's wishes almost before they realized it.

"I tell them and tell them," muttered Hilary, wincing in pain as she rummaged through her handbag, "the unit secretary is the professional representative of the— Okay, here it is."

"Hilary, honestly, there's plenty of time for—"

"No, there's not." Hilary jerked her head toward the tall, white-uniformed woman marching smartly down the patient corridor at them. "You're about to get chucked out of here."

She shoved a scribbled scrap of paper into Edwina's hand. "Listen, call this girl and tell her what you told me. She used to work in Blunderbutt's office. Ouch. Oh, *damn* it all, now I remember why I said two kids were plenty."

Edwina glanced at the scrap of paper, and then at the nurse now bearing imperially down on them. The nurse wore a starched white dress, white stockings and shoes, and a white linen nurse's cap with a narrow midnight-blue velvet ribbon on it. Also, she wore an expression of determined competence Edwina thought boded well for Hilary's health, if poorly for her disposition.

" 'Blunderbutt?' " Edwina asked as the tall nurse seized the handles of the wheelchair. Her namepin proclaimed that she was Clarissa Schmidt, R.N., Head Nurse, Obstetrics Division, and her face, which was attractive by comparison with, say, your standard woodsman's hatchet, said she brooked no nonsense from anybody and especially not from patients.

"So, Mrs. Bendel," said Clarissa, beginning to wheel Hilary away, "we meet again, hmm? How are we doing? Beginning to have a little twinge, are we? Doctor has left us orders to call the anesthetist, to give you the painkiller. Although," the nurse added disapprovingly, "it is *early* for that, in *my* opinion."

Hilary cast a help-me-Lord look back at Edwina, managing a grin. "Tell her," she called, "that I said to spill her guts."

"Goodness," said Clarissa Schmidt, "such language."

"Oh, shut up, Clarissa," said Hilary, vanishing behind the doors of the delivery room, "and get that anesthetist in here, pronto."

* * *

"Blauderbundt," corrected Karen Russo, "his name is Gerhardt Blauderbundt. Doctor of medicine, professor of forensic pathology, and medical examiner for the state of Connecticut. Ex–medical examiner, I mean. Also a senile old fool, although you couldn't tell that from his hands when I was there."

Karen, a tall brunette beauty with flawless skin, pale-green eyes and the fat-free body of a long-distance runner, looked up from her plate of noodles Alfredo, her side dish of cheese-baked potato skins and deep-fried eggplant cubes, her salad with croutons and blue-cheese sour-cream dressing, and her buttered croissants.

"His hands?" Edwina asked as Karen dug into the plate of noodles. After dialing the telephone number Hilary had given her, Edwina had wondered why anyone would give up an evening's plans to have dinner out with a stranger, especially since Edwina had been honest with Karen, explaining that the dinner was in trade for answers to some questions. Also, Karen didn't seem to have a spiteful bone in her body, which made her an unlikely gossip.

Now, though, Edwina knew the answer: Karen was hungry. She had already demolished two appetizers, a basket of rolls, and most of a dish of black olives and baby gherkins, and she showed no sign of slowing down. To judge by the extreme leanness of her figure, meanwhile, Karen apparently metabolized calories almost as fast as she could shovel them in.

"He put his hands," Karen explained, "in all the places where a younger man would put them. For example, on the arms and legs and chests and backsides of any young woman who happened to be around, when no one else happened to be around to see him do it."

She reached politely for the rest of her croissant; an instant later, it had vanished. Edwina took a bite of her own broiled garlic shrimp, chewed, swallowed, and reached for her glass of water, noticing as she did so that half Karen's noodles Alfredo had also disappeared.

"Didn't any of the women complain?" she asked, as Karen began devouring potato skins.

"Mm-mm." Karen shook her head, swallowed, and bit into an eggplant slice. "Well, they did"—the eggplant slice seemed to evaporate—"but it didn't do them any good. Blunderbutt had connections, see. The minute anybody complained about anything, it would turn out they'd been stealing office supplies, or calling in sick too many times, or making personal long-distance phone calls on the office phones. You know, just something to make them look bad, like maybe they'd complained to try to take the heat off themselves somehow."

Karen drank some wine. "So Hilary's having her baby, huh? She's a good kid, Hilary. I mean, I don't know where I'd be now, without her."

Having finished the eggplant and her salad, she began on the bread again. "Actually, there was one woman who made something stick on Blauderbundt. Not officially, and she didn't get to keep working there. But I heard she got something out of him, which was only fair, after all. I mean, he did get her pregnant."

"I beg your pardon?" Edwina sipped some more water, to wash down a bit of roll that seemed suddenly to have stuck in her throat. "How old is Dr. Blauderbundt, and was he married?"

"Well," said Karen Russo, "he's ancient, at least sixty."

Edwina swallowed hard; the stubborn bit of roll went down. To Karen Russo, who was perhaps twenty-five, she herself no doubt seemed well on the way to decrepitude. Just wait, she promised silently and uncharitably, until that calorie-burning apparatus of yours slows down for the middle-age stretch.

"And," Karen went on, "oh, boy, was he ever married. Not only that, his wife's brother is some famous divorce lawyer, one of those guys who gets enormous settlements for women, and he's on the TV news anytime some wife decides to stick it to some rich famous guy."

Karen smiled in appreciation of this idea. "Anyway, I heard Blunderbutt paid the woman a bunch of money to go away and never talk about it to anyone. She was just a kid, I heard, a high school kid in one of those summer intern programs? Only none of it stopped Blunderbutt's wandering fingers. That's why I left. I used to clean house for Hilary, but she helped me get a new job, or I'd still be cleaning houses now."

Karen attacked her zabaglione with gusto. " 'Course," she added, "he couldn't pay *other* people not to talk about it, which was how I heard about it. I guess it must have been about a year ago, and then right after I left, Blunderbutt retired all of a sudden. In June, I think it was. Yeah, about five months ago he split."

She took a deep breath, laid down her napkin, and sighed. "Wow, that was delicious. What a great place this is, I really appreciate you bringing me here. Anyway, was that what you wanted to know? I mean, about Blunderbutt?"

"Actually, I just have two more questions," said Edwina, signaling for the bill before Karen could digest her meal and decide that she was getting hungry again. Considering her long, narrow shape and the amount of food she had consumed, the girl should have resembled a python that had recently engulfed an antelope, but instead she looked just as bright-eyed, energetic, and comfortable as she had when she first sat down.

Also, just as ravenous; quickly, Edwina pronounced her final questions before Karen's slender hand could flash out and snatch some further delicacy from a passing tray or, God forbid, from a nearby table.

"Did Blunderbutt—that is, did Dr. *Blauderbundt*—make many mistakes? You said earlier that he seemed senile. Did he ever make professional errors, that you know of? And do you happen to know the name of the girl with whom he was said to be involved?"

"Mistakes?" Karen looked thoughtful as they walked out of the restaurant. "I never heard of any, not that I necessarily would have. When I said senile, I meant the way he acted in the office. I really didn't know much about his work."

Darn, thought Edwina. Well, maybe Karen would know someone who could comment on Blauderbundt's competence. The bet-

123

ter his work was, the less likely that he would have made an error—as opposed to a deliberate misstatement—in Ricky's autopsy. Still, the doctor's willful participation in a fraud was looking less probable by the minute.

Karen popped an after-dinner mint, a handful of which she had scooped from the bowl by the restaurant's exit, into her mouth. "I know the name of the girl, though," she said. "Some of the other clerks still talked about her sometimes. Let's see, her name was . . ."

Edwina gathered her coat about her. It was after nine in the evening, and beyond watching Karen Russo take nourishment, she felt she had accomplished little. If Dr. Blauderbundt was wealthy, he would have small incentive to take a bribe, and he had apparently already paid off his own personal embarrassment factor; that pretty well ruled out blackmail. She supposed Harry's idea about threats could be correct, but it sounded farfetched. So, even if Karen remembered the young woman's name, Edwina didn't see how that could—

Karen Russo snapped her fingers. "Got it. The girl's name was Carlotta Zimmerman."

EIGHT

"It's simple," said Edwina as she poured her coffee the next morning. "Of course, I'll never prove it. But I'll bet Carlotta Zimmerman sent one of Ricky's friends to see Dr. Blauderbundt, to let him know the deal with Carlotta had sprouted a few strings now that the Zimmermans needed a favor. All Blauderbundt had to do was stipulate a time of death that let Ricky out of Riordan's murder, and everything would stay nice and quiet. Otherwise . . ."

McIntyre's eyes had taken on the glaze that meant he was appearing to be listening while thinking about something else.

"Otherwise," said Edwina, testing this theory, "Blauderbundt would turn into a giraffe, and the moon would become a balloon."

"Yes, dear," said McIntyre, laying down his newspaper with a bemused smile, and of course she did not roll it up and beat him about the head and body with it. At least he wasn't angry with her anymore—which, considering the way things had been going on that score lately, she counted as an improvement.

"What would actually happen, of course," she told Maxie when McIntyre had gone off to work, "was that Blauderbundt's wife would find out about his dalliance unless he agreed to fake the autopsy report on Ricky."

The black cat blinked, either comprehendingly or in an excellent imitation of this, and followed her to the back hall, where she began pulling on her coat and gloves.

"And what that means," she went on, struggling into her rain boots—the weather, while warmer, still threatened to be stormy, and the melting snow would ruin her shoes in any case—"is that Ricky Z. probably could have killed Tom Riordan, or whoever was in that car when it exploded. And I'll bet Ricky did, too."

"Pffft," remarked Maxie, eyeing her mistrustfully. He did not like being left alone in the house. Home, to Maxie, required the presence of at least one human being and if possible two; otherwise the place was merely a large, fancy cage to which an animal of his unusual intelligence ought not to be confined.

To communicate this message more effectively, he stalked out into the kitchen, planted himself determinedly before one of the cabinet doors, and began sharpening his already needlelike claws on a linen dishtowel hanging from a hook there.

"Oh, all right." Edwina gave in. "But you're going to have to wait in the car a lot. And if you try that clawing business on the seat covers, I'll have you made into a fur hat."

This Maxie regarded as an empty threat, to judge at least by the speed with which he presented himself for bundling into the front seat of the Fiat. Meanwhile Edwina loaded the trunk with the animal's food, collar, leash and—in case of emergency—his wire carrying crate, since it was perfectly possible to send a cat somewhere in a taxi, and even possible to phone Walter, the building superintendent, to ask *him* to send Maxie somewhere in a taxi, which upon occasion really was the only sane alternative.

There was the time, for example, when Edwina had discovered, moments before a new client was due to arrive, that the client claimed to have been mauled by a psychiatrist's pet ocelot while

126

waiting in the doctor's office to be treated for the belief that he—the patient, not the ocelot—was a vampire. Under the circumstances it had seemed only prudent to bustle Maxie off for a little jaunt. (The neighboring office tenants were all starchy types with their eyes on the prize and their hearts, apparently, stashed in cold storage somewhere, for none of them liked cats.)

Once the client arrived Edwina was convinced of the wisdom of her action, for by the time the client finished his obsessive investigation of the foyer, the bathroom, the kitchenette, the wastebaskets, and all the furniture in the consulting room—he could not, he insisted, divest himself of his secrets without first making sure no animals were hiding and listening—Edwina had begun wishing she were out on a taxi ride, too.

But it was impossible to send Maxie anywhere unless he was first confined to his travel crate. Taxi drivers and office-building superintendents alike, in Edwina's experience, shared an unreasonable fear of domestic animals, most of whom did not possess Maxie's perfect riding manners, his love of car trips, and his bred-in-the-bone reluctance to claw the eyes out of any human being whatsoever, no matter how rude, unfriendly, or superficially unattractive (this being a special problem with some of the taxi drivers), unless that person did something nasty to him first.

"Anyway," said Edwina once she had loaded the cat, the cat's equipment, and herself into the Fiat and gotten the Fiat started, "that means somebody hired Ricky Z., since the last time I looked professional killers didn't go around giving it away for free."

Frowning, Maxie sniffed at the air inside the Fiat. His small round black nostrils dilated and shrank as he received the information, not yet perceptible to Edwina, that something about the atmosphere here was wrong. Something, in fact, was horrid about it. From some wellspring of unhappiness deep in his chest, a guttural moan began issuing, as he sprang from the bucket seat onto the floor, where he crouched in wide-eyed misery. Human assistance, he conveyed, was required, but unfortunately he possessed neither the physiology nor the vocabulary to communicate the reason for his distress.

"Maxie?" Setting the hand brake, Edwina leaned over to pat the animal and, if possible, to lift him to the seat again, but Maxie was having absolutely none of that. His eyes resembled two smoky yellow beacons: the hairs on his neck were standing up straight, and his tail was the size of a bottle brush. Had he been able to back through the Fiat's firewall and escape through the engine compartment he most certainly would have done so. But since he could not, he went on glaring, moaning, and generally signaling discontent at the presence of something under the car's right-hand bucket seat.

Now that the car was warming up, Edwina began to suspect the nature of that something, herself. It had definitely been alive at one time, and now was not. Snarling, Maxie jabbed at it. It had not attacked him, he apparently reasoned, so it must be a wimp, and he might as well attack *it*.

"Oh, no you don't, buster." Seizing him by the scruff, Edwina imprisoned him long enough to open the car door and propel him out into the snow, slamming the door as he reversed himself in midair—how, she had time to wonder, did he *do* that?—and came barreling back at her, the look on his face pure feline *lemme-at 'em* and his yowls heartfelt.

By now she was breathing heavily, and that was a mistake. As the temperature inside the Fiat continued rising, the atmosphere continued thickening. Maxie leapt up and crouched on the hood of the car, glaring and uttering feline swear words, while Edwina sat behind the wheel, uttering the very same swear words only in a different language. But she did not sit there for long, since being gassed to death by the fumes of a dead animal placed under her car seat was not high on her list of projects for that day.

What *was* high on her list was getting the animal out of the car, preferably by saying "Presto!", since any other method she could think of would require her to touch it. But "Presto!" did not work, so she went into the house, thrust her hands into plastic bags, and removed from beneath the car seat what turned out to be the body of a headless rat.

This time, the rat had not been preserved—or, if it had, it had been *un*preserved again some considerable time ago—and came equipped with dozens of the unpleasant organisms generally associated with advanced biological decomposition. Plucking these from the carpeting with tweezers and the aid of a flashlight, Edwina eventually got the car cleaned out and aired out, and got herself and Maxie back into it.

"No note," she said tightly, swinging the Fiat around and aiming it down the driveway. "I guess someone thinks this little prank was message enough by itself. Dead rat—pretty plain in the symbolism department, wouldn't you say, Maxie?"

The cat sniffed the air, now redolent of pine soap, but offered no comment on the possible deeper meaning of dead rats.

"It means that's what I'll be," Edwina added. "Dead."

One of Maxie's eyebrows lifted; since he had begun obedience training, he seemed to listen with special care to all single-syllable words. After a moment, realizing that this one was not a command, he looked bored and disappointed.

"But," said Edwina, still fuming over the *nerve*, the utter *arrogance* of someone's daring to desecrate the Fiat, her single most prized possession—at age sixteen, it had not a single spot of rust and its oil was so clean a newspaper could be read through it—"I don't think it's going to turn out that way."

Shifting into third gear, she listened with pleasure to the throaty roar of the Fiat's carburetors and felt the little vehicle strain forward as if begging to be unleashed. Zipping up the entrance ramp to I-95, she shifted briskly again, glanced into the side mirror, and accelerated once more, neatly inserting the car between a Pontiac Grand Am and a Greyhound bus.

Moments later she had left the other vehicles behind and was tooling happily along in fifth gear, the little Fiat gobbling the miles up joyfully, as it was designed to do. Nothing like a burst of unreasonable speed to clean the valves out, she thought. But she was a veteran of too many nursing shifts in the emergency room to disregard the speed limit for long; reluctantly she slid back over into the right lane and let the speedometer drop back to a sensible fifty-five again.

"Because," she told the cat, "this all *started* over a dead rat. I mean a *human* rat, by the name of Thomas Riordan. And now, a human rat has succeeded in making me extremely angry—angry enough to get to the bottom of this nonsense."

Fifteen minutes later, Edwina pulled the Fiat into a parking spot in front of Riordan's Jewelry on Whalley Avenue. It was a low concrete-faced building with no windows for thieves to break and no shrubs for them to skulk behind; it looked as if it had just recently shouldered its way out of the earth, and now it hunkered, grim, ugly, and impregnable, its front door protected by an iron-spiked portcullis.

Pacing before the portcullis with the alert, why-don't-you-come-and-try-me seriousness of an often-kicked junkyard dog was a young man with forearms the size of mutton roasts and a chest whose hugeness made custom tailoring of his uniform imperative; probably, Edwina thought, they just nail it onto him. He sported a blond brush haircut no strand of which was long enough for an opponent to get an effective grip on, and atop his short, thick neck sat the blocky, faintly toddlerish face of the confirmed steroid abuser.

Shutting off the Fiat's engine, Edwina remained in the car a moment just blinking at this creature, none of whose attributes would have given her much pause were it not for the equipment—

as if this weapon shaped like a guy needed *other* weapons—his employers apparently felt it was necessary for him to carry.

It was a Smith & Wesson Model 1026, the heavy, top-of-the-line semiautomatic with the five-inch stainless-steel barrel, fixed sight, and decocking lever. Two pounds, six ounces of high-class professional weaponry, it carried nine 10-mm rounds in the magazine and one in the chamber; the decocking lever allowed the weapon's level of readiness to go from "safety" to "fire" with the twitch of a finger.

As he paced, the guard's gaze kept turning and returning, while he wondered who the woman in the Fiat was. Different, he thought; threat, his instincts reported to him. Finally he approached the car, his hand unconsciously caressing his weapon in the suggestive way that Edwina always found revolting.

"Ma'am," said the guard, his left hand rising with the habit of the old, remembered gesture. A flicker of irritation showed in his expression, as he realized that the brim of a state trooper's hat no longer shaded or concealed his eyes; retired on disability, Edwina realized, noting the barely visible limp. "Ma'am, this here is a no-parking zone."

He was thirty or so, beautifully exercised and nourished like some prize specimen of mule. With his irritation came a shadow of puzzlement, as if he remembered another, better life before this one and wished he could recapture the details of it.

"I'm going to open my bag now," Edwina told the guard, "and then I'm going to show you my checkbook."

The guard's eyebrows knitted suspiciously. He didn't like people reaching into bags of any kind to bring out items he had not seen before. He didn't like it at all, his expression said.

Edwina noted that the guard's weapon was held in a black basket-weave thumb-break security holster, that the holster hung from a basket-weave duty belt, and that belt and holster were of

Don Hume manufacture, all of which said plenty for the guard's taste in equipment, not to mention for his pocketbook.

Or for someone's pocketbook. There was no sense carrying the 1026 if you couldn't get at it quickly, and for professionals the ability to do that was supplied almost exclusively by Don Hume. The cost of the equipment was exotic until it saved your life; then suddenly the Dom Hume price list started looking cheap.

But an ex-cop on disability couldn't afford it: not and buy all the tiger's milk, protein powder, and vitamin and mineral supplements this guy was swallowing, not to mention all the very illegal but—for the right price—highly available steroid preparations he was shooting into his buttock muscles every few hours or so.

Up close, he had the telltale piggy-eyed look; it meant his body was starting to lay down inappropriate fat deposits. It also meant he was at risk for steroid psychosis; slowly, Edwina opened her bag and removed her checkbook, making no sudden moves, keeping her hands and the contents of her bag in plain sight. Meanwhile, she contemplated the motives of an employer who hired an obvious steroid freak, armed him with the equivalent of a rocket launcher, and set him to pacing out in front of the store, where a glimpse of him would scare off all but the bravest, most determined customers.

Assuming, of course, that there were any customers. In ten minutes, not a soul had walked in or out of Riordan's or even approached the place. Edwina held up her checkbook so that the balance in the register was visible to the guard.

"I mean to buy some earrings," she said. "Diamond earrings. And I don't see any no-parking signs around."

The guard's eyelids flickered. "Sorry, ma'am. My mistake. Press the white button alongside the gate. Somebody inside will buzz you in."

After a pause, somebody inside did, whereupon Edwina saw the reason for the bunkerlike building, the lack of windows, and the guard, as well as for the scarcity of customers. Riordan's did not cater to casual foot traffic, unless of course the drop-in trade happened to be impulse-shopping for a diamond big enough to choke a Clydesdale. One of these, ensconced on a pillar-shaped pedestal made of some space-age glasslike material, glimmered haughtily at Edwina as she entered the severe, beige-walled and track-lit display area.

On the walls were some Matisse sketches; these, Edwina intuited, were not for sale. Rather they were to establish the tone of the proceedings, and perhaps to prepare the younger, less experienced customer for the sort of heavy-duty financial commitment that would be required in order for those proceedings to go forward. In short, people did not shop at Riordan's; they invested.

"Good morning." A tall, gray-haired woman in a good black linen suit, pale silk stockings, and mid-height black heels stood up from behind a Queen Anne writing table at one corner of the room.

"Good morning." Edwina extended her hand; the woman held it briefly, and smiled. As she did so Edwina smelled the vodka on her breath, but the luminous gray eyes were clear and the woman's gaze was steady.

"I've come . . ." Edwina began, and then faltered. It was not so much that she did not want to lie, as that she knew it would be useless. This woman knew precisely why she had come; it was almost as if she had been expecting her. Her lovely face was made up with the sort of not-from-the-drugstore-counter cosmetics that promised to bring out, as the advertisements euphemistically put it, the mature woman's full-blooming natural beauty, and in this case it seemed they had done their job marvelously. But the rose-tinted mouth was pinched even as it smiled, and the clear gaze was spoiled by a glimmer of cunning.

"I am Edwina Crusoe," she began again. "I'm investigating a murder."

133

Instantly, she regretted saying this; by telling the truth she had surely done little more than shoot herself in the foot. Now this woman, whoever she was, would see Edwina out, murmuring whatever polite phrases she had in the past found effective for getting non-diamond-buying intruders out of the showroom and onto the street amongst the common herd again.

But the woman's face did not stiffen in shock or suspicion; only a look of heightened wariness passed over it. Once again Edwina felt the woman had been expecting her.

"Ma'am?" The muscular guard materialized at Edwina's elbow, his expression now actively hostile.

"It's all right, George," the woman said. "Miss Crusoe is my guest." Her nostrils flared slightly with dislike, or perhaps fear, of George, but her voice remained commanding. "You can go back outside now."

George's blocky forehead wrinkled in consternation. "But, Mrs. Riordan, she's—"

"I know who she is, and I know why she's here," Mrs. Riordan told the stocky hired gun. "That will be *all*, George."

"Yes, Mrs. Riordan." George turned away obediently, but not before firing a smoldering glance at Edwina.

The suit, she saw as Mrs. Riordan turned, was Chanel, and the perfume in the air was Shalimar. From hidden speakers a Bach prelude sprang sweetly. But there was nothing sweet in Mrs. Riordan's voice when she turned again in the doorway of a small office and beckoned Edwina in.

"I suppose you've come about my husband," she said. "I read in the papers that the girl had been killed, and when the article mentioned you, I knew I ought to begin watching for you. Do you want a drink? No, probably not. But I do."

The office was a utilitarian cubicle, furnished with a gray metal office desk and gray metal folding chairs. In the corner stood a battered gray filing cabinet; waving Edwina to a chair, Mrs. Riordan pulled a bottle from the back of the bottom drawer and unceremoniously filled a chipped china teacup. Swallowing a slug, she stood still and let the stuff hit her, and smiled disconcertingly again.

"It was what I prayed for, you know. That the girl would die. Horribly, if possible: trapped in a car crash, or thrown out of a high window. Buried in a box, running out of air. I used to put myself to sleep, imagining different deaths for her. From the minute I found out about her, I prayed for it. And it's happened, and do you know what? I miss the wretched creature."

The smile began cracking. Mrs. Thomas Riordan sat down heavily in the metal folding chair behind her desk. "Without her, I haven't a single thing left to live for. Losing what you hate is as bad, in its way, as losing love. Don't you agree, Miss Crusoe?"

Before Edwina could answer, a tall, impeccably suited man with silver hair, buffed nails, and wire-rimmed glasses appeared in the office doorway. As he caught sight of Edwina his long nose twitched as if he were trying to identify an unpleasant odor.

"Mrs. Riordan," he said, his voice combining deference with silky threat in a way Edwina found immensely disagreeable. You wouldn't last ten minutes in my employ, you stuffy old clothes-horse, you, she thought emphatically.

"Yes, Jeffries," Mrs. Riordan said; the small nameplate on her desk said her first name was Madalyn. "What is it now?"

Jeffries smiled, exposing even, white teeth. The better to bite you with, Edwina thought, liking Jeffries less by the minute. "Young Mr. Riordan asked me to come and remind you of your conversation with him," Jeffries said.

His silver head swiveled smoothly until his gaze rested on Edwina. "I'm afraid Mrs. Riordan has another appointment now," he intoned, and of course he did not giggle, although Edwina got the clear feeling that that was what he very much wanted to do. Instead he contented himself with touching his slim fingertips together in satisfaction. So intent on his triumph was he, in fact, that the china cup made him duck reflexively as it sailed past his head and smashed against the door frame, inches from his skull.

When his head came up again, it was with a lurch of cold-blooded fury. His hand flew inside the front of his coat in a smooth, lightning-fast gesture that betrayed not only what he kept there, but also what he was—which made, thought Edwina, two professional weapons handlers on the place, and wasn't that an interesting bit of information? One hired gun might be prudent in a high-class jewelry store, but two was . . . curious.

"You can tell young *Mister* Riordan," Madalyn Riordan grated out, "that if he ever grows up, I'll be glad to start listening to his advice. For now, Mr. Riordan is my stepson and my employee. I'm still the boss around here, I do all the hiring and firing, and if you persist in spying on me, Jeffries, I'm sure you can guess which one of those is going to happen to you."

Jeffries's eyes, at the conclusion of this speech—which Edwina thought was a remarkable one considering how drunk Madalyn Riordan was—had narrowed to two little glittering slits of hatred. "Mr. Riordan is merely concerned about you, ma'am," he managed from between clenched teeth.

Madalyn Riordan's face expressed contempt. "Mr. Riordan worries that his father's stupidity is about to become common knowledge. And he worries not out of any respect or affection for his father but because he thinks it might be bad for business. A business he's greedy for and expects to grab away from me—and *you* all expect he will, too—any minute. His only concern for me is that I be shut away in some ritzy drunk tank as soon as possible, so he can get power of attorney. That's all Mr. Riordan wants."

She turned to Edwina. "I'd better say this fast, before my dear stepson gets here, now that this traitor has alerted him. He's turned Jeffries against me by promising him a share of the business, once I'm put away. And Tommy Junior is the sort of man who can convince others of that kind of thing, the sort other men adore—to his face. Behind his back they despise and fear him, but they'd never dare say so. Isn't that right, Jeffries?"

Jeffries finished blotting vodka mingled with bits of smashed teacup from his forehead, but made no move to go. With the grin of a naughty child, Madalyn Riordan produced another teacup and filled it.

"My husband was besotted with the Whitlock girl the moment he saw her, the day she came in to look at cocktail rings. Such a vulgar sort of jewelry, it suited her perfectly, but of course he didn't see that."

Outside the office, there was a small commotion, and heavy feet came stomping across the showroom.

"It wasn't the first time Thomas had strayed," Madalyn said. "But this time was different. He was mad about her. He gave her gifts, very valuable gifts. Things even he couldn't afford to give." As she spoke, Jeffries glanced over his shoulder at the approaching noise, and a look of relief appeared on his face.

"So I waited," Madalyn went on. "I still thought he would tire of her, as he had of all the others. He wasn't a bad man," she added. "But he'd made some bad decisions."

"Mrs. Riordan," Jeffries said warningly as a tall dark-haired young man appeared behind him. His face, which might otherwise have had the sort of cookie-cutter attractiveness often seen in failed film actors and successful mail-order catalogue clothing models, was frightening in its fury as he strode into the office, seized Edwina by the arm, and yanked her toward him.

"What do you mean by coming here bothering my stepmother?" he shouted. "Who the hell do you think you are? I've heard of you, you're nothing but a cheap busybody." His face purpled; small white flecks of spittle flew from lips. "You get the hell out of here"—he propelled her toward the door—"and stay—"

"Tommy," said Madalyn Riordan, and something about her voice made everything stop. Edwina turned her head, her body being immobilized by the steel-trap grip Tommy Junior had on her arms. Jeffries blinked as if touched by the flick of a whip, and turned his attention also to Madalyn. Even Thomas Riordan Junior paused momentarily, long enough for Edwina to wriggle free.

Everyone stared at Madalyn Riordan, who was holding a small revolver to her head. Specifically, she was aiming it at her left eye, smiling meanwhile as if this were the most natural and indeed the most pleasant activity in the world.

"Why don't you invite Miss Crusoe to sit down?" Madalyn's index finger tightened perceptibly on the trigger of the little weapon. "The whole place goes to charity if I die, you know; no one's managed to browbeat me into changing that yet. And I have nothing to live for. A dead philanderer husband, treacherous employees, a stepson sharper than a serpent's tooth. Appropriate for a boy with all the finer feelings of a reptile. Tommy, you apologize to Miss Crusoe."

Tom Junior's handsome face had gone slack with shock; Edwina took a perverse pleasure in seeing this. Jeffries's hate-filled eyes were fixed on the gun, but he winced as Tommy's glance raked him.

Madalyn caught the glance and laughed at it. Her words were beginning to slur a bit, but she was a long way from passing out and she'd have to be unconscious to miss her mark at the distance she was aiming from.

"Tommy, you mustn't punish Jeffries. He couldn't have stopped me from having the gun, no matter how impertinently ever-present he made himself. You see, your father gave me this as a wedding present. You remember the wedding, the day you set fire to the summer cottage? You thought I was going to be in it, but we'll let that go. Now, I asked you to apologize."

"I'm sorry. Sit down," Tommy pronounced. Each word sounded

as if it were being pried out of him with a crowbar. "I'm afraid my stepmother has had—"

"—has had it to the eyes," Madalyn put it succinctly. "Now, Miss Crusoe, let me tell you a few things before the boys in the white coats get here. No doubt George is summoning them right now, the horrid muscle-bound dope addict. He's the result of my letting Tommy do any hiring."

She shrugged, her gaze wavering for an instant. "That's what I get for trying to give Tommy responsibility: water that's sought its own level. At any rate—"

Jeffries made a sudden lunge across the desk. As he wrapped his arms around her, Madalyn fired the .25 into the ceiling and he sprang away, his hand clapped to his right ear. He staggered back and sagged against the wall.

Madalyn resumed speaking as if nothing had happened. "My husband was involved in some shady dealings, and after he was gone there were a number of stones I couldn't account for."

"You mean, gemstones were missing?" Edwina asked.

"Some were missing," Madalyn agreed. "But there were also some that were there, only I couldn't find where they had come from. Ordinarily there are papers on purchase and delivery of gems: certificates of inspection, insurance affidavits, bonded delivery records, all that sort of thing. For these stones, nothing. And there was a good deal of cash missing—although the police told me later what they thought had happened to that. It was burned up in the explosion that killed my husband."

But McIntyre had said the police didn't believe it was Tom Riordan who had died in the fire, and that more cash was gone than had been burned. Edwina wondered if they had kept their suspicions from Madalyn; the doubt must have showed on her face.

"Oh, I know they think he's not dead, that he's run off with the money," Madalyn said. "The police didn't say so, but it was just the sort of thing Tom would do. Only, I don't think that's all there was to it. For one thing, if Tom were going to run, why not take the undocumented stones? There were some quite valuable diamonds, and no one knew about them until afterwards, not even Tommy. Too bad *he* was there when I opened that safe."

"Do the police know about the diamonds now?" Edwina asked. Madalyn shook her head. "No. Those stones are my insurance policy. And no one knows where they are now, except me. That's why these gentlemen take such good care of me," she added with potent venom. "Except when Tommy gets angry. Poor Tommy has a problem with his anger, don't you, Tommy?"

She lowered the weapon, smiling murderously at her stepson. "Dear," she said, "you'd better go and speak with George. He's probably in touch with whatever doctor you've bought for yourself by now. And if anyone signs me into an institution, you'll never find out where those diamonds are. I'll go to my grave first."

Tommy's lip curled with frustration and contempt. "Bitch," he uttered, and hurried from the office. Jeffries remained, as if suspecting that Madalyn might tell Edwina where the gemstones were, but from the way he continued nursing his ear, Edwina suspected he could not have heard the information even if Madalyn were to reveal it.

"What sort of shady deal would a person have to do," she asked, "to acquire the sort of stones you found? That is, I assume if they could have had the proper paperwork, they would have had. So—"

"Quite right," Madalyn replied. "Jeffries, why don't you explain it to Miss Crusoe? I think poor Jeffries was in on it," she added, "even though he will go on denying it. But you have all sorts of useful contacts, don't you, Jeffries? You introduced my husband to high-level, low-life scoundrels from all over the world."

Jeffries squinted at her, trying to make out what she said by reading her lips. Once he understood, he replied reluctantly. "Unpapered stones might be stolen, but if they were they would be difficult to resell. More likely, they were smuggled in, either because of some other difficulty in their provenance, or to complete some transaction neither party wished to have noticed."

He was careful not to admit any involvement, Edwina noted. "So Mr. Riordan might have taken some of the cash he'd been skimming off the books, and used it to pay for smuggled diamonds. He would get the gems, and the other party would get a lot of clean, untraceable cash."

"Precisely." Jeffries spat the word like a prune pit. His hearing seemed to be returning—at least, he was no longer shouting—but his disposition had not improved. In his pique he resembled an elderly child, angry at having been thwarted, and plotting his retaliation.

"What," Edwina asked, "could Theresa Whitlock have had to do with such a thing? From what I understand, she was quite an accomplished little thief, but this was rather beyond her scope."

"I don't know," said Madalyn Riordan. "But I know she was there the day he died. He said he had business in the city, but I didn't believe him. I knew he'd be seeing her. So I followed him. I even stayed at the same hotel."

She took a deep breath, remembering. "The next morning, after he had gone downstairs, I saw her leave his room and go back to her own. I suppose he thought if he registered two in his room, I might learn about it. I meant to confront her, but at the last minute I lost my nerve. I remember she was wearing a blue summer dress, and carrying a briefcase like my husband's."

"Did you tell this to the police?"

"No." Madalyn's face closed tight. "If I had, they'd have asked me what else I knew about his business jaunts, and by then I'd found the diamonds, you see. I didn't want to trip myself up by talking too much. So I kept quiet, except about the missing cash; I knew they'd find it ought to be there when they went over the books. When you're a woman, it's easy to make people think you're ignorant," she finished acidly.

"But now," Edwina pointed out, "you've told me. And I may not be able to keep silent about it, you know. So far all I have is your story that you saw Theresa at the hotel, and that you've a cache of diamonds somewhere. But if any of it is important to my showing the police who killed Theresa—"

Jeffries's breath came out between his teeth. "You *stupid* woman, now you've ruined it for everyone."

Madalyn Riordan's eyes were wide, clear and amused. "Oh, Jeffries, don't be an idiot. There's nothing to ruin; neither of you will ever get those stones in any event. You'd be happier if you forgot them. And Miss Crusoe doesn't care about diamonds, do you, Miss Crusoe? She's above all that sort of thing."

And, Edwina thought, you know you can deny you mentioned any diamonds to me, if it should come to that.

Jeffries muttered an oath and stalked out, his manicured fingers clenching as if he wanted to wrap them around someone's throat. Madalyn watched him go, then turned to Edwina again.

"I suppose I should get rid of them all," she said, "but I'm afraid to. Tom really did try to burn me up in the cottage, and there've been other incidents. If I made him angry enough he would kill me, even though I'm the only one who knows where the stones are. He might not remember that until afterwards. I wouldn't mind dying, but Tommy's methods would surely be unpleasant."

She sighed. "Anyway, when I saw you come in here this morning, something finally clicked with me. There you were, free to come and go as you please, no one threatening you or spying on you. I wanted to be like you—to be able just for once to tell the truth. So I thought, I'll tell her. If she asks me, I'll tell her. And I have. You can understand that, can't you? That I would want to *tell* someone?"

Madalyn's eyes were beseeching, her breath reeked of vodka, and her hand closed tightly on Edwina's arm in the moment before she forced herself to let it go.

"Yes, of course I can," Edwina said, privately not so sure how much of this to believe. "But have you any idea where your husband might be, if in fact he is still alive? Have you heard from him, or *of* him, since the day he was supposed to have died in that explosion?"

It was the question she had come here to ask, not expecting to get a useful answer but feeling that at least she must try; more and more, it seemed that Riordan was behind it all, and now that the official search for him was not so fresh and hot, he might be letting himself relax a little. He might even be after the gems he had left behind; the whole thing, Edwina thought with a burst of frustration, just got murkier and murkier.

"No," said Madalyn Riordan. "Not a glimpse, not a word, and I have no desire for any. I have no idea where he might have gone, and with the amount of cash he supposedly took with him it might have been anywhere. But I still think he died that day, I don't care what they say. As far as I'm concerned, he did."

Moments later Edwina took her leave and went out, past the glowering Jeffries and the sullen, dangerous-looking Tommy Junior. On the sidewalk, George stood scribbling in a notebook as he watched her drive off, an act she felt certain was meant to intimidate her; he must have run her plate number through the Motor Vehicle Department's computer the instant she'd entered the store. It was why he'd come hurrying in after her and why, when he'd failed to get rid of her, he'd alerted Tommy Junior and the immensely unpleasant Jeffries: He'd recognized her name from the newspapers.

Well, something was rotten at Riordan's, all right, but it was still entirely unclear just what; meanwhile, it occurred to Edwina that Perry Whitlock had mentioned nothing about his wife's having had an affair with Thomas Riordan, Sr. Pulling into traffic headed downtown on Whalley Avenue, accelerating as the light at Whalley and Norton turned green ahead, she wondered if Perry had even known about it.

And as the lumbering garbage truck ran the red light coming out of Norton across Whalley, appearing like a ten-ton bad dream directly in front of her and much too near to steer around—

—"Damn," Edwina breathed, hitting the brakes; in response the brake pedal sank floppily to the floor, meeting no resistance and providing no braking action whatsoever—

—as all these events occurred in rapid succession, Edwina wondered suddenly and urgently just what the hell was going on here, and whether or not she would survive it.

NINE

"You see, the Fiat 124, she's gotta front and rear power disks," said the parts manager at Worldwide Motors, "so to get alla four brakes to fail at once, usually you gotta either mess with the hydraulics or foul up the master cylinder. Easiest way, cut the brake line, alla fluid leaks out."

The parts manager snapped his fingers to demonstrate just how easy this would be. He was a short dark man with sad brown eyes, a thin mustache that looked penciled on, and the name Gerry embroidered in red script across his white shirt's breast pocket. "Only," he said, "that's not what happened here."

Edwina stood before the parts counter at Worldwide Motors, her hands clenched on the scarred wooden surface. At what had seemed the last moment, the garbage-truck driver had noticed her hurtling at his vehicle and had put on a startling, sudden burst of speed while swinging his steering wheel sharply right.

Edwina, seeing his purpose, had swung her own wheel, aiming the Fiat at the tiny space the garbage-truck driver was trying to create between the rear of his truck and the lamppost at the corner.

145

But the space had not widened enough by the time she reached it; as a result, the Fiat's front fender peeled back, detached itself, and tore a gash in the car's black fabric top. Along with the shriek of ripping sheet metal had come the crash of shattering glass; an instant later, the Fiat halted.

On impact, Edwina had felt her chest slam solidly into the seatbelt, which operated perfectly in terms of keeping her body from being hurled up and out through the windshield. It did not, however, restrain her head, which continued moving forward for a fraction of a second and then snapped back, clicking her teeth sharply together. The resulting burst of pain from her front tooth made the rest of the collision feel like a minor inconvenience; only her grab to keep Maxie from scrambling out the hole in the Fiat's top stopped her from simply sitting there, howling.

"See," said the parts manager, "I putta car up on the rack myself. I gotta fellow does that, but this time I do it. Because, Miss Crusoe, I smell something funny here. I know you keep this car nice, you bring it in, what, every three thousan' miles or so." He kissed his thumb and fingertip together. "Is perfection, the way you maintain this car."

In the face of the parts manager's praise, Edwina forbore to mention that anyone owning a Fiat 124 Sport Spyder was pretty well forced to maintain a nearly fanatical maintenance schedule, just to keep the body from collapsing into a heap of rust flakes, or the crankcase from dropping out onto the garage floor.

"So," she said, speaking with some difficulty through the numb, floppy-feeling aperture that was her mouth; the resident on call at Chelsea Memorial's emergency room had turned out to be an old friend of Harry Lemon's, and upon examining her and hearing her story he had summoned a cooperative oral surgeon carrying a syringe full of enough novocaine to freeze a side of beef.

"So, what did you find when you checked out the car?"

The parts manager looked troubled. "Miss Crusoe, you know I

like you, I don' want you to get mad when I tell you this. But it's for your own good, okay? Because I think you got some kind of bad enemy, somewhere."

Having an hour ago been released from the emergency room wearing an itchy, bulky, uncomfortable foam-rubber neck brace, and having been equipped with muscle-relaxant tablets for the neck spasms that, according to the emergency-room resident, were inevitably going to develop, Edwina had already gotten mad and doubted she could get any madder. Also, she knew she had a bad enemy somewhere.

"Go ahead, Gerry," she said. "It wasn't the brake line, was it?" If it had been, she would have felt something sooner; even an exploded brake line gave you at least one last fading pump, before all the brake fluid spewed out of it.

"No," Gerry said, looking almost as unhappy as he had the day the Fiat had been towed in, after its timing belt broke and its engine seized up. "Not the brake line, and not the power pack. You'd still have brakes, with that, just not power brakes. So I keep looking, you know? And what I found—"

Gerry held up a piece of metal. Attached to it was the Fiat's brake pedal. The piece of metal had been filed almost all the way through; the final thin shred of it had broken.

"This," Gerry said, "is a push rod. You push the pedal, the pedal pushes the rod, the rod sends a message to the brakes, see. It makes the whole big braking system go, just this little push rod."

"But not if someone cuts through it." Distantly, Edwina noticed that her hands had stopped shaking. "I can see somebody cut through it, enough so that eventually it would—"

Behind Gerry, the work in the auto shop went on. A teenaged boy chattered in Italian to another young man while he watched the hydraulic lift raise a red Alfa Romeo sedan off the concrete floor. Somebody dropped a tire iron and snatched it up hastily again, cutting off its metallic clangor. A hydraulic wrench attacked

147

the lug nuts on a black Lamborghini with a sound like a monster dental drill, in between blasts of rock and roll music from an Italian-language radio station. Over it all hung the sweet smells of motor oil, gasoline, and expensive leather upholstery.

Gerry nodded. "Thing is, that takes a while. Somebody file through this rod, maybe forty-five minutes. This is not an easy thing, here. Also, this is not a simple part to get at. Takes a lotta time, a lotta patience, to do a bad thing like this."

"What about with some kind of power cutting tool?"

Gerry shook his head immediately. "First of all, you start cutting around down there with the kind of tool you're talking about, you got sparks. Also, down there you got gasoline. You get the picture? No, you don't want to be doing that. Besides, even if you did, you could see it on the metal. See, this is all black and grubby here, it's only bright where the file cut it."

He put the pedal and the snapped push rod on the counter. "No, Miss Crusoe. If I know you, the only place you leave that car for very long is inna garage. All nice and safe, overnight. Only, while you sleep—"

He held up his index and middle fingers, crossing the index finger of the other hand over them in the warding-off-a-hex sign. From his crate at her feet, Maxie growled his distress and backed into a corner of the wire enclosure.

"Ssh, Maxie," she said. "It's okay, we're going now."

Gerry peered over the counter at the cat. "Hey, you gotta black cat, huh? You let him cross your path? Maybe you better get nice big dog, put him in the garage with the car at night."

"Right. Maybe I'd better. Right now, I think I'd better go down to the police station, and tell them what you just told me. Put that part somewhere safe, will you please? And Gerry, when can I have the car back?"

Gerry looked more mournful than ever. "Okay, look, first I gotta fix the brakes, the suspension, the tie rod, everything. After that I send it over to my brother, he does the body work so we got something to put the headlight in. He's gotta get a new fender, the front chrome and hood, plus he's gotta put a new top on it. Then you got your painting, for sure he's gonna paint the whole thing, otherwise it don't match right, you gotta two-tone."

He glanced up. "Also, Miss Crusoe, I gotta tell you I never checked yet, see if the frame's bent. The Fiat, she's no utility vehicle, you know, she's a precision automobile."

The Fiat, thought Edwina, is an excellent little car on the occasions when it is running. But the rest of the time, it might just as well be constructed from tissue paper stuck together with airplane glue. Expensive tissue paper, and expensive airplane glue.

Fifteen minutes later, having extracted from the parts manager a promise to call her with an estimate just as soon as possible—assuming she ever wanted to drive the car again at all; if the frame was bent, a hay wagon would be more comfortable as well as tighter in the turns, even after the repair job—Edwina was in a rental car, headed back across town.

The white Ford Escort had no radio; it had plastic seats, an automatic transmission, and a four-cylinder engine whose oomph suggested it was powered by a squirrel cage attached to a rubber band. Its only advantage was that it was not, at the moment, mashed between a light pole and a garbage truck.

She had called Arthur. He had been sympathetic, but he already had an emergency patient who he expected to take up his whole afternoon; could the tooth wait? Yes, Edwina told him, she thought it could.

Which left the police to see—she'd already explained the circumstances of the accident to a traffic cop, but the filed-through push rod was certain to interest them, and she still had the Polaroids of the rat's head, the note, and Jennifer Warren's handgun to deliver—and Perry Whitlock to visit. Tomorrow, after all, she would probably have a stiff neck and a sore mouth, and be doped up on muscle relaxants and painkillers. That made today the day to ask Perry if he'd known Theresa was seeing Thomas Riordan, a conversation for which she would need all her wits about her. Besides, she wanted to get it over with.

* * *

"I don't believe it," Perry Whitlock said. He sat across from her in his private office, which was decorated in hearty, masculine style: hunting prints, oversized leather chairs, and a pair of antique dueling pistols in a glass case on the wall behind his head. There were also a dozen or so small framed photographs, all of people in costumes and makeup, some signed. But all the things with which he had surrounded himself seemed to overpower him, almost to swallow him up.

"It's an insult," he went on stoutly. "Theresa'd had some troubles. But we never kept secrets from one another."

Except, thought Edwina, for that fifty thousand dollars. Whitlock slid forward in his chair, which was too large for him; she found herself wondering if his feet could touch the floor, then returned her attention to what he was saying.

". . . I would have known. You saw Theresa's face; imagine it trying to lie to you. My God, first someone murders her, and now this? I tell you, it's impossible. And," he insisted, "I'll sue anyone who says differently without proof positive."

From some of the photographs beamed the heavily madeup face of Perry Whitlock himself. In one he was a pirate; in another, a clown; in a third he strutted improbably in what looked like the title role in *Hamlet*.

"I'm sorry, Perry, of course I don't mean to distress you. But when I heard this story, I thought I'd better ask—"

"No, no, don't worry about me. I'm glad you told me. A man needs to know when rumors are going around, and I'd rather hear it from you than anyone. It's just . . . well."

Perry managed a brave smile. "It's just that the house is so empty, and the evenings are very long. I'll get used to it, I suppose. But the police haven't come up with anything. They say they haven't anything to go on, really, and they don't hold out much hope. Your husband's been awfully kind, and honest, too; it isn't his job to bother with me, but he does, and he doesn't try to pretend the other officers are getting anywhere."

Whitlock got up and began pacing, pausing to adjust the venetian blind at a big window looking out onto an alley. "Awful view," he commented, lowering the blind and closing the curtains. As he did so, the buzzer on his intercom sounded; irritably, he pressed the "speak" button.

"What is it, Jean? I said I didn't want to be—"

"It's Mr. Granger," came the disembodied voice of Perry's office receptionist. "He says it's urgent."

"Oh, all right," Whitlock replied. "This'll just take a minute," he told Edwina, and picked up the phone.

"Jack? Right, you too. What's the— No. I don't care, Jack, I told you what I want to do, and that's— What? Yes, I do know what it'll do to my premium, and I— Yes, I know we could fight it. I know that, Jack, but—"

Edwina concentrated politely on examining some of the knick-knacks on Perry's bookcase, as if by turning her back on him she could keep from overhearing his conversation. But she could not.

"Look, Jack," Whitlock said, "maybe they *don't* have a case, and maybe we *could* get it thrown out. The guy she's got lined up to testify isn't even a practicing dentist anymore, he practically makes a living being an expert witness. But I have my reasons, Jack, I just can't take any more of anything right now, what with losing Theresa, and I— Yes."

He paused to listen. "Yes, I understand. Jack, I've got someone here with me at the moment, and I— No. No, I wouldn't let you try telling me how to be a dentist. But my mind is made up on this. Clear?"

It was certainly clear to Edwina, whose own practice of medical sleuthing had taught her to comprehend such oblique monologues. Perry Whitlock was being sued for some sort of dental malpractice and against his lawyer's advice had decided to offer a settlement rather than fight the accusation, apparently because he did not want to go through a courtroom battle. She supposed she could understand this, even though it was going to cost him, insurance-wise. Such things could be hugely expensive in time and energy, even for the winning side, and Whitlock was already emotionally drained.

She waited a moment for Perry to finish his conversation. Before her on one shelf sat a cassette player; on another, a Harvard mug with a collection of small tools—a screwdriver, pliers, a tackhammer—standing in it. Then she turned.

"I suppose Theresa met Riordan in the office," she said, "when she worked for you? I understand he was your patient."

Whitlock blinked. "I don't know how you know that, but yes, he was. Probably she did meet him, but only in the office. I tell you, I'd have known if she were having an affair."

Obviously he wasn't going to budge on this, and Edwina felt that he really believed what he was saying. Unhappily, he picked up the photograph of himself as Hamlet, turning it over and over in his small, clean hands. "I'd have known," he repeated stubbornly.

"Yes. Well, I had to ask. And when the authorities asked you for Tom Riordan's dental records—"

"I supplied them," Perry finished the sentence for her. "I didn't— Wait a minute, what are you saying? You think Theresa had something to do with his death? But that's ridiculous."

"Perry, I'm sorry. I didn't come here to upset you. But I do need to know these things. You sent the records off, and that was your only involvement in the matter?"

He spread his hands. "Yes. I'm a family dentist, not a forensics expert, as I told you. There was no reason for me to be involved further. And I know you're trying to help, Edwina. I'm sorry if I . . . Well." He bit his lip and tried very hard to look brave, bringing it off unsuccessfully.

A long moment of silence passed. "So," Edwina tried, "what do you do with yourself to keep busy now? When you're not here, I mean."

Perry gave a wretched wave. "I tried last night to tinker around. I have lots of hobbies, I guess I've mentioned. But I couldn't stick to anything, so I tried reading. That didn't work, either. I suppose things will improve in time. I hope they will." Sighing, he climbed down from his chair.

"I've got a cancellation, by the way, I could have a look at that tooth for you," he offered. "No charge, of course. I appreciate your concern." He walked with her to the office door. "It can't have been easy, telling me what you had heard."

Edwina smiled as well as she could without being able to feel her upper lip. "You were good to listen so well. And thank you for your offer, but I have an appointment with Arthur."

Perry Whitlock nodded approvingly. "Fine man. He'll take care of you." He opened his office door to let her out ahead of him.

While Perry's private chamber resembled the den of a real man's man, the atmosphere outside it was pure dentist's office: the tang of rubbing alcohol mingled with the scent of clove mouth rinse, the faint reek of instrument-sterilizing solution, and the burning smell, just perceptible, of tooth enamel being vaporized by a high-speed drill.

"Do you know," he asked suddenly and apropos of nothing, "why your anesthetized upper lip seems to feel so enormous? It feels the size of an elephant, doesn't it?"

"Yes, it does," she laughed, pleased that he was able to lighten the conversation even in the midst of his obvious grief. "Only, *this* elephant is clinging to the front of my face. I suppose now you're going to tell me why it feels that way."

Whitlock's tone grew pensive. "When your lip or any part of you is numbed by a local anesthetic," he said, "it's not only the pain messages that are blocked."

He straightened, cleared his throat, and went on. "All the sensory messages from the area vanish; suddenly, the brain gets no more signals. Something that had been there is abruptly gone, vanished like a plane from a radar screen. And the reaction from the brain is very remarkable: It *needs* to have a whole organism to manage. It expects and wants it. It *must* have it."

Suddenly Edwina realized that she was being told something important. She wasn't quite sure what, only that Whitlock was giving her the key to something, perhaps without knowing that he was. She listened carefully.

"The organism must exist, whole and entire," Whitlock went on, "or the brain becomes uncomfortable. And to avoid that discomfort, it supplies the missing element."

"You mean, I'm not feeling anything from my lip. No signal is being transmitted. I could put a hot match to it and I would not feel anything."

"Not a blip," Whitlock answered, looking gratified. "Your lip's whole nerve-system network is blocked. That's why they call it a nerve block; it's as if your lip weren't there at all. But as a replacement, your brain has created a new lip—or at least supplied its best guess at one. Your brain is delivering lip feelings to itself—only it's got the proportions wrong."

"And that's why my lip feels so huge, so swollen and wrong? Because my brain is trying to supply the sensations a whole, undamaged body would be sending, and not doing it quite right?"

The idea, she had to admit, was remarkable: a phantom lip. A sort of brain mirage. When the brain did not receive sensory signals it was expecting, it created them for itself.

"Precisely." Following her as far as the reception desk, Whitlock laughed wanly. "There I am, up on my teaching horse again. Maybe I should give some thought to an academic job." But he didn't sound as if he meant it.

"Perry," she said, "just one more thing. You said whoever was saying Theresa had an affair with Thomas Riordan would need proof. But what if there is proof? What then?"

He paused as if trying to think how to reply to this. In the corridor between the desk and the treatment rooms a nervous young man was being escorted toward a door labeled PROPHYLAXIS. At a counter behind the desk, a technician scrutinized the contents of a manila folder.

"You can file this again," the technician said, handing the folder to a clerk. "I've sent everything her insurance company will need, so we should be getting the check soon." The clerk scanned a long bank of filing cabinets, located the proper one, and replaced the folder among hundreds of other folders.

"Perry?" Edwina asked again. "What if it turns out that way? Would you want to know? I mean, if I did come across any actual proof?"

Whitlock shook his head as if to clear it. "No, I don't suppose I would. Theresa was perfection to me. I'd like to keep that memory." He managed a smile. "If I can. Thanks for asking, though. Have you found out anything else? Anything that could show who might have . . . killed her?" He forced the last words out.

"Not yet. But I think I may be making some headway. I'll keep in touch, shall I?" She clasped his hand, which was cold and damp, and went out through the lobby into the side parking lot of the office building, just off York Street.

There she found that Maxie had managed to wriggle out the passenger-side window of the rental car; to provide ventilation she had opened it an amount that she would have sworn was less than the width of his head. Now he was stretched on the Escort's roof, lazily washing himself in what remained of the weak autumn afternoon sun.

"I suppose I should be glad you're only an escape artist and not a runaway," she grumbled, lifting him with unusual ease—for once, he did not squirm or protest—and depositing him on the car's front seat. There, looking not the least bit guilty, he settled and began purring loudly, for Maxie dwelt secure in the notion that if he followed the spirit of whatever law Edwina laid down for him, the letter would probably take care of itself.

"Prutt," he pronounced, composing himself for sleep as the Escort's tires spun for a moment in the dirty slush, then caught hold. A new sort of weather seemed to be moving in, with a hint of warmth in the air despite the oncoming early dusk.

"Easy for you to say," Edwina told the cat. But he knew she liked his hardheaded independence, so there was really no sense in wasting time scolding him, especially as he was here now and the day did seem to be disappearing fast.

Edwina steered the Escort into traffic. There was just time to get to the police station—she would, she hoped, not have to spend *too* much time explaining things to them—and then to hurry to Arthur's for the revolting matter of the tooth repair.

Thinking this, Edwina grimaced, glancing into the Escort's outside mirror. When she glanced back the car ahead of her had stopped, flashing brake lights.

"Blast," she said to the cat, "this car is— Maxie?"

Later, of course, she would come to realize that Maxie was, after all, only a cat. There were millions, maybe billions of cats in the world; but at the moment there was only Maxie, whose limp, senseless body slid from the car seat as she hit the brakes, landing floppily and heartbreakingly upon the rubber floor mat of the rented Escort as the vehicle slammed to a halt.

"Maxie? Oh, no, please." Reaching down, Edwina seized a handful of black cat fur and hauled it desperately upward. The black cat's head bobbled bonelessly as his body slid back up over the seat's edge. Maxie was half-conscious, his eyes bluish-white slits, and a thin line of foam showed horridly on his lips; when she pressed him to herself she felt his heart racing thinly.

Behind the Escort, vehicles began honking as drivers of all kinds began demonstrating the one trait they could be depended upon to share in an emergency: the strong, genetically ingrained belief in their own inalienable right to behave like Neanderthals, combined with the deep, unswerving certainty that anyone who got in their way deserved torture.

Edwina slammed her foot onto the Escort's gas pedal. This, predictably, only made the Escort's transmission whine while it decided whether or not to engage. Next the vehicle lugged slowly forward, as if mustering up the courage to accelerate.

What happened then, however, was startling. The Escort did actually possess some motive power; it merely needed time to gather it. Once it had, it sprang forward, differential howling and skimpily treaded tires scrambling, like the runt animal of the litter who has, after some final, insupportable humiliation, at last decided to show its stuff.

"It's okay, Maxie, it's okay, boy," Edwina murmured to the animal lying across her lap as she passed slow vehicles on the left, faster vehicles on the right, and ran yellow lights with abandon. Flooring the Escort unapologetically through the barest beginning flicker of a red light. she hammered the horn steadily as she raced toward the New Haven Veterinary Clinic on Pearl Street.

"Okay, buddy, we're here, now," she whispered, cradling the black cat to dash up the red brick building's steps and through its big glass front door.

"Edwina," said the woman behind the desk, with a smile that vanished at once as she spied Maxie. Leaping up, she raced around the counter and snatched the lifeless-seeming animal from Edwina's arms; slamming her palm onto a red buzzer on the desk, she departed down a corridor at a trot, with Edwina behind.

"What was it, a car?" Shouldering her way into a treatment cubicle, she laid the animal on a metal examining table. "What happened to him, do you know?"

"No," Edwina admitted helplessly as the veterinary resident came in through the door at the back of the cubicle. Taking in the scene and general situation at once, he examined Maxie's eyes and ears and listened to his heart while looking grim.

"No," Edwina went on, "I don't know what happened. Nothing *did* happen. He was waiting in the car for me and when I came out he'd gotten up onto the roof and was sunning himself, looking lazy."

The vet was drawing a syringeful of blood from the inside of Maxie's left hind leg. "What's he eaten, anything different? Catch any birds, insects, any trash off the street?" He examined Maxie's ears, pried open his mouth, and peered down his throat.

"He . . . Wait a minute. Someone could have given him something while I was inside. The car door was unlocked. Maybe he didn't get out by himself. Maybe someone poisoned him?"

Sprawled on the metal examining table, the black cat looked small and helpless. His velvet flank rose and fell very slowly with his breathing. The vet pushed a button on the wall and a buzzer sounded back in the kennel area, summoning a veterinary technician. The vet lifted Maxie with both hands and gave him to the technician.

Please, Edwina thought, restraining the urge simply to grab the animal back.

"Set him up with an IV," the vet said. He was young and tired and all business. "Just run it at keep open for now, and stick one of the cardiac monitors on him, will you? I'll run this over to the lab myself, and we'll see what shows up. Because," he went on as Maxie was carried out, "this cat looks drugged to me."

158

"Drugged," Edwina repeated stupidly. "So what will you do?"

"Find out if it is, and what it is," the vet said, "and see if it's treatable. He might come out on his own with fluids and support. Worst case, if it is a drug, we might have to dialyze it out."

But from the vet's face she saw that wasn't the worst case at all. "Look around the car," he went on, "see if you might have dropped something on the floor that he could have picked up. You didn't have an open Tylenol bottle around, by any chance?"

She shook her head. "No. Nothing."

"Good. Tylenol's fatal for cats, you know." He picked up the syringeful of Maxie's blood. "You can call us in an hour, see how we're getting along, all right?"

Without waiting for an answer he went out, leaving Edwina unsure whether to resent his failure to offer reassurance, or to be glad that he had hurried off to care for Maxie; the latter, she decided. Nothing he could have said would have made her feel better, anyway. Slowly she walked back to the lobby, not wanting to leave Maxie but not knowing what else she could do.

"You can wait here if you want, instead of calling," the nurse at the desk said, "but I'm sure Maxie is going to stay here at least overnight, Edwina. I'm so sorry about this."

If he lives the night. "Thank you," Edwina said. "But I'd better go check the car. It's a rental, someone else might have dropped a pill or something on the floor. If I do find anything I'll come and let you know what it is, and of course I'll call to check on him. If anything . . . happens, meanwhile, here's my card."

She didn't want Maxie in a cage with needles in his veins and monitors hooked up to him. She wanted him purring in her lap. Outside it was dark, and through the clinic's big glass front doors the lights of passing cars blurred into multicolored spangles, as Edwina's eyes filled with tears.

Angrily she blinked them away, and she glimpsed a woman staring at her from across the street. The long, bony face with its

159

slightly protruding teeth and frame of dark hair bore a strong resemblance to Wilhelmina Zimmerman's, as well as to the photographs in newspaper accounts about Ricky Zimmerman.

Straightening, Edwina forced down the rest of her tears. There was nothing wrong with a good cry, but now was not the time for it. Someone had scared her, threatened her, and injured her in the car, and she disliked all those things immensely. But trying to hurt Maxie was a whole different ball game, and now she knew who the woman across the street must be.

She straight-armed the glass doors. It took ten minutes to find a working pay phone, two to get the number she wanted, and forty-five seconds to convince Gerhardt Blauderbundt to tell her absolutely everything she wanted to know, immediately.

"Or," she told the doctor, "I'll ask your wife."

Bingo.

*   *   *

"Talk to me, Carlotta, or I'll make sure you go to Niantic Women's Prison for blackmail and extortion at the very least, and I'll make sure you stay there. Why were you following me and what did you feed my cat while I was in Perry Whitlock's office?"

Carlotta shrugged. "I didn't do nothing. What do I care about a cat? I don't know what you're talkin' about, extortion. You got some nerve comin' here, try pushin' people around."

She turned from the greasy stove where she was heating a bottle of milk in a battered pan filled with scummy water. The mineral rings on the inside of the pan showed it had been used again and again for this purpose, apparently without benefit of washing.

Edwina resisted the attractive but unrealistic notion of making Carlotta drink the water. At the moment, she was angry enough to consider making Carlotta eat the pan.

But never mind; poor old frightened Dr. Blauderbundt had given

160

her all the bludgeon she needed for Carlotta—along with her address, which curiously enough turned out to be right here in New Haven—and besides, the baby was hungry, judging by the fretful wails it was emitting from its crib in the next room.

"I mean," said Edwina, "you forced Blauderbundt to give you ten thousand dollars by threatening to tell his wife what a jerk he was if he didn't pay you. Small potatoes, though, wasn't it, Carlotta? I don't think Ricky would have approved. On the other hand, Ricky was out there murdering people for only ten thousand, from what I hear, so maybe—"

Carlotta whirled. "You shut up about my brother. If that little Whitlock bitch had just kept away from him—"

She stopped, and sullenly squirted a few drops of milk from the baby's bottle onto her wrist, then plunked the bottle back in to heat longer. "I mean, I guess it was her. She got killed and now you're here sticking your nose in. It must've been her," she finished unconvincingly, "wasn't it?"

"Ten thousand didn't go very far, did it?" Edwina asked, ignoring Carlotta's question in her pleasure at just having gotten an answer to one of her own. "Not with medical bills, a baby, food and clothes and a roof over your head. And whatever your friend in there takes when he's short on cash. Which I gather is most of the time."

She angled her head at the kitchen doorway; beyond it, oblivious to the baby's screams, which were steadily increasing in volume, the boyfriend slumped in front of the TV set. Each time the baby howled, the springs of the chair creaked and the television's volume went up yet another notch.

"He's lookin' for work," Carlotta said. "It ain't easy, you know. He's good with cars but nobody wants to hire a guy's been in prison." But her tone in his defense was not particularly spirited.

"Besides," she added, "that's all old Blunderbutt could get, ten thousand. I had him scared, he wasn't lyin', so I took it. What was

161

I gonna do?" She tested the bottle again and left the room; plugged off by the rubber nipple, the baby's howling stopped.

Edwina waited at the chipped wooden table, in the horrid little kitchen with the old grease splatters on the walls. Several days' worth of dishes lay jumbled in the sink, and the color of the linoleum could no longer even be determined through the layers of grime. A rank odor drifted from the garbage pail, packed to overflowing with kitchen refuse and disposable diapers; bottles and cans lined the countertops, including one small vial that looked medicinal; Edwina was about to get up to examine it when Carlotta came back in again.

"I don't know what you want," the young woman resumed complaining at once. "I got enough troubles, without snotty strangers like you coming around hassling me."

"I didn't come to you. You came to me. You were following me today. I saw you," Edwina explained patiently, resisting the urge to take this slatternly princess by her bony shoulders and shake her until her eyes rolled back. The baby was beautiful, and Edwina suspected that it had spent the afternoon howling—and that this hadn't been the first time.

"I want to know *why* you were following me," she said. "And if you don't tell me, or if you don't tell me the truth, I'll do exactly what I said I'd do—but first I'll call the Department of Family Services, and report you for neglecting that child."

Which I still might do anyway, Edwina added silently, seeing Carlotta's quick guilty glance. And it had to be Carlotta: Tom Riordan, Jr., and his pair of ugly pals hadn't known of Edwina until this morning, and Edwina could not imagine Madalyn Riordan poisoning Maxie: For one thing, she'd been too drunk to do the complex following required. Willie Zimmerman simply wasn't in the running—no one was *that* good an actor; besides, Willie was too far away—and Edwina had begun doubting Tom Riordan Sr.'s

162

ability to accomplish anything at all. And, just to quash the long shot, Perry Whitlock had been in plain view at the critical time.

So: Carlotta, with her masses of stringy black hair and her looks, which had once been spectacular, but now resembled the colors in some ruined wall painting, lovely until the elements had gotten at them. Carlotta, with a chip on her shoulder, and her obvious need for money.

"It must have been a big disappointment for you when that insurance policy of Ricky's didn't pay off," Edwina said. "You told Blauderbundt he'd better fix that time of death, or you'd make his life miserable. Ricky must have told you what he was up to— against whom, and for whom."

"He told me," Carlotta agreed reluctantly. "I knew he was s'posed to kill the Riordan guy. But," she added with a burst of resentment, "he didn't tell me he lied on the application for the insurance. He should've just said he wasn't working, not made up some bigshot job. But that was Ricky. What a jerk."

"Did he tell you who hired him?"

"Yeah," Carlotta admitted. "He said it was her. She was sick of this Riordan guy, and she had some way of getting money out of him, a lot of money he'd be carrying, she said. But Ricky had to kill him, otherwise he'd take the money back. That was what she was going to pay Ricky with, see, part of the money she was going to steal from the Riordan guy."

"Only," Edwina said thoughtfully, "she never did pay."

"Or that kid got it," Carlotta said. "The one killed Ricky, that they picked up in Ricky's car. *Somebody* got it."

"No, I don't think it was Maurice. He didn't have money on him when they arrested him," Edwina replied.

But that must have been why Ricky had gone to the rest area in New Jersey: It was the payoff spot. He'd intended to meet Theresa there. The thought made Edwina remember what Maurice had said about a blue car.

"Anyway," Carlotta mumbled, as if the effort of telling the truth had completely exhausted her, "you're out there, doing who knows what. Maybe your husband doesn't know, or you've got something on the side. I bet you do," she added slyly. "So I thought I'd have a look, see what you do, places you go. But I didn't do nothing to any cat."

"Uh-huh. You were in your mother's house the other night; that's how you knew about me. And it worked on Blauderbundt, so maybe it would work on me, is that it? A little more blackmail, fatten up the bank account again? Seeing as your hero doesn't appear to be climbing out of that easy chair any time soon."

As if triggered by this comment, a hoarse voice bellowed from the living room. "Hey, Carlotta! Where the hell's the sandwiches you were gonna make me? Tell whoever that broad is you're busy, goddamnit, you ain't got time for her bullshit."

Edwina got up and smiled as sweetly as she was able. "Nice fellow. Hope he'll let you out, later."

Dully, Carlotta pulled Wonder Bread from a cabinet and began smearing it with margarine. "I ain't goin' nowhere."

"Yes, you are. I'm having a party and you'll be there, ten o'clock, or I'll have that baby in foster care and you in Niantic so fast, none of you will know what's hit you."

For the first time Carlotta looked really frightened. "He ain't gonna let me go anywhere," she whined, "he don't like when I go out at—"

Edwina pressed a card into Carlotta's hand. "You should have thought of that before, because I've had it with an entire group of sneaky, lying, not-to-be-trusted people, and you've put yourself among them by your own behavior today."

She put the end of her index finger in the center of the other woman's shirt front. "So if I were you, Carlotta, I'd try convincing him, I really would. My address is on that card. Be there, and don't be late."

She gave this last instruction extra emphasis with the tip of her fingernail. Carlotta didn't flinch, only stared with wide brown eyes that once had been pretty. Now they were gummy with the strain of the lies she'd had to tell, or thought she'd had to: to stay alive, to get some money, to keep what had come to pass for freedom.

Carlotta nodded, up and down like a plastic doll. "Why?" she whispered. "Why are you doing this? He'll kill me if he finds out I sneaked out."

Just for an instant Edwina felt sorry for Carlotta. Her own desire to leave this appalling hovel grew by the moment; what must it be like to wake up here, to have to sleep, eat, and exist here?

Then she remembered Gerhardt Blauderbundt, speaking to her on the telephone. Her call had unnerved him, which from the sound of him was not difficult to do. Quaveringly, he had answered her questions; it was clear that Carlotta had scared him half to death, and that however disreputable and unpleasant he might once have been, he was now a broken man.

"Just be there," Edwina repeated, and left the house.

*   *   *

Jennifer Warren looked younger, skinnier, and tougher out on the street than she had in Edwina's kitchen. At the sight of the Escort she skittered down the sidewalk, pretending not to notice the woman beckoning to her from behind the wheel.

"Jennifer," Edwina snapped, cranking the window down, "get over here, it's me."

The girl paused, checking out Edwina's reflection in a store window before turning to catch a sideways glimpse. Only then did she saunter to the curb. "Hey," she said, "how's it going?"

"Fine, just fine. Get in, I want to talk to you."

The girl took a hasty step back. "I gotta meet somebody. My boyfriend, he's—"

On the street, Jennifer was like a small wild animal, cautious and alert. Her foxlike face and bright eyes radiated a wild creature's vitality; she moved with wiry grace in her tight jeans, high-heeled leather boots, and a blue denim jacket over a spandex tank top.

"Jennifer, cut it out. I've got something important to say to you, about Theresa, and I don't have much time."

Edwina shut the Escort's ignition off, and got out of the car. Just then a tall, black-haired fellow with a pockmarked face and thin lips eased from the shadows between two buildings, disguising his intentness with a smile as his glance flicked from Jennifer to Edwina. He lit a cigarette, cupping his hand around the match, and tossed the match away.

"You got a problem with my girl?" He slung his arm around Jennifer, gave her a brief squeeze and then a sharp shove, back out to where the cars cruised and slowed on the avenue. Their headlights mingled with neon from the storefronts to gleam in the dirty slush puddled by the curb; Jennifer's fur-topped boots were spattered with it.

"Go on, honey," he told her, "I'll take care of this."

"There isn't anything to take care of," Edwina told him. She looked at Jennifer, who stared out at the passing cars, and up again at Jennifer's pimp, whose eyes were about as full of normal human feeling as a pair of steel ball bearings.

Jennifer had lied about being on her own; what else had she lied about? And Mr. Congeniality here looked plenty capable of pulling the trigger on Theresa Whitlock—only why would he want to? Edwina revised her guest list upward.

"In that case," he advised softly, "you should take a walk." His voice was full of practiced menace. "I don't like people who bother my girlfriend."

"Right," said Edwina, who by now had had just about enough of dancing around with this bozo. He was the type who talked tough as long as he was bigger, and as long as he was in good health, but after a poke between the ribs from an angry, coked-up

166

girlfriend's suddenly produced switchblade—this being a common occupational hazard for fellows who pimped seriously and professionally—he was also the type who rolled howling into the emergency room, cursing anyone who got near him and begging hysterically for morphine, his mom, and God's mercy, in that order. And that was exactly what he had done, one night a few years earlier when Edwina had been working an extra shift in the Chelsea trauma department.

"You don't recognize me, do you?" she asked him. "Let's see, I think your name is . . . Timmy. That's right, Timmy DiNardis, and you've got a scar about this long right down your middle."

His eyes narrowed further; then suddenly he broke into a grin. "Hey, sure, I remember you now, you got me the painkiller and some ice chips to chew, couple years ago when I got stuck. Man, I was thirsty." He shook his head, recalling it. "What're you doing, this part of town? They runnin' short of patients for their torture chambers, send you out to round up a few?"

On the evening in question Edwina would happily have stuffed a block of dry ice into Tim's mouth and shot him up with enough painkillers to stun a moose, if only they would have shut him up. She remembered his name only because it was what the girl who had stabbed him kept crooning as she sat blubbering in the minor-surgery room, having her own wounds cleansed and stitched; Timmy, it seemed, had gotten a few licks in himself before the cops and the ambulance arrived.

"I came to talk to Jennifer," Edwina said as the girl sidled cautiously nearer again and Timmy's face hardened with suspicion. Jennifer flashed a look of frightened warning as his hand shot out and seized her collar, and gave her a shake that was supposed to look playful but didn't.

"Oh, yeah? What's my girl been up to, that a nurse's gotta chase her down?" He shook the girl again, harder. "You sick?"

"Cut it out, Timmy, that hurts," Jennifer complained. "I'm not up to anything, and I'm not sick of anything but you." She winced, squirming from his grasp.

"I just wanted to chat," Edwina put in quickly. "But I know your time is valuable so of course I'll make it worth your while. Can I buy you both a drink?" She slid two twenties from her bag. "We'll let the gentleman handle the money, shall we?" she added to Jennifer, holding out the bills.

Timmy, his suspicions now thoroughly aroused, pocketed the cash grudgingly as his glance flicked like a knife tip from the girl back to Edwina.

"Yeah, sure," he said. "I could use a drink. I could use some straight answers, too. You," he told Edwina, "ain't here to talk girl talk with this one." He nudged Jennifer hard with his hip, to get her moving. "She don't have any classy friends like you."

Jennifer's face clouded as she frowned down at her cheap clothes and slush-soaked boots, her fingers blue with cold under the clutter of junky rings she wore. "Whose fault is that?" she asked bitterly. "If you had your way, I wouldn't have any—"

"Never mind," Edwina interrupted, struck by the notion that if Timmy had his way, Jennifer would have no friends; considering the manner in which she had just lost one, it was an interesting idea. Maybe running into Timmy wasn't such bad luck after all.

"I'll meet you across the street." Edwina pointed at a bar whose window displayed a sign promising CHILLED WINE SANDWICHES. "I've just got a quick phone call to make."

"Yeah, right," Timmy agreed sourly, giving Jennifer's arm a yank that nearly pulled the girl off her feet. Watching as he pushed Jennifer ahead of him into the slushy intersection and propelled her across the busy avenue, Edwina thought DiNardis was a bullying creep; seeing the way he shoved Jennifer made her want to stick a knife in him, herself.

"So whatta you want to chat about?" he demanded ten minutes

later when Edwina entered the dingy saloon and sat down on one of the imitation-leather stools at the bar.

She had reached the animal hospital from a pay phone on the corner; Maxie, the veterinarian had reported, was no better and no worse. The first group of blood tests showed high levels of a tranquilizer, but there was no specific treatment for an overdose and since the cat's condition was not deteriorating, a wait-and-see approach was best; Edwina was to call back in another hour.

On top of her already simmering dislike for Tim DiNardis and her growing suspicion of Jennifer, the information had heated her temper back up to a boil. "Theresa Whitlock," she said flatly.

Beside her, Jennifer stiffened and began babbling. "I just needed somebody to talk to. I just wanted somebody to—"

Timmy turned toward Jennifer, his pockmarked face coldly furious. "Quiet. The lady and me are talking here, okay?"

The girl's mouth snapped shut like the jaw of a ventriloquist's wooden dummy. Miserably, she toyed with her cocktail napkin, pushing it around in a puddle of water on the bar.

"Jennie here has a bad habit," DiNardis said, smiling in a way he apparently thought was charming. "I try to explain to her, people don't like it, but she don't listen to me. Now, what I think is, this Whitlock chick who got herself whacked, who Jennie says she remembers from the old days—"

Edwina glanced at Jennifer in the cloudy, yellowed mirror behind the bar and wondered how this child could even have old days; seated between herself and DiNardis, Jennifer appeared to be no more than fourteen. Catching Edwina's eye in the glass, the girl returned to her sullen manipulation of the cocktail napkin.

"What I think," DiNardis went on, "Jen here saw some kind of way, run a little sympathy number on you, see if there might be any advantage in it. Because the truth is, Jennie hardly knew this Whitlock bitch, only she—"

"Woman," Edwina said, watching in the mirror as DiNardis's

mouth moved. Any moment she expected a long forked reptile's tongue to come flickering out of it. "Not 'bitch.' Woman."

"Yeah, right, whatever. The important thing is, and we was talkin' about it just now, right, Jennie? The important thing is, Jennie's sorry what she told you, like, if she caused you any trouble or anything. Right, Jen?"

His elbow moved sharply; Jennifer winced, biting her lip. "Right," she murmured. "I'm sorry if I caused you trouble."

DeNardis's thin lips stretched upward in an imitation of good humor. "Hey, can't fault a girl for trying to get ahead, right? Only from now on, honey, you listen to me. You try thinkin' for yourself all you do is screw things up. Your equipment ain't in the thinkin' department, you know?"

He slid from the barstool. "So, now we got that little misunderstanding all cleared up, the two of us will just be—"

"What about the ten thousand dollars?" Edwina said.

DeNardis froze in the act of downing the last of his watery beer. Jennifer bit her lip hard but her chin kept on quivering.

"What ten thousand dollars?" DeNardis's glance at Jennifer was bright and interested, almost friendly.

Almost. "I'll explain it later," Edwina told him, "at my house, ten o'clock tonight. You'll both be there," she stated, noting DiNardis's clenched fists, "and neither of you will be suffering any accidents, minor or otherwise, in the meantime."

DiNardis reached past her to grab Jennifer's shoulder and spin her around on the barstool. "What's she talking about?"

"No bruises," Edwina cautioned him. "No black eyes, no split lips. She'd better look wonderfully healthy when you get there, Timmy. She'd better look pink and pleasant."

Jennifer blinked from Edwina to DiNardis, not certain by this time which one scared her most. In her fingers she crumpled the sodden cocktail napkin, reducing it to shreds.

"I didn't—" she began.

Furious, Edwina whirled on her. "Liar," she snapped. "I don't know what happened between you and Theresa, but I know it wasn't what you told me. How old are you, Jennifer? Never mind all the fake ID cards in your wallet. How old are you really?"

"Hey, folks," said the bartender, a paunchy, balding fellow with a stained white apron and fleshy, liver-colored lips. "We don't want any trouble in our fine—"

"Oh, stuff a sock in it," Edwina told him, stepping up very close to Jennifer. "You can tell me," she said, "or you can tell it to the juvenile courts."

Jennifer paled. "Seventeen," she whispered. "I was twelve when I met Terry. She didn't know. I looked older."

"Jesus," said Timmy DiNardis.

"Get her out of here," said the paunchy bartender, "before I lose my—"

"Ten o'clock," Edwina told DiNardis. "She knows the way."

"What if we don't?" By now DiNardis wanted nothing so much as to get away from Jennifer, whose extreme and felonious degree of youth he had apparently not realized.

"If you don't, I'll mention to a friend of mine that a guy named DiNardis is selling teenaged girls, and something ought to be done about it. And if *you* don't," she added to Jennifer, "you will find yourself confined to a detention home for wayward young women, and if you think I'm not sincere about that, just try me."

The bartender snatched the beer Jennifer had been drinking and toweled the bar energetically, as if to remove evidence of her having been there. "You get outta here, the three of you, or I'll call a cop," he said.

Edwina moved toward the door. The smells of smoke and beer competed with the rancid stink of the kitchen's deep-fat fryer; the music from the jukebox was a relentless burble of self-pity, accompanied by synthetic steel guitars. From behind her came the angry click of DiNardis's metal heel cleats, and the squishing of Jennifer's sodden boots.

The two of them, Edwina thought as she stepped onto the sidewalk, deserved each other, and either could have had reason to kill Theresa Whitlock. Still, she felt sorry for Jennifer, whose life was in all probability spoiled for good.

At least, she felt sorry until she had started the Escort, pulled it out into traffic, and made a U-turn at the corner to head back down the avenue toward her last stop of the evening before going home. After the revelation of Jennifer's age, and the hint of ten grand that DiNardis might have gotten his hands on, but somehow hadn't, Edwina was not expecting to see the two together. If they were together, they would be arguing, with Jennifer getting the worst of it.

Instead, as Edwina moved slowly up to the traffic signal, she glimpsed them in a battered blue Dodge parked at the curb. DiNardis's match illuminated the front passenger compartment of the vehicle just as the Escort pulled alongside, so Edwina's sight of them, although brief, was revealing.

They were not arguing. They were conferring, urgently and so intently that neither noticed Edwina. A final glance showed a flash of something metal clutched in Jennifer's ringed fingers. That was when Edwina remembered: Jennifer Warren was in the habit of carrying a gun. The girl's first weapon was still locked in the trunk of the Escort, but now it seemed Jennifer had gotten another weapon in short order, most likely from the despicable Timmy.

DiNardis, too, was almost certainly equipped with some sort of weapon; the night he had come into the emergency room he'd been carrying a switchblade, an ice pick, a steak knife, and a set of brass knuckles, and Edwina doubted he had become a fan of personal disarmament since then.

Carlotta Zimmerman's personality suggested that she tended to pound the table when the argument went against her; the fellow she lived with probably had a varied collection of guns from which she might choose, even if surreptitiously.

Finally, Edwina suspected something small and pearl-handled probably fit nicely into Madalyn Riordan's handbag; certainly the pistol she had displayed earlier could be concealed, and with the kind of employees and the sort of son she had, it was a wonder the diamond merchant's supposed widow didn't walk around swinging an axe.

That didn't even count what Jeffries, Tom Riordan, Jr., and George the steroid-monster security guard probably packed when *they* went on social calls: bazookas, Edwina imagined, to judge by their personalities. She wondered whether any of the Riordan-connected creeps would decide to show up: At least two, she thought, probably would.

In short, each of the guests who would soon arrive at her house was potentially dangerous, probably armed, and possibly Theresa Whitlock's killer. Thinking this, Edwina aimed the Escort back out Whalley Avenue. It had been an interesting day.

And it was going to be an interesting evening.

TEN

"The Riordans, funnily enough, were easiest to persuade. One mention of the IRS, and my comment about where I think all that extra cash really is, and they scurried to accept my invitation. Now, Perry," Edwina said into the telephone, "I need only persuade you."

It was nine in the evening, and another call to the vet had produced the same information as before. Maxie had not regained consciousness, and there was no way of knowing when—or if—he would. He was breathing, and his heart was strong; that was all that could be said for certain. But in the veterinarian's slow, calm voice, Edwina heard another, darker message, one she refused utterly to consider—at least for now.

Tomorrow, she thought; he would wake up tomorrow. "Perry," she said, "the thing is, I didn't know Theresa. And all these people are lying about something. When they get here they're going to lie about her, most of them for their own crummy little reasons, but one of them about her murder. Only I might not know it unless you're here to point the lies out to me, you see."

"I understand," Perry Whitlock said reluctantly. "I do, and I hope you don't think I'm a coward. But—" His voice broke. "It's not getting any easier. Being without her, I mean. And if I have to hear things about her that aren't true, even some that are true . . . I mean, I know Theresa's life before we met wasn't any bed of roses, and I'm beginning to realize she wasn't perfect, but that doesn't mean I like thinking about it."

He sounded miserable. "Of course," Edwina said, "but I hope you'll change your mind. I can't seem to catch them out in anything specific, one on one, so I'm hoping that when I get them together they'll start to contradict one another. Maybe that way I'll find out who's lying naturally—there's not, I must say, an attractive personality in the bunch—and who's lying out of desperation, to avoid being arrested for murder in the matter of Theresa's death."

"You're really sure," Perry Whitlock asked hopefully, "that one of them did it?"

"I'm certain," she said, "that one of the people who will be here tonight is responsible. I just don't know which one."

Yet, she added silently. Around her the empty house seemed to yawn with lonesome hollowness; Maxie, at this moment, should have been gobbling his cat food, to line his stomach and prepare it for the many bits of human food he would cadge throughout the rest of the evening. He should have been jingling his collar and dancing through his training session, or curled watchfully upon his mat in front of the stove.

Where he should not be was comatose in a cage, miles away and under the observation of a trained veterinary technician who, although certainly competent and probably concerned enough, could not be expected to love him.

Still, she could not very well tell Perry Whitlock that while she regretted very much the murder of his wife, what she really wanted now was revenge for her cat.

"And when I find out which one it is, I'm going to come down on that person like a load of stones," she assured Whitlock. "So I hope you'll think again about being here; it would help a great deal."

"I . . . I don't think so," he replied; his thickened voice told her he had been weeping, perhaps was even weeping now. At any rate, she would not press him. He must decide for himself what he could and could not do.

"All right, Perry; don't worry about it. I'll let you know what happens, shall I? I'll keep you informed."

"Yes, thank you," he said gratefully, "I'd appreciate it. And Edwina—"

She heard him move away from the phone for a long, honking blow. When he returned, his voice was steadier. "Thank you so much for staying involved," he said. "The police—well, I'm afraid when the police learned about Theresa's background, they seem to have put her on the back burner. It's almost as if they don't think it's—"

Disposable girls, Edwina thought again. That, of all the things Jennifer Warren had said, was probably true. "I don't feel that way about it," she told Perry Whitlock gently. "Not at all. I'm going to keep on working at this until I get some answers."

And that, for the moment, was that: The stage had been set, not as well as Edwina would have liked, but as well as possible in the face of Perry Whitlock's grief. And if she could not get the truth from the individual players, perhaps the small ensemble she had arranged would provide a bit of extra prying power.

Edwina set the coffee perking and put out cups and saucers. Now, she thought sourly, pouring half-and-half into the cream pitcher and placing it beside the sugar bowl, if there were only some way of filling the room with poison gas, I could do humanity a service.

But this attitude was hardly proper for an ex-nurse, nor was it likely to stimulate the sort of confidences Edwina was looking forward to eliciting: gently if possible, somewhat forcefully if need be, and in the end—although this, she reflected, was a long shot—perhaps by trickery. The sort of benevolent tyranny exercised by the better class of dog trainers, she decided, was likeliest in this group to produce the desired effect; the whip and chair, after all, would have brought them here, and could be put aside for awhile.

Only, not too far aside; retrieving the .38 from its place in the top drawer of her bedside table, she loaded it and snapped the cylinder shut, and dropped the weapon into the pocket of her bulky woolen cardigan. Thus equipped, she sat down to wait for her guests, who began arriving forty minutes later.

* * *

"First of all," she told the assembled company—Carlotta Zimmerman, Madalyn Riordan and Tom Junior, the chilly-eyed Jeffries, Tim DiNardis, and Jennifer Warren—"first of all I think we can assume Ricky Zimmerman killed Tom Riordan, Sr."

Carlotta Zimmerman opened her mouth to object, but a rap at the back door interrupted her. "Excuse me," Edwina said, with a mentally muttered oath that she retracted when she saw it was Perry Whitlock.

"Hope I'm not too late," he mumbled. "I thought it over, and figured I'd better come if it could help."

She took his hand and led him in, noticing that he was not wearing the zircon pinky ring she had seen on the night she first met him; he caught her questioning glance.

"Damn thing slipped off," he explained. "I've lost weight since Theresa . . . well, I haven't eaten much since dinner with you the other night. Feel sort of naked without my ring, though," he added. "Have to have it made smaller, I guess."

"Yes, of course." He did look thinner. "Everyone, this is Perry Whitlock, Theresa Whitlock's husband."

Nodding and looking as if he wished he could disappear into the upholstery somehow, Perry seated himself at the end of the sofa, as far as possible from Carlotta Zimmerman. She, dressed in raggedy jeans, moccasins, and a faded, oversized plaid shirt, eyed his buttoned-down neatness with ill-concealed dislike. The others simply avoided looking at him.

"As I was saying," Edwina began again, "Ricky killed Thomas Riordan by blowing up his car."

"He didn't," Carlotta said fiercely, "he was dead when—"

"No," Edwina said, "he wasn't. You'd already terrified Dr. Blauderbundt into giving you some money, payment to you for his sexual indiscretions. Then Ricky died, and you were furious. You wanted to know who hired him, believing—quite reasonably, it seems to me now—that whoever it was had also killed him. But how were you to find out? Ricky told you it was the mistress of the fellow he was going to kill, but not her name."

Perry Whitlock looked rebellious. "Theresa didn't—" he began.

"I'm sorry, Perry, but she did. Theresa hired Ricky to kill Thomas Riordan, for reasons I will shortly make clear to you. I want to get back to Carlotta's part in it now, though, because Carlotta took the first steps that made Theresa's eventual death inevitable."

Carlotta's face expressed contempt. "What would you know?" she snarled. "You're just guessing about all this, and besides, I didn't kill her. I wish I had," she added defiantly to Perry, who cringed at her tone. "And Ricky *did* tell me her name."

"No," said Edwina, "Riordan's lawyers had no way of finding out about Ricky's insurance so fast—not without your help."

Carlotta looked uneasy, while the rest pricked their ears up alertly. "You mean," demanded Thomas Junior, "she told them? That's stupid. Why'd she help my dad's lawyers make a claim against that little punk's insurance when if she'd have just shut up, she'd have got it herself? She's his sister, isn't she?"

"Very good," Edwina commented. "Why? I wondered it myself, until I realized the other side of the coin. She was safe in telling them about the policy because she was also blackmailing Blauderbundt again. It didn't matter what Riordan's lawyers did; if Ricky was already dead when Riordan died, they had no claim on the money. And good Dr. Blauderbundt made sure Ricky *was* already dead—on paper, at any rate, on his autopsy report. It was wasted effort, because the policy never paid—but as a result of it, Carlotta got the name she wanted. Theresa's name."

"Hey, I get it," put in DiNardis with a glance of admiration for Carlotta. "She wanted information, so she made as if she had some to trade. If they told her the name of this Riordan guy's main squeeze—who hired Zimmerman and then probably killed him afterwards, right?—she'd give 'em the straight stuff about the Zimmerman guy's insurance, they could slap some claim against it, get some for themselves."

"Somehow I knew you'd understand, Tim," Edwina said drily.

"That's ridiculous," Jeffries snapped. "Assuming any ethical lawyer would reveal such a thing, how would he know it in the first place? Miss Zimmerman is right, Miss Crusoe: You are guessing, weaving a tissue of half-truths, suppositions, and utter nonsense."

"Come, now, Jeffries, you know the answer to that. You were probably the one who told the lawyers about Theresa so they could investigate her background. Somehow I don't think Thomas Riordan, Sr., did much that you didn't know about; he was your meal ticket, after all, and God forbid some love affair of his should put a wrench in that little monkeyworks."

There, Edwina thought; you can dish it out, but can you take it? "Leaving aside the question of ethics," she went on, "I notice that my supposition of earlier this afternoon—that more cash remains in the coffers of Riordan's Jewelry than the IRS is aware of—held together pretty well. And I think perhaps fewer gemstones are in Mrs. Riordan's possession than she is letting on."

180

Jeffries stiffened; Thomas Junior stared down at his expensive Italian shoes; and Madalyn Riordan blanched. The effect, Edwina reflected, was all she could have hoped for.

"But again I'm getting ahead of myself." She smiled at the group, all of whom appeared acutely uncomfortable, torn between the desire to leave at once and the need to find out what further bombshells Edwina might be preparing to drop.

"You can stop pretending you don't recognize Carlotta now," she told Perry Whitlock. The result confirmed Edwina's guess.

"You son of a bitch, you probably killed her yourself and now you're putting it on me," Carlotta screeched, hurling herself at the hapless Whitlock. "Son of a bitch, son of a bitch," she wept, pummeling him while Tim DiNardis and Thomas Junior struggled unsuccessfully to drag her off.

"I'm sorry," gasped Whitlock, but his remark cut no ice with Carlotta. Not until Madalyn Riordan got to her feet, crossed the room in three strides, and seized the young woman by the hair did Carlotta cease her onslaught.

"Stand up, you silly girl, and stop that nonsense," Madalyn Riordan ordered. Yanking mightily, she snapped Carlotta's head back. "You've got worse things to worry about than him, in case you hadn't noticed. She's got something on all of us, don't you see? That's how she got us out here."

"Ouch!" Carlotta whined, jerking around with clenched fists to confront this new tormentor. But Madalyn Riordan stood her ground, looking unmussed in a green wool suit and high heels and gazing contemptuously at Carlotta. After a moment the younger woman sat down, with daggerlike glances at Whitlock, and Madalyn resumed her seat as well, her hands folded primly in her lap.

"Very nice," Edwina commented. "Now, where was I?"

"You were about to explain," Jeffries put in acidly, "the connection between these two . . ." His lip curled, which surprised Edwina since until now it had seemed so stiff that she suspected it of being

181

reinforced with cardboard. Apparently her second mention of the Riordan financial situation had taken some of the starch out of him.

"Yes," said Edwina. "Well, the thing is, once Carlotta knew who Theresa was—"

"She set out to torture her," Perry Whitlock finished. "I advertised for household help, and this woman answered."

Edwina nodded. "That's how she got a sample of Riordan's handwriting, to send Theresa ugly notes—Theresa must have kept some of his letters around, and Carlotta searched the house. It's how Theresa's pill bottle got spiked, and how the notes disappeared, once Theresa had read them and hidden them. Carlotta was right there *in* the house, for weeks, every day."

Whitlock shook his head in dismay. "I invited this . . . this viper into our home, gave her honest work, paid her a salary. And this is my repayment."

Carlotta laughed bitterly. "Honest work? Cleaning up your messes? I'd have been better off working at the zoo."

"But you did take the job to find a way to frighten Theresa, didn't you?" Edwina interrupted. "You did write the letters and make them vanish mysteriously, and do other unpleasant things, or arrange for them to happen. I suppose when Perry advertised for help, it seemed like a heaven-sent stroke of luck to you. But how did you know it was him, advertising?"

Carlotta shrugged. "I recognized the phone number. I'd been watching for a long time, calling sometimes. You know, call and hang up, breathe into the phone. Just stuff to make her nervous, but I was always looking for housework jobs, too. So when I saw the ad, I knew it was them."

She looked around defensively. "She killed Ricky, I know she did. But I didn't kill *her*. I was just starting to have fun, getting her really scared. Why should I spoil things by killing her? Dying fast—no way. That was too good for her."

"I don't know, Carlotta," Edwina said. "Maybe you found out

she was coming to see me. Maybe you realized your revenge had gone too far and I would find out about you. You, and the numerous crimes you'd committed in your obsessive quest to avenge your brother's death. Or maybe you just lost your temper."

"No," Carlotta said stubbornly, "I didn't, and I'm not going to say any more."

"You could have gotten a weapon," Edwina persisted. "You could have followed Theresa up to my office. And I saw a little bottle of what I think was probably chloral hydrate on your kitchen counter. I'll bet you're dosing that baby at night, to keep it quiet, aren't you? Is that what you gave my cat, too?" Edwina watched Carlotta carefully as she said this, but Carlotta only clamped her lips shut and refused to answer.

"Never mind, Carlotta," Edwina said, "you'll like this next part better. It's about how Theresa killed Riordan, and why."

"She didn't," Perry Whitlock insisted again. Meanwhile Tim DiNardis and Jennifer Warren began to look more comfortable, as once again the proceedings had not focused on themselves; just wait, Edwina promised them silently.

"I'm afraid Theresa was telling the truth about that," she said gently to Whitlock. "She killed him for the money."

"But she had plenty of—"

"Plenty of *your* money," Edwina finished for him. "You kept her like a fabulously indulged pet bird—and she felt the cage. That was why she got involved with Riordan: for the freedom, and for things he gave her. Things that hadn't come from you."

Whitlock looked crushed. "She loved me," he insisted.

"Theresa was probably planning to leave you as soon as she got money enough together. Money she intended to steal from Thomas Riordan while they were together in New York. He meant to buy a shipment of smuggled gemstones, and he'd brought along a hundred and fifty thousand dollars to do it. He had the cash in a brown briefcase; Theresa secretly brought along one like it, meaning to use it in a switch. Why should she settle for only the jewelry he'd given her, when she knew he was carrying all that cash? Madalyn saw her with the case, returning to her own room just after Riordan left."

Whitlock shook his head slowly. "She said she was visiting a girlfriend. I just can't believe she—"

"Believe it, Perry," she said less gently than before. "In her own room, she opened the briefcase, and found that Riordan had gotten wind somehow of what she planned, or perhaps saw her making the switch. On that, of course, I am only guessing, but he'd switched the cases back, so the one Theresa had was empty."

For a moment Edwina imagined Theresa's baffled rage, and her horror when she realized what was about to happen to the money.

"What Riordan didn't know," Edwina went on, "was that she also planned to kill him—or, at any rate, to have him killed. So he toddled happily off to his appointment, which turned out to be an appointment with murder."

They were listening intently. "Anyway, the briefcase in the car that exploded contained all the money," Edwina said, "part of which Theresa had meant to use to pay Ricky for his services. So you can see her dilemma, can't you, Tim?"

"Dunno what you're talkin' about," DiNardis replied stoutly. "Never met the girl. You ain't gettin' me to blabber a lot of stuff like these other ignoramuses, here. In fact, I think I'm just gonna take myself off, and you can—"

"Sit down." Her sharp tone froze him. "You did meet her. Jennifer introduced you. Come on now, Tim, Theresa wouldn't know how to hire a hit man. Ricky wasn't exactly listed in the Yellow Pages, you know, and she'd been off the street too long to hear about him by chance. It was you who got them together, after Theresa talked to Jennifer about her plans."

DiNardis's eyes hardened; he seemed about to speak. Edwina got in ahead of him. "No, no, forget the denials. You're in it, buddy. It was your blue car that pulled into the rest area where Ricky died that day. So just sit back down, and if you think of any facts that are significant please feel free to share them."

Tom Riordan, Jr., mulled it all over for a moment. "The woman had no cash but she'd promised to pay Ricky Zimmerman for killing my father. So then she killed Zimmerman, too? And this guy and maybe the girl with him—they helped?" He glanced about as if expecting praise for his insight, but in this, as in so much else, he was disappointed.

"Shut up," said Jeffries. "We should all leave here this instant. Any word we speak could incriminate us."

"Yes," said Edwina pleasantly, "but if you do, I'll just go straight to the police and tell them all I know about all of you, and let them sort out which one of you really killed Theresa. I don't think any of you would like that. But patience: I'm almost finished. And in answer to your question, Thomas—I'm not sure who actually pulled the trigger on Ricky.

"Maybe," she added with a severe look at Tim DiNardis, "someone who had more practical experience than Theresa did in the violence department. Someone who knew Ricky Z. might get angry if he weren't paid precisely as promised, and decide to get rid of the promiser. Of course, if that's true, then anyone involved in killing Ricky had a good motive to kill Theresa, too, when she threatened to get talkative. To stop her from telling exactly what went on."

"This is ridiculous," Madalyn Riordan said. "First you say one person did it, then another. The fact is, none of us could have done *all* that was done. No one here could be guilty." She lifted her head in triumph.

"That's been troubling me, too, Madalyn," said Edwina. "Until I realized that no one person has to be guilty of it all. Each of you did something to contribute to Theresa's death. Only one of you pulled the trigger, but you're all involved, either in her murder or in blocking my investigation of it, for reasons of your own."

Now Jennifer, who seemed to feel she might yet get out of this unscathed, opened her mouth. "I didn't block you," she offered. "I came out here to ask you to go on."

"You came," Edwina retorted, "to find out how much trouble I was going to be to you and Tim. Encouraging me couldn't harm you and might help you, by allaying any suspicions I might have of you. You even brought a gun with you, in case there was no help for it but to get rid of me. You hadn't planned on my taking it away from you, right off the bat."

Edwina turned once more to the group. "Ricky would have gone after Tim *and* Theresa, and Jennifer, too, if he thought they were welshing on the deal; each had a perfect motive for being in on killing Ricky. Afterwards, Jennifer or Tim might have wanted to silence Theresa, to cover up their part in the matter—as accessories to Riordan's murder *and* participants in Ricky's."

"You said my mother hasn't got the diamonds she says she has," Thomas Junior put in. "How would you know that? And even if it's true, what would it have to do with any of this? I mean, hell, we all hated the Whitlock woman. She got my dad way off the track, got him killed. But we don't go around murdering people." He sat back, proud of his little speech.

"Don't be stupid, Tom. You know and I know your father gave jewelry to Theresa. He wasn't just in love with her—he was crazy about her. Probably he meant to get the valuable things back, after she tried switching those briefcases."

Madalyn Riordan looked very uneasy indeed, Edwina saw with satisfaction, and Jeffries appeared not much more comfortable. "But he never got the chance," Edwina went on, "and when Madalyn opened up that safe, there *were* gems in it. Only not as many as she thought there would be. Am I right?"

Madalyn nodded grudgingly. "My husband," she grated out,

"was a complete fool. But your *wife*," she spat furiously at Perry Whitlock, "was a lying, thieving, murdering little—"

"And that," Edwina went on calmly, "explains the attempted mugging, a purse-snatching, which did succeed, but which did not produce the gems the Riordans thought Theresa still had, since by then Theresa was not carrying any valuables around with her, and it explains the rash of burglaries and vandalisms the Whitlocks suffered."

Thomas Riordan, Jr., shifted unhappily as Edwina went on: "The bunch of you—Madalyn, Tom, Junior, and Jeffries—all cooperated in it, trying to get back what you thought Theresa had. Most of the hostility you display toward one another is another lie, to throw me off the track. Although I suspect that if one of you were to find the stones—or perhaps just one especially valuable one— you wouldn't rush to share your good fortune with the others."

Jeffries sat up, about to speak, but Edwina cut him off. "Too bad you didn't bring your hired guard," she said. "I've an idea he could say a lot about Riordan family attempts at getting the goods back from Theresa, assuming the steroids you keep him stoked on haven't rotted out his higher speech functions yet. He might even know where you've hidden the rest of the cash Tom Senior was supposed to have taken with him."

"Slanderous!" Jeffries hissed. "I'll see you in court over those remarks, young woman—"

"Oh, shut up," she advised him, feeling tired and irritated. The gathering was not working out as she had hoped; they were all so accustomed to lying, they probably couldn't tell falsehood from the truth. Among them, a killer would be well camouflaged.

"I'm sick of the lot of you," she said. "Dead rats, sabotaged brakes, one of you has even poisoned my cat. None of you should be sitting here drinking my coffee, trying to look respectable. You should be out in some stagnant, polluted little slime pond, where you'd all feel a lot more comfortable."

She set down her own cup with a sharp, disgusted click. "I hoped to get the truth out of you, or some of it. But now I see I might have saved myself the trouble. Get out of here. And," she added, raking them with a gaze full of as much contempt as she could muster—which was plenty—"if anyone is thinking about harming me to keep me from talking about the things I know about you all, well, I've taken the precaution of writing it all down and locking it away, so don't bother."

She turned and stalked from the room.

*　　*　　*

"I'm sorry, Perry. That can't have been very pleasant for you, and it didn't work out as I'd hoped, either. The idea was that when they realized how much I did know—or had guessed—one of them might drop some little tidbit I *didn't* know. Nobody did, though."

Edwina sighed. "I guess tomorrow I *will* have to go to the police and hand everything over to them. I've done what I can, but this time my best just isn't good enough."

The others had all gone, gathering their coats and marching out in chilly silence, their cars filing down the driveway like vehicles in a funeral procession. Edwina stood at the kitchen sink, rinsing cups, while Perry slumped in the rocking chair. It was late, but she did not wish he would go; sooner or later she would have to confront him, too, and it might as well be tonight.

"It's all right," he said, gazing mournfully into his empty coffee cup. "I guess there were a lot of things about Theresa I wasn't seeing, but there's no sense fooling myself now. You must wonder why I didn't say I knew the Zimmerman woman."

"No." She wiped her hands on a towel. "You were stunned at the sight of her, I could tell. And horrified, I suppose."

He laughed weakly. "There's an understatement. I was sure you'd start suspecting me of hiring her on purpose or something. You don't think that," he added in anxious tones, "do you?"

"No. I know you didn't realize who Carlotta was when you hired her. Even I was only guessing—but I knew she was short of money and might try cleaning houses. I also knew you had a new housekeeper. And a housekeeper would have the kind of access those nasty pranks would require."

She sighed, feeling discouraged. "That's the thing, you see. No one knew what anyone else was doing, and everyone has something to lie about. Carlotta didn't know the Riordans were trying to get back the valuable jewelry Tom Riordan had given Theresa. The Riordans didn't know Carlotta was busily torturing Theresa, harassing and frightening her."

Hanging the dish towel on its hook, she went on. "None of them knew about Tim and Jennifer's involvement in what Theresa had done, and that it was probably the three of them together who killed Ricky Zimmerman. The police didn't know Riordan couldn't have run off with money to live on; he only took a hundred and fifty thousand, and that was blown up in the explosion. The Riordans found the rest after the explosion and hid it, saying he'd taken it. And of course," she finished gently, "no one knew about your part in the whole matter."

Whitlock looked up from between his fingers. The line of whiter skin where he usually wore his ring showed sharply on his pinky. "My part? But you just said you didn't—"

"I said I knew you didn't know who you were hiring when you took on Carlotta as your housekeeper. But Perry, there's another thing: Tom Riordan's dental ID. You faked it, didn't you? You sent someone else's X rays with a dental chart to match. Riordan is dead; he died in the explosion that day. Only, with the wrong dental records supplied by you, his body couldn't be identified."

He paled. "What . . . what makes you think that?"

"I see you don't deny it. Your conversation with the lawyer the other day—I didn't mean to eavesdrop, Perry, but I was right there. I suppose you thought I wouldn't understand. But I do, and when I called Arthur to cancel my appointment with him this evening, I asked him just how much your malpractice premiums would go up, if you were to settle the case a patient is bringing against you. The answer told me you had a reason stronger than fatigue and grief to want to stay out of court—and the reason is, you don't want your recordkeeping investigated."

Whitlock gave a mirthless little laugh. "I guess you've got me. But look, I wasn't hurting anyone. And I've got to cover my expenses somehow—what I get from the government doesn't begin to pay what it costs me to take care of some of my patients, and the patients don't have the money, either. So sometimes I send in claims for more procedures than I actually do. I say I put in two fillings or three, when sometimes I only did one. So what?"

"Not sometimes. Often. And you do it on patients with private insurance, too. Patients like Tom Riordan, for example."

"All right," he said sulkily, "pretty often. And sure, I hit up his insurance. Why shouldn't the fat cats help out?"

Edwina refrained from pointing out that the money Perry was skimming from government entitlement programs and insurance companies did not go into the pockets of the poor people he was pretending to champion; it went into his own.

"The point is," she said, "that if you'd sent Riordan's own X rays, they wouldn't match the records his insurance company has on file—records you'd faked, to get paid for more work than you actually did on Riordan's teeth. You could have mocked up a record to match the X rays, but you couldn't risk the possibility that somewhere along the line, the two sets of records might be compared. Your only chance to stay out of trouble was to make it look as if the teeth weren't Riordan's at all, but those of some unknown other person. That way, Riordan's records would cease to be of interest—and your own fraud could go on, undetected."

Whitlock shrank into himself. "I don't see," he said, "how you could know all that from overhearing one phone call."

"Oh, Perry. It wasn't just the one call. It was everything I knew or suspected—especially when I began thinking Riordan really had died in the bombing. Because, look: No one had seen him or heard a word from him. A dozen kinds of agencies were on the hunt for him, and they know how to hunt. There was nothing at all to say he was alive, except the things that began to happen to Theresa—and then to me—and I began to see lots of other people with reasons to do those things. Then I told the Riordans I thought *they* had the money—they hid it, and told the police Riordan had taken it—and saw them flinch. That was when I knew I was right: Riordan's dead."

Whitlock got up, looking beaten. "What are you going to do now?"

"I don't know," she admitted. "I don't feel bad for the others, but I do for you, somehow. Not," she added, "that I can approve. But—"

Perry Whitlock shook his head slowly. "No, I don't suppose you would approve. Well. And to think I believed the worst had happened. I could go to jail, you know."

"Perhaps it needn't come to that. Look," Edwina said, "why not come up to my office tomorrow. We can talk about your situation, see what it really is. I have lots of legal friends who can help you, too. Will you do that, Perry? I'd like to help somehow."

He considered for a moment, then nodded. "All right. Yes, I will do it. Thank you, Edwina." He gave the mirthless laugh again, like a painful little cough, and moved toward the door.

The telephone rang as he was entering the hall; McIntyre, probably, calling to say when he would be home. She turned toward the instrument and felt rather than heard Whitlock's sudden rush at her. Snatching at the receiver, she felt his hand clamp down on her own; with a vicious twist he wrenched her arm around and up hard behind her, while the telephone continued ringing.

A second later came the sting of the hypodermic; the last thing Edwina heard was the click of the answering machine, somewhere in the gathering darkness.

*   *   *

A bright white light bored into Edwina's eyes as, painfully, she forced them open. She lay on her back, her arms restrained behind her, in a sort of reclining chair. Smells of antiseptic and medicines made her feel nauseated and something on her left foot itched maddeningly.

A thump of fright passed through her as she realized where she was: The reclining chair was a dental chair. Worse, it was Perry Whitlock's dental chair.

"I'm sorry, Edwina, but I can't let you go on," Perry said as he came into the room. "You've already figured out way too much. It's only a matter of time until you realize the rest of it, and I can't let that happen. Not before I get away."

Along one side of the room was a built-in sink with jars of cotton balls, alcohol wipes, and a container of sterilizing solution. Against the other wall leaned small twin tanks of oxygen and nitrous oxide.

"I had to be there tonight, to find out what *you* knew," he went on. "But I also knew the Riordans were going to be there and they'd recognize the stone; even if I put the zircon back in, that alone would give them too many ideas. But when you noticed I wasn't wearing the ring, I knew my plan hadn't worked. You'd made the connection, even if you didn't know yet that you had."

"She'd told you the whole story, hadn't she?" Edwina guessed. "She was so scared, she finally leveled with you. She told you she was coming to see me, and when. But you weren't just enraged over her affair—you were scared." Cautiously, Edwina tested her restraints; he mustn't notice her trying them.

"She could ruin you," Edwina went on. "Your fraud would

192

certainly be exposed if she confessed to Riordan's murder. So you followed her and shot her. But you—and you alone—knew precisely what it was that Riordan had given her as a love gift. She'd told you about the one really valuable diamond, probably in an effort to placate you."

"Big fat diamond," Perry snarled. "Big fat nothing. As if it was okay she was running around, up to all her old tricks, if she got something valuable out of it and offered to share."

"But you weren't going to waste it, were you? You took the diamond out of her bag after you'd shot her, and in your thorough way you put a thousand dollars in, so no one would even begin to suspect that anything had been taken. Later, you replaced the zircon in your ring with the diamond."

The restraints felt a bit soft, as if they had been padded, perhaps with rolls of gauze. She tested the bonds once more and felt them stretch a bit, but not enough. No, not nearly enough.

"I suppose she was carrying the diamond because you'd said she should? You told her you would meet her after her appointment with me—the two of you would rent a safety deposit box—or some such story," Edwina said.

"That is correct," Perry Whitlock replied jovially, his good cheer returning as he fussed with something behind the chair. Craning her neck up, she saw that her shoe had been removed; the itchy thing on her foot was a swatch of adhesive tape, holding the IV needle in a vein.

"Now, don't worry," he assured her, "I'm not going to harm you. I only want you to talk to me, to tell me anything more that you know. I must know everything, before I go. Otherwise, some small fact I don't realize you have might make it easier for them to find me."

Delay him, she thought. Get him interested; slow him down. "Carlotta sent the letters, and took them away again," she said. "She did it to frighten Theresa, to torture her, without knowing that other people hated Theresa, too. A lot of people, including you."

Whitlock smiled. "Yes, little Theresa seemed so innocent, didn't she? It was that way with everyone she met. To look at her, you'd think she was some angel come down on a cloud. But after a while . . ." His expression darkened.

"After a while, Theresa began lying to you the way she lied to everyone," Edwina finished for him. "She lied as naturally as breathing. She didn't tell me she'd killed Ricky Zimmerman, or had him killed, for instance. She was frightened enough to come to me with part of the truth, but even when she feared for her life she didn't tell me all of it. But Perry, where did you get the rats? That interests me."

He swung his head around, startled. "How do you know it was me? Anyone could have done that." In his hands he held a glass syringe; the print on it read SODIUM PENTOTHAL, USP.

Firmly, she averted her eyes from it, feeling the fear sweat break out on her body as she realized what he intended.

"You have the high-speed drill with the tiny drill bit," she replied, "for making the hole the hatpin went through. You could trap a rat right out in the alley. I suppose you fed it some tranquilizer to kill it. Is that what you gave Maxie, too? Only *how* did you? You were in my sight all the time."

But Whitlock ignored her question, concentrating instead on injecting the drug into the bottle hanging from the IV pole, which he wheeled into her view. It was a half-liter bottle and the drip was running slowly, Edwina saw with a twinge of hope. Still, with a twitch of his fingertips he could turn it up, and within minutes that would be the end of her—the idea that he meant her no harm being ridiculous.

She tried again. "The note to me was clever. Riordan must have written letters to Theresa and both you and Carlotta found them and imitated them. And the rat head *was* artful, if not quite to my own taste."

Whitlock preened. "Yes, I thought so, too. I only wish my discouraging tactics had worked. The tampered brakes were also my doing. Oh, not directly, of course. I've a patient with a talent for that sort of thing, and I make it my business to know as much about my patients as possible. Once I explained to this fellow that I knew how many times he'd committed grand theft auto, he was eager to do a favor in return for my silence. And my friend's the kind of fellow who wouldn't care if a dozen policeman husbands were living in the house," he added smugly.

He didn't mean, she saw, to question her about anything. He didn't need to know anything; probably he didn't even mean to leave town. What he meant was to deceive her, to keep her from struggling, so his job of killing her would be easier. Later her body would be found, perhaps looking like a suicide, and while Perry Whitlock might be suspected of involvement in her death—he had, after all, been the last to leave her house, as far as the others knew—suspicion was not proof, a fact that had so far served him very well.

"Actually, killing Theresa was even easier than I thought it would be," Perry went on conversationally. "The timing was dicey but I knew what time her appointment with you was, and about when she'd probably be leaving. If things didn't work out, well, nothing forced me to go through with it, so I gave it a try and got lucky. I went out through the window into the empty alley—the Dumpsters shield it from the street—came around and in through the lobby doors, and took the elevator up. No one paid any attention. Afterwards I sprinted down the service stairs, walked back out through the lobby, and nipped in through the office window again. I'll bet I wasn't gone fifteen minutes."

He turned to drop the syringe in the sharps box by the sink; as he did, she strained once more against the gauze restraints and felt them give another fraction. Her sweat-slick palm slid against the padding, which was meant of course to keep her from bearing any marks of having been bound. Where would he leave her, she wondered? Perhaps in her own bed, or out in the car, or in a motel room somewhere.

"But just to be sure," Perry added, "I'd put a tape of a two-sided conversation on the answering machine, on the private line in my workshop at home; I knew the housekeeper wouldn't answer that one. When it came time, I dialed my own number to start the tape playing, so even if someone picked up my line at the desk, it would sound as if I were on the phone. I ran my own side of the taped conversation on an audio deck inside my office, too, so my voice could be heard through the wall. That's why my receptionist could say so convincingly that I was in the office when Theresa was shot. It all," he finished, "worked very well."

Across the room the heavy stainless-steel gauges on the oxygen and nitrous tanks winked merrily in the overhead lights, while nearer by a clear solution of IV fluid continued flowing, droplet by silvery droplet, toward the IV needle in her foot. The droplets looked like teardrops, and the adhesive tape didn't itch anymore. The room began turning.

"Yes, it's beginning to work now," Perry Whitlock said in a soft, wonderfully soothing voice. "Soon you'll begin feeling sleepy. Edwina, did you really write it down? Is there a record somewhere of what you think I've done? Did you, did you write it down?"

The drug made her answer. "No. I was just saying that, to scare the others."

But the drug had not yet done its worst, and she must fight it. I *must*, she thought, suppressing a giggle followed by a shiver of despair. Oh, please let me stay awake.

Perry's back was turned. Probably he thought he'd won; nothing left but cleanup. The idea made her furious. Not on your tintype, buster, she thought through a cloud of increasingly weakening dopiness, and gave a ferocious, last-ditch yank at the restraints.

Whereupon, to her immense surprise, her hand came free. But this would have been more helpful had the hand not weighed, apparently, more than all the other parts of her body combined. *Drugged.* Overhead, the lights had grown haloes; Whitlock's voice sounded far away. Whatever he put in that IV, it was more than sodium pentothal.

"She'd made a fool of me. She'd have ruined me. And she *did* have the diamond," Whitlock said, beginning to turn toward her again.

Hide, Edwina thought at her escaping hand, which had managed to make its way only halfway across her lap; its spirit was willing, but its flesh was sedated in the extreme, and this impeded its progress.

"Hey," said Whitlock, catching sight of the hand just as it managed to reach the safety of her bulky woolen sweater pocket, where to its delight it encountered the friendly, familiar bulk of the Smith & Wesson .38-caliber Police Special revolver Edwina had placed there, hours earlier.

I'll be darned, Edwina thought.

"Oh, no, you don't," Perry Whitlock began.

"Oh, yes, I do," she told him, and fired the thing.

The shot tore a hole in her pocket, missing Perry by a mile, but the report did not sound like a gunshot. Edwina turned her head and watched with mild, muzzy-feeling amusement as a chunk of the steel regulator from the small yoked oxygen and nitrous tanks by the wall sailed brightly through the air at Perry Whitlock.

A look of consternation appeared on Whitlock's face. His legs went out from under him, his body dropping as if he had been chopped off at the knees. Almost at the same moment, something struck the base of his examining chair with an enormous metallic clang.

That tank, she realized. I shot it. It's spinning around loose, and it knocked him off his feet. Or . . . cut them off.

Meanwhile Whitlock's head continued sinking, his eyes glazing as if he were tired of the whole proceeding, until his skull intersected the trajectory of the sailing regulator chunk, which was being propelled by—Edwina remembered, in the sudden useless way an irrelevant fact will pop into one's mind—the instantaneously released force of twenty-two hundred pounds per square inch.

The impact sent Perry lurching suddenly forward; he sprawled across the lower part of the treatment chair, then slid back. Edwina watched as he sank lower and lower, until his now lifeless face disappeared below the foot of the chair. A thud signaled his arrival on the floor, and it was over.

Only not *entirely* over. There was, Edwina felt sure, still something she should do. Something urgent and important. But the lights kept getting blurrier, and the room kept turning faster.

Dizzily she stared at her foot where the IV needle was, then up at the brightly falling droplets.

Something. Important. Faster.

ELEVEN

"So Whitlock had no idea Theresa was involved in Riordan's death when he supplied the phony dental records to the coroner?"

"None at all," Edwina mumbled around the cotton wads, plastic lip retractor, bits of astringent cord, and other items of equipment with which Arthur had filled her mouth like the bargain bin at a dental going-out-of-business sale. "He just wanted to spare himself a devastating fraud charge."

"That creep," Arthur pronounced, preparing to drill.

"Urngh," Edwina agreed; then Arthur began to demolish what was left of her right front canine tooth. When he had finished, the tooth felt to her cautiously probing tongue like some bombed-out building, a ragged-edged crater of its former self.

"And," Arthur said, "all that stuff about how heartbroken he was—that was just a crock?"

"I'm not so sure," Edwina replied. "I think he loved her once. But when she didn't match up to his image of her—when she wasn't perfect, and threatened unwittingly to expose his fraud—he killed her, not being able to stand the conflict."

She shifted in the chair as Arthur, behind her, went on preparing another set of instruments. "And then," she said, "he made up a new Theresa, the way the brain will supply an image for itself of something that's not there anymore. Only a not quite accurate image, you see."

"He was an actor, though," Arthur said skeptically. "The newspapers made a lot of that while you were still so sick, that he'd been a drama major before switching to pre-med. Only he was a bad actor. Good at it, but bad."

He fiddled with something on a tray, frowned, and readjusted it. "And the money?" he asked. "What about the money Theresa Whitlock gave you—where *did* it come from?"

Edwina answered quickly, while she still could; Arthur, she could tell, was gearing up for a cheery romp through the wilds of endodontal therapy, and soon would have no thought to spare for any other subject.

"She'd sold some of the smaller things Riordan gave her. The ten thousand Jennifer said she'd lent Theresa was a lie—she just said it because it was a nice round number, one there was a chance I'd believe. And when by chance it coincided with an entry I'd seen in Theresa's checkbook, I did almost believe it. Just not enough to give it back to her."

Edwina sighed; Jennifer, she thought, might actually have been rescuable. Anyone who could get that kitchen wood stove lit single-handedly couldn't be all bad. But Jennifer had been an accessory before the fact to Tom Riordan's murder: She had put Theresa in touch with Tim DiNardis, who helped Theresa hire Ricky Z. She had waited with Tim outside the hotel on the morning Riordan was killed; the plan was for all three to drive in Tim's car to New Jersey, where Theresa would pay them *and* Ricky Z.

But when there turned out not to be any money in the briefcase, the plan had to change. If Ricky Z. didn't die, he would find and kill all three of them, Tim DiNardis knew. Ricky just wasn't the kind of guy who would wait for his pay, or listen to explanations about the lateness of it, either; Ricky Z. was an animal. And *that* was why Jennifer had had to find Edwina and cozy up to her so fast: to find out how much Theresa had said about Jennifer and Tim's involvement in Ricky Z.'s murder, and Tom Riordan's, too.

"It serves Timmy DiNardis right for thinking he could handle something like this," Edwina said. "Doing business with Ricky Z. probably looked to him like running General Motors. It made him think he was big-time, a real important bad guy. Now the bunch of them are going away for all the things they've done—except for Perry, of course."

Madalyn Riordan was up for tax fraud, as was Tom Junior, while Jeffries had already confessed his part in Tom Senior's business misdeeds, and the horrid guard had been arrested for possession of enough illicit drugs to fill a pharmacy. Carlotta Zimmerman was under investigation for crimes including malicious mischief, extortion, and endangering a child, and for harboring her boyfriend, who turned out to be a wanted burglar.

Maurice Underhill III, by contrast, had been let out of his prison cell, and was certain to have his conviction reversed; what the result of this would be, Edwina was not sure, but it had to be better than leaving him where he was. Maurice, according to reports from John D. Maxwell, had taken heart from Edwina's visit, and had begun cracking smart remarks in company where he ought not to, so that if he had not been removed from prison society soon, his dim wit surely would have become fatal to him.

Finally, the Fiat was a total loss; Edwina had bade it good-bye with the feeling that she was leaving behind her youth. Then Gerry had stepped from behind the parts counter at Worldwide Motors.

"Miss Crusoe," he said, "I got this friend, and he's gotta real nice car. Alfa Romeo sedan, he can't keep it, but he don't want to get rid of it to just anybody. You want to take a look?" The car was a pale champagne-colored vehicle, square and stodgy-seeming until one drove it; it sat now outside Arthur's office.

"Good riddance to Perry," Arthur said. "I've got absolutely no sympathy for a guy like that. And you're lucky to be alive, is all I've got to say about it. Who'd have thought old Walter could move so fast? He's a real hero, in my book."

"Grmsh," said Edwina, for by now Arthur had begun fitting an appliance approximately the size of Rhode Island over the tooth that interested him, in order to create a sterile area within which he might perform root-canal surgery upon said afflicted tooth.

She remembered nothing of Walter's actual heroics: By the time the elderly building superintendent had heard the gunshot in Whitlock's office, phoned the police, run down to his workroom for his set of master keys, and dragged Edwina from Whitlock's treatment chair—dislodging the IV in the process—she was unconscious and barely breathing. But after four days in the hospital and six recuperating at home, she had recovered entirely from the near-fatal event; in fact she thought she was in some ways much improved because of it.

For one thing, nothing that could be done to her in a dentist's chair could ever again hold any terror for her, as long as the dentist doing it was not Perry Whitlock. For another, her escape had been so narrow that she felt her outlook permanently altered by it.

"Let me know if this bothers you," Arthur said.

Don't worry, Arthur, Edwina thought. I will.

It seemed she had been doing little else for days. She had, for example, let McIntyre know that it bothered her to live out in the country in a house she despised, whereupon to her surprise he had merely lifted an eyebrow at her and said:

"Good heavens, Edwina, why didn't you tell me so? Sell it. I don't care about it—I thought *you* did. We can find a place in town that will suit us, don't you think?" Then he had gone back to his sports pages and to stroking the sleek black fur of Maxie, who according to the vet's report had been regaining consciousness at just about the time Edwina was losing hers.

No one, it turned out, had poisoned him. The toxicology tests had been run a second time, and the first tests shown to be in error. Instead, the cat had probably been grazed by a passing car after escaping from the Escort; at any rate, once the mild swelling in his brain receded, he'd woken up all by himself and seemed little affected by the loss of at least one of his nine—or perhaps eight or seven—remaining lives.

Blinking at the mildness of McIntyre's first answer, Edwina had tried again, expressing her desire to continue snooping as a profession, and in fact her determination to do so. She knew it worried and even upset him at times, but she saw no other choice; she steeled herself and told him so.

At this, McIntyre had laid down his newspaper. "My dear," he said, "I didn't marry you by mistake, you know. I'm sure I shall manage to tolerate your occupation, as long as *you* manage not to blow my head off in your pursuit of it."

He tipped that very head, the corners of his eyes wrinkling in the way she loved. "And," he added gently, "I'm sorry if I've given you some other impression. I have been a bit preoccupied, I know. Now, is there anything else?"

"No," she had replied in a small voice, thinking how irritating it was for Harriet to be so blasted right all the time. "Only, isn't there something you want *me* to do? A favor I could do for you, a habit you'd like me to acquire, or break?"

"Well, now that you mention it, there is," he had answered. "If you must chase murderers, I'd appreciate it if you'd get to the firing range oftener. Missing Whitlock at ten paces doesn't say much for your marksmanship, drug swoon or no drug swoon."

He raised his newspaper. "Oh, one other thing," he added. "What if I took early retirement, to go to law school?"

Edwina had stood there for a moment, wondering how she, a

person who so little deserved it, had managed to become so fortunate. "That would be fine with me," she told McIntyre.

"Good," he said, "because I put the papers in last week." And with that he had raised his newspaper again, not lowering it until she began persuading him—as prettily as she knew how—to give up reading altogether for the remainder of the evening.

"Almost done here," said Arthur now. "You okay?"

"Nh-hn." The novocaine had kicked in hard, so that Arthur's labors—what *was* he doing in there?—proceeded painlessly.

Meanwhile the overhead lights in Arthur's treatment room shone whitely down onto trays full of clean bright instruments. Smelling of breath mints and bay rum, Arthur hummed as he worked, daubing the inside of her tooth with something astringent and pungently creosote-tasting. Had she not been holding obediently so still, Edwina would have laughed aloud at all of it.

Alive, she thought, grasping the arms of Arthur's treatment chair with affection and enormous gratitude. *Alive, alive-oh.*

"Count three and it's done," said Arthur.

And as always, when Arthur said it, it was.